STRAWBERRY MOON

A Mystery Novel

STRAWBERRY MOON

Robert Underhill

Arbutus Press
Traverse City, Michigan

Strawberry Moon

ISBN 10 - 09766104-4-2
ISBN 13 - 978-0-9766104-4-1

Arbutus Press
Traverse City, Michigan
editor@arbutuspress.com
www.Arbutuspress.com

This book is a work of fiction. Names, characters, businesses, organizations, and incidents are the product of the author's imagination and are used fictitiously. Any resemblance to actual persons, living or dead, is entirely coincidental.

Library of Congress Cataloging-in-Publication-Data

Underhill, Robert
Strawberry moon / Robert Underhill.
p. cm.
ISBN 0-9766104-4-2
1. Leelanau County (Mich.)--Fiction. I. Title

PS3621.N343S77 2006
813'.6--dc22
2005033249

Printed in the United States of America

PROLOGUE

1963

THE MOONLIGHT WAS AS BRIGHT as he'd ever seen it. That wasn't good. He wanted to walk right up to the house and look in a window. Not wise. There were no lights on in the front room, and if anyone were there they'd see him approaching as if he were on stage. Instead, he settled down to wait in the tall weeds across the road from the small frame shack. He laid the tractor crank on the ground by his feet. He had only brought it along because an angry impulse had made him reach out and lift it from the nail on his garage wall. Covered with cobwebs, it had hung there for many years. It was only an impulse, no more than that. He had no intention of doing anything—not tonight anyway. Tonight he'd only come to get a good look at the guy. He'd parked his truck down near the highway and walked the half-mile back on the dirt road to the house. He'd sit here a while, and then drive the fifty miles back home to the Leelanau Peninsula. Now, at least, he knew where the bastard lived.

A light went on in the front room. Shit, there he was. He was big, dark skinned, wearing a white T-shirt, long black hair tied back with something yellow. He looked just like he'd expected the damned Indian to look. A woman came into the room. Was the guy married? Kids? Those questions made no difference to his rage. He still wanted to kill the son-of-a-bitch.

The front door opened suddenly. The man stood there, a husky silhouette against the light from the room. He looked back, talking loudly to the woman. He stepped outside, slamming the door and stood for a moment on the stoop, his white shirt brilliant in the moonlight.

In spite of the tall weeds, the watching man felt exposed. He held his breath, still as a stone. A tense few seconds, then the Indian turned and walked toward the woods at the side of the house. For a few moments, his white shirt remained visible, caught by moonlight breaking through the trees. He was moving at a good pace. He must be following a path through the woods, thought the watching man. He relaxed.

He thought he knew where the guy was headed. Earlier, when he'd driven by to locate the house, he'd passed a rundown tavern a mile or so farther down the dirt road. The path must be a shortcut through the woods—-a well-worn path, he'd wager. Leaving his hiding place, he ran along the road and reached the tavern just in time to see his man enter it. The windowless old building was dark against the gravel parking lot. A neon Miller High Life sign and a bare light bulb over the entrance cast the only light.

He had unconsciously changed his plans while running. He was no longer an observer; he was now lying in wait. He hoped the Indian would leave the tavern before it closed. At closing time, other people would be leaving with him. He settled behind a pick-up truck the guy would have to pass on his way home along the path.

He'd never come close to doing anything like what he planned to do now. He was a God-fearing man, an elder in his church, but he felt no guilt. He had been given leave by his Lord to right a wrong, to punish a mortal sin. "Thou shalt not covet thy neighbor's wife." He glanced up at the full June moon, the one the Chippewas call

Strawberry Moon. The man up there smiled an approval. Heaven was on his side.

During the next hours, half a dozen cars came into the lot and the people went inside. One couple came out and left and a while later a single guy followed them. Half an hour before closing time, the tavern door opened and closed noisily, and the Indian stood unsteadily in the circle of light at the entrance. He attempted to light a cigarette with the exaggerated, deliberate efforts of a drunk. Swaying, he took his bearings toward the path and began walking across the moonlit parking lot.

Behind the truck, a waiting hand closed around the hard steel of the tractor crank.

CHAPTER 1
2004

THE MAN IN THE GRAY ITALIAN suit moved nervously from one small routine task to another to quell his excitement. It was sexual excitement he felt and his pounding heart wouldn't be calmed. He'd made his desire clear to her at her last appointment - in terms she couldn't possibly have misunderstood. Hadn't she responded positively? Yes, he was sure she had. He'd smiled suggestively and talked of "a more intimate form of therapy" and she'd smiled back.

His unaccountably strong desire for her began that first day she came to his office. It was immediate. He'd wondered if it was some undefined thing about her expression, sad but hopeful, or something about the way she handled her body, offering it seemingly unaware? He didn't know. He only knew that on the day he'd opened the door to his waiting room and saw her timidly standing there, soft gray eyes looking up to him for the help and understanding she hadn't found elsewhere, his desire flamed and his goal was set - his yearning wouldn't be denied.

Neither uncontrollable passion nor uncertainty was typical of his relationships with women, but there had been exceptions. Two came to his mind.

In an attempt to relax, he continued the small tasks of opening the office for the day: starting a pot of coffee, watering the three ivy plants and the large ficus, and checking the tissue dispenser on the table next to the chair across from his desk.

These things done, he came to stand behind his desk and glance down at his open appointment book. Hers was the first name, Barbara Wilson. His gaze drifted to the couch. It had a special meaning this morning. He went over to it and picked up a bit of lint.

❍

Earlier the same morning, alone at the crest of Kalcheck's Hill, the Sheriff of Leelanau County greeted the day.

"Damn it, Hoss, you're one stupid son-of-a-bitch."

He'd just stopped his car on the dirt track at the hill's highest point and turned off the ignition. He shook his head in disbelief. Why had he let it happen? He knew Marti's tricks. She'd always treated him like a large, harmless bear she could lead about by the nose.

He heaved his near three hundred pounds and six foot four frame up and out the door and stood beside the patrol car. The car's springs groaned gratefully. Reaching back inside, he got the thermos of coffee K.D. had made for him and walked to the front of the car. With his back to the grill, he slid up onto the hood, the car bowing down deeply under his weight like a camel kneeling to take on a rider.

Here he was again on Kalcheck's Hill. At earlier times, he'd come up here to ponder the important decisions of his life - which football scholarship to take, the U or State, dare he ask K.D. to marry him, should he run for sheriff. The broad panorama from the hill always helped him put things in perspective.

He unscrewed the top of the thermos and poured the steaming coffee. Sipping it, he scanned the Lake Michigan coastline to the north, where the yellow sand of Gill's Point fell three hundred feet straight down into the cold, blue water, then on along the wooded hills broken by the lighter green patches of the cherry orchards, to the village of Leland, where he'd lived all his life save for the college years. His gaze rested here. He couldn't see the village itself—intervening hills blocked his view—but the long, rounded hill called the Whaleback placed it. From out on the lake, the whale looked like it was about to devour Leland and all those living there.

Hell, he admitted to himself, once again it was a decision that brought him up to the hill. He didn't like to admit it, but there was a question on his mind--could he allow himself to cheat on K.D.?

Hoss Davis finished the coffee and automatically poured another cup. Thoughts of the previous night intruded even as he tried to close the door on them. Marti had called the Sheriff's office asking for him, claiming she'd seen a prowler run across her yard and duck behind the barn. Learning that Hoss wasn't at the office, she'd called him at home. He'd answered and listened to her plea for him to come immediately to her place. With misgivings, he'd gone, not telling K.D. where he was going.

Driving last night to Marti's farm he'd thought about how unpredictable she'd always been when they were kids, saying or doing something aimed at making him uncomfortable. The memory of the ninth grade sex-ed class flashed to mind, Marti asking in mock innocence, "Mrs. Moore, is the size of a man's penis proportional to the rest of his body? If it is, Hoss must have a whopper!" A shock of embarrassment still ran through him after all these years.

At that time he didn't know that her taunts were as close as she could let herself come to open affection. He'd only felt diminished by her agile mind, thinking he was a prototypical "prove" - a name she'd coined for intransigent provincials.

Marti left town immediately after graduating from high school. A couple of years later her father, mother and younger brother moved to Texas. Four months ago, everyone who'd known

Marti was very surprised when she returned and paid cash for the old Johansen farm on Swede Road. She lived there alone now and painted.

Last night, not knowing what to expect, he'd parked next to her frame farmhouse and got out of his patrol car. The nearly full moon lit the scene except for deep shadows alongside the barn. He shined his flashlight at an elevated shape near the barn door but saw that it was only long grass growing around part of a long-abandoned hay rake. He spent the next ten minutes searching the inside of the barn. There was no sign of an intruder.

As he searched, he became more suspicious that he'd been called there for a purpose other than the one Marti claimed. Hesitantly, he climbed the steps to the screened porch. Marti, watching him from the darkness of the porch, pushed the door open before he could knock. She was as exotically beautiful to him as ever, so different from any other woman.

"Evening, Hoss. Thanks for coming."

Not knowing what else to say, Hoss remarked on the obvious. "Hi Marti, I didn't see anyone around the barn."

"Must have been my imagination. C'mon in."

This was what he had feared—and, in part, why he'd come.

Marti turned on the light switch and Hoss saw that she was on crutches, her left leg in a cast. He also noticed a number of paintings lined up on the porch along the outer wall of the house. He had never seen any of her paintings before and they caught his attention before he could frame a question about her leg. He let his eye travel from one canvas to the next. She waited, watching him for his reaction. Hoss took several steps along the line.

"I like these," he said, meaning it.

Each canvas produced a feeling difficult for him to define, a yearning for something lost. Each was an incomplete statement reaching out to the viewer for help with its completion. Hoss felt this strongly and was visibly moved and it pleased her.

"Do you sell them?" He asked and immediately felt foolish. "I mean are they for sale?"

Marti smiled: the same old Hoss, painfully uncomfortable in her presence.

"When I need money, I pack a couple of them up and send them to a gallery in New York that shows my work. Believe it or not, there are actually a few people who are collectors."

"You don't sell them locally, then?"

"No. Well, actually, I did sell one, or rather the Suttons Bay Rotary Club sold one at a fund-raising affair. But, the answer to your question is really, no. And, they're not for sale to you either." She couldn't help teasing him; it came naturally.

Hoss searched her face, afraid he'd just been rebuffed.

"I'd like to give you one. That's what I mean."

Hoss laughed lightly, relieved. Their eyes made a warm contact, reviving old feelings between them. She turned and entered the house, swinging gracefully on the crutches and saying, "You'll have to choose one … in the daylight."

He picked up the meaning in that easy statement. It said that he would be coming here again, coming to take a part of her and carry it away. He next thought of K.D. She didn't like Marti - had not liked her since school. People came down hard on either side of the line about liking Marti Jensen. The majority thought that liking her was like making a pact with the devil. Hoss saw no evil in her, only an inability to compromise, but if devil she was, the devil had a lot to offer.

Marti paused at the doorway to the living room and flipped the switch. She stood so that Hoss had to brush against her as he passed. She smiled up at him as he uncomfortably edged by. Hoss noticed there were fine wrinkles now at the corners of her dark brown eyes. This was the only sign that her age was the same as his, forty-two. Her hair was still jet black, without any of the gray that was rapidly gaining a majority share on his head. One thing he was sure of: she'd made no effort to cover any gray. To shun artifice had always been Marti's salient attitude.

Hoss turned from her dizzying closeness and saw that a bottle of wine and two glasses were on the table in front of the couch.

"I can't stay," he said quickly, "I've got to get on home."

She'd swung around to face him. "Oh come on, not one little glass?"

"I'm sorry, I can't." His head spun with the possibilities and the dangers.

She knew this, of course, and moving closer to him while looking into his eyes, reached forward at the level of her waist and touched him.

Hoss didn't move. He felt paralyzed, only conscious of her touch and his growing erection. Here were both the realization of countless hours of adolescent dreaming and the most dangerous threat to his present life.

"I can't," he choked and put out his arm and gently but firmly pushed her away. He left after that, with Marti talking comfortably about his coming back to pick out his painting.

This morning, on Kalcheck's Hill, the memory of the night before caused him to move uneasily, to put the cup down and lean forward with both hands on the hood of the car. His thoughts turned to K.D., at home earlier in the morning, how she moved about the kitchen making breakfast. There had been nothing in twenty-three years about which he couldn't be completely truthful with her. He didn't like his furtive guilt as he watched her unguarded devotion to their partnership. He poured more of the hot coffee and brought the cup to his lips, steam momentarily obscuring the unsullied landscape before him. As the view cleared, so did his thinking. What he had with K.D. was too precious to risk on a few adventurous moments. To drive Marti from his mind, he deliberately turned his thoughts to the distasteful job that lay ahead of him.

During breakfast, David Wick, his youngest deputy, had called to tell him that the clerk at the Mobil station in Suttons Bay had reported to Kate Schott, the night dispatcher, that someone had driven away from the station without paying. Seventeen dollars worth of gas. The deputy on duty hadn't done anything about it because he thought Hoss might want to handle this himself.

"Why so?" Hoss asked.

"Because the guy the clerk fingered is your buddy, Swifthawk."

Hoss felt instant irritation. "She was sure he was the guy?"

"Kate got the plate number and checked it out. Swifthawk's car all right."

"But, did the clerk actually see him?" Hoss persisted.

"No. She said she looked out and saw someone pumping gas, but he stayed down low behind the car."

"That's what I thought," Hoss sighed. He looked at his watch. It was a quarter to six. "I'll go out there myself before I come in to the office. Anything else?"

"Sam Bostick drunk and disorderly at The Happy Hour, and Mrs. Marcie Crawford reported that one of Frank Bishop's German shepherds took a crap in her vegetable garden."

"In the middle of the night?"

"She said she'd been debating all day whether or not to report it. She made up her mind at one A.M."

Hoss chuckled. "See you in a while, Dave."

Kalcheck's Hill was on the way to the Chippewa reservation where Harry Swifthawk lived. That's what had started Hoss off in the direction of the hill; the need to sort through his conflicting feelings over Marti's offer was what had him, now, perched on the hood of the Leelanau County Sheriff's car. Nothing had happened last night— nothing on his part—except not stopping her right away. That and leaving the door open for another time.

Hoss shook out the remains of the coffee from the cup and screwed it back on the thermos. He felt better having decided to decline Marti's offer, but deep down he sensed his decision was malleable. She would have something to say about it, yet. He was not an irresolute man, but Marti Jensen was a worm in his brain.

From the crest of the hill, the land of the Leelanau Peninsula slopes gently away from Lake Michigan eastward five miles then rises in a long sandy ridge before falling sharply to the shore of Grand Traverse Bay and the reservation. The countryside of the peninsula alternates between deep hardwood stands and cherry, peach, and apple orchards. At regular intervals neat, old, white clapboard farmhouses give evidence that the beautiful and varied landscape came at the price of very hard work. Hoss knew this well. He had grown up in a four-generation family of farmers. He glanced now with a critical eye along the even lines of cherry trees that he passed. The spring had been slow in coming and so was the development of the fruit, but there had been no late, hard frost and the blossoms had set well. The prospect was solid for a good crop. A fruit-damaging hailstorm still remained a possibility, but the odds were against it.

Hoss loved this place and his job. Privately, he thought of himself as the protector and friend of every person in the county - all of those who'd allow it. Some didn't. At the head of that short list stood Harry Swifthawk, a guy who seemed to take a special delight in provoking Hoss. The book on Harry was he'd been a troubled kid whose father had been murdered by an unknown killer. Hoss wondered what it would be like growing up with that baggage.

A new, elaborately painted sign on Highway 22 proclaimed to the world and to Sheriff Davis that one was entering the reservation of the Grand Traverse Band of Ottawa and Chippewa Indians. In all, the reservation covered about one square mile, with most of the five hundred or so tribal members living in the village of Peshawbestown. For many years that sleepy village had consisted of only one small store, a five-room school, a church, a garage for the fire truck and a scattering of small, frame houses and mobile homes, many in need of repair. The non-Indian community that surrounded it, a community which, for the most part, knew little of and cared less about the Native Americans living in their midst, had dismissed the reservation as irrelevant.

Then came the gambling casino and with it came radical change. Hoss passed this way often, yet each time the new construction surprised him. This morning he scanned the main street for any familiar member of the Tribal Council. Through an understanding between tribal and county law enforcement, Hoss could question people on the reservation without the permission of the Tribal Council. Still, he preferred to touch base with one of the members before proceeding to Swifthawk's place. The reservation was not his jurisdiction. A few tribal cops took care of the small stuff; serious matters belonged to the FBI. The scene of the gasoline theft, however, was in Hoss's territory. If he were to arrest Swifthawk or even bring him into Leland for questioning, he'd first need to get a warrant. Sometimes getting cooperation from the Tribal Council involved much foot-dragging—not that he didn't understand their feeling. How many hours in the past had Chippewas stood in line waiting for their rightful claims to be heard? But today Hoss only intended to pay Harry Swifthawk a "social call."

Standing outside the new Gaming Commission building were just the men Hoss needed. He pulled the patrol car off the pavement, rolled down the window and waved. Charlie McNab and William Blackbird walked over. Blackbird was the Gaming Commissioner and both men were on the Council.

Hoss pointed, "Armani sunglasses? Give me a break, Charlie!"

"I'm just beginning to find the style that suits me, Hoss."

"What about you, Will, I suppose you're wearing Ralph Lauren undershorts."

"Those are for my kids, man. I get mine tailored in London. My tailor could do a lot for that drab uniform of yours, Hoss."

"Speaking of kids," Hoss said, "I read in The Clarion that your daughter has gone on a dig in Peru for the summer."

"Isn't that something. The things a kid will do to dodge a little digging right here in her mother's garden." His tone became more serious. "Where you headed, Hoss?"

"I need to have a talk with Harry Swifthawk, if I find him at home."

"What's he charged with now?" asked Charlie McNab.

"There's no formal charge at the moment. It's just that his car was identified as a non-paying drive-away from the Mobil station in Suttons Bay last night. I'd like to talk to him about it—informally. If I need to go further, I'll bring it to the Council, of course." He hesitated for a moment, and then said, "I've always wondered if that's his real name. I mean, Swifthawk is kinda, well…."

"Heroic?" supplied Will Blackbird.

"That's the word."

Charlie laughed, "If a man says it's his name, then I guess it's his name."

"Hey, why not," Hoss agreed. "See you guys later, I've got to go see me a Swifthawk."

"Good luck," chuckled Charlie.

That had been easy. He had checked in with the Council and got a tacit blessing to interrogate Harry without having to disturb the waters. He turned left off the highway and onto a dirt road passing the empty shed that had once served as everything to do with the government of the reservation from meeting hall to fire engine garage. Its various functions were now carried on in several state-of-the-art structures nearer the casino.

The road narrowed to a mere sand track and off to the right stood the weed-embraced, decrepit trailer where Harry lived with his former brother-in-law, Buddy. Hoss had been here many times before.

As soon as he turned off the ignition, Hoss heard Harry's mongrel, Yellow, coming at him. It had been lying in front of a sagging, wooden garage, but sprang up and dashed at the patrol car, barking and snapping at the air, a most convincing warning to anyone with an idea of setting foot in the yard. This loud threat of flesh tearing segued gradually into a general baying at the sky accompanied by stolen glances at the patrol car. Anyone in the trailer would know Hoss was here, but no one called off the dog. Hoss got out and stood. Yellow continued his threat, but moved away just enough to make a slow walk to the trailer possible. Hoss knocked on the screen door, while his eyes were drawn to the cigar butt being used to plug a hole in it.

Harry slowly emerged from the gloom of the trailer's interior and faced Hoss through the tattered screen, wearing only drooping jockey shorts, socks and a reversed cap. "Hoss Davis! What would bring so much man out to my pore little house so early in the morning?"

"Good morning, Harry. I think you know why I'm here."

"I think I do at that. I was just sayin' to Buddy here," he glanced back into the dark room. "I said, the only thing'ud bring Hoss out here at six in the morning is ta tell me those folks in Leland have voted me Grand Marshall of the Fourth of July parade this year."

Hoss smiled. "Maybe they have, Harry, but I'm here to have a little talk about gasoline."

"Gasoline? Well now, I can't help you there. We never use that stuff here on the rez. Rub sticks together. Make'em much fire." He raised his hand and Hoss saw that it held a can of Bud. "Step in, Hoss. I'll get you a beer an' you can tell me about this…fire-water."

Hoss knew better than to go inside. Once there and out of sight, Harry could and probably would claim the Leelanau County

Sheriff had beaten him up right in his own home. Buddy would confirm it. Hoss looked around. Outside another mobile home not fifty yards away, an old woman, who'd probably been unable to sleep longer, hoed a flowerbed. She'd make a better witness to their meeting.

"C'mon outside, Harry. It's too nice a day to sit inside. I'll skip the beer, too."

"Suit yourself. Be a minute." Harry stepped away from the door.

Hoss knew the next part would be what Harry relished-– the real reason he had stolen the gasoline—it would be Harry's attempt to make a fool of him. Hoss reminded himself that Harry was good at provoking impotent anger.

Harry came out of the trailer door pulling on a pair of dirty jeans. He'd looked better behind the veil of the screen. In the morning light, his bare skin had a sickly pallor. His powerful physique had gone slack, yet there was haughtiness in his erect posture and his long hair, held together by a leather band, was as clean, black and shiny as obsidian. He motioned toward a flimsy aluminum lawn chair.

"Sit down, Hoss."

Hoss eyed the chair. His three hundred pounds had once flattened a chair just like it. "Let's lean. Come over to the patrol car and we can lean."

"Hey, cool. I can tell the guys at the casino that Sheriff Hoss Davis came by and we leaned together."

Harry followed Hoss to the car, where Harry hoisted himself easily onto the hood. Despite his self-neglect and abuse, Harry was strong and agile.

Hoss took off his sunglasses and rubbed his eyes. "We got a report that you filled up at the Mobil station in Suttons Bay and drove off without paying."

"Report from who?"

"The clerk at the station."

"I guess that little gal made a big mistake," smiled Harry.

"I didn't say anything about a gal. How'd you know the clerk was female?"

Harry shot back, "Don't pull that Detective Columbo shit on me, Hoss. Everyone knows a woman works the night shift at that station."

The Sheriff grinned at Harry. "Who said it happened at night? What were you doing last night, by the way?" Hoss knew Harry had a story ready to cover, and Harry knew he knew it.

"Here. Partying all night with Buddy."

"Small party."

"Coupla them gals came down for a while." Harry gestured with the beer can in the general direction of the casino.

"Those women have names?"

"Sure. Debbie or Darlene or Donna or Diane. Didn't pay much attention. They don't use their real names, anyway."

Hoss decided to end the useless interrogation. "You didn't do any driving—that's what you're telling me?"

"That's it." Hoss knew what was coming next. "Couldn't have gone far, anyway. Tank's empty." He gestured toward the red '93 Bonneville. "You can check the gas gauge if you want. I'll get the keys." He slid down off the patrol car.

"Don't bother, Harry." Hoss knew the gas had already been siphoned into Buddy's pick-up. The hose was still hanging over the tailgate where a careless throw had left it.

"Too bad you didn't think of using Buddy's truck. I'll bet the tank's full."

Harry's deed was intended as a provocation. Nothing could be done; there was no one who could identify him. Just a plate number, and it would be elementary courtroom procedure to make the station attendant admit she could have been mistaken. "Was it dark outside, Miss?" etc. The thing Hoss wanted to do was to spoil Harry's fun.

"You're really wasting yourself on this petty shit, Harry. It doesn't take a 'swift hawk' to steal gasoline from a little girl at night." He opened the door of the cruiser and got in. "You could be using your brains to help solve some of the real problems we got here."

Harry's anger flared. "That'll be the day—when you want any help from a lazy Indian!"

"You said it, I didn't. And just try me some time."

Hoss backed the patrol car up and turned it around. As he headed back out the sandy track, Harry let the can of Bud fly at the side of his trailer. Glancing up at the rear view mirror, Hoss saw Buddy come to the door to see what was happening.

Frustrated, Hoss drove south along the water toward the village of Suttons Bay. What had he accomplished? He admitted to himself that his crack about it not taking a swift hawk to rip off a little girl was childish. Harry had gotten to him once again. Now, Harry, stung by the remark, might just feel obliged to retaliate. Great!

Hoss decided he'd better drive by the Mobil station and explain the situation to Wes Haldeck, the owner, before heading toward the Sheriff's office in Leland. Wes would have to take the loss. Seventeen dollars. It was small, but it would stick in his throat. Hoss had known Wes a long time and knew him to be a volatile guy, one who could easily turn his frustrated anger against a messenger of bad news.

He certainly didn't need that today. A lot of dumb complaints had been lodged against him and the Sheriff's Department lately. K.D. was philosophical about it. She put it down to some people needing to cast a wide net to find someone to blame for their displeasure. The problem for Hoss was that he was facing re-election.

The main cause of the growing displeasure in the county was the conflict between those who saw the peninsula's bucolic beauty as a great opportunity for land development and those who were determined to keep it pristine and unchanged.

Hoss had ridden into office when just such a wave of dissatisfaction had swept Leonard Potter from his job. There couldn't have been a more dedicated public servant than Len, smart and effective too. It was at a time when things began changing in Leelanau County. An increase in population had brought with it an increase in crime. Leonard Potter, the sheriff, must be the one to blame, and here, running against him, came Hilyard "Hoss" Davis— young, university-educated, local high school sports hero, well liked, from good local stock and an impressive physical presence. Goodbye Leonard Potter.

A joke circulated at the time that two deputies could be laid off just because of Hoss's intimidating size and strength. Because of his size, his schoolmates had long ago hung the nickname of the character from the old Bonanza TV series on him. Hoss had welcomed it. He never saw himself as a Hilyard.

As Hoss approached the blinker light at the northern end of Suttons Bay, he imagined how Wes Haldeck was going to react when told he was out seventeen bucks. It was one thing to be alone with Wes as he poured forth his anger, but quite another to have this happen in front of the gas station's early morning customers, ones who were sure to repeat the story at the barber shop or over a Rotary lunch. Abruptly, Hoss turned the car sharply to the right at the intersection and onto the road to Leland and the Sheriff's Office. He'd call Wes later. If there were only a way to do it, he'd gladly take out his own wallet and pay for the gas.

Leland traffic had doubled in the last month and would triple by July fourth. Some residents wanted a light installed at the main intersection to handle the summer congestion. It would make only the second light in the county, the other was at the southern border with Traverse City, a city of forty thousand.

Winter slumber shaken off, Leland hurried to get ready for the summer influx from the hot and crowded cities to the south: Detroit, Chicago and Cincinnati.

Hoss spotted Jack Taylor walking along Main Street and waved. Jack had fled from a harried life in a leading Chicago law firm and set up a gourmet bread bakery here in town. When he turned into River Street, Hoss noticed that Barclay Scott, back from wintering in Ecuador, had the "Open" sign out in front of the Riverside Inn. The inn, a two-block walk from the Sheriff's Department, was Hoss's favorite place for lunch. On a fine day such as today, he'd eat a sandwich on the bench down beside the Carp River.

Hoss's territory was home to a lot of good people. Sometimes, though, even these good people got themselves into trouble. He wanted to go on helping them get untangled from those troubles as long as they'd let him—hopefully well past the coming primary election.

He parked in the reserved space at the rear of the new office building and, entering through the rear door, walked straight through to the dispatcher's desk where he placed both hands flat on its surface and began reading the log of the previous night.

Deputy Wick came and stood beside him. "How'd it go with Harry Swifthawk?"

"Not much I could do without positive ID, except let him know we know he did it. That, of course, is just what he intended, thumb his nose at us while we can't prove a damn thing. If he were anyone else, we could haul him in for questioning. That scares most people into a confession, but Harry would love to have us try that. The son-of-a-gun knows we have a weak case and we'd come out looking like the bad guys."

"Haldeck's called already to see what's being done," Wick interjected. "I told him you were going up to the reservation personally. He told me he was going to call Dreisbach's office too."

Peter Dreisbach was the County Prosecutor. Hoss wanted to talk to him about the situation with Haldeck, but he knew that Pete, a night person, wouldn't arrive at his office for at least another hour.

"Good ole Swifthawk," Hoss thought, "If you only knew just how much trouble you were already causing me you'd be throwing another party."

David interrupted these thoughts. "There's a note that a woman named Jensen was trying to get in touch with you. She thought there was a prowler on her property. Did she reach you?"

David didn't know that Hoss had gone to high school with Marti. Hoss stiffened. He'd heard Wick's innocent question, instead, as a knowing reference to his lust. He caught himself and tried to make his reply sound detached.

"Yeah, and I went out there and looked around. Saw nothing. I guess a woman living alone can get spooked from time to time."

He thought of what he'd just said. Had he unintentionally set up an excuse, here at the office, to go to her farm again?

David, young and eager to be a good deputy, idolized Hoss and hung on his every word as a revelation of wisdom. He filed away Hoss's observation on womanhood.

"Morning, Hoss," sang out his secretary as he walked toward her desk. "Mr. Kammer from Alliance Radar is waiting to see you."

Matronly Florence Schaub was very pleasant in person and on the phone. Her other secretarial skills were plain lousy. Hoss had once considered replacing her but discovered she had built up such a fan club among those who had regular business with his office that firing her would have been very unpopular—as big a mistake as the firing of long-time Detroit Tiger radio announcer Ernie Harwel.

"At ten, you have to be available for Judge Burdick's court." She looked up from her notes. "That's about the boy who set fire to the school bus. The file is on your desk."

Hoss was pretty sure it would be the wrong file.

"At eleven you have an interview with Keith Hansen for the job of inland lake deputy. Then you have nothing until three, when there's a hearing on the widening of Bingham Road. Howard wants you to attend."

"Bingham Township Hall?"

"Yes."

A normal day. He moved his massive body through the doorway to his roomy new office, leaving an invisible wake of air turbulence behind him.

❍

Again he looked at his watch. Barbara Wilson was five minutes late. Had he been mistaken? He had hoped she'd be early, and just as eager as he was. He paced back and forth across his inner office, glancing absently out of the large window at the expanse of Grand Traverse Bay. Was that…? Yes, it was the outer door leading into his waiting room. She was here. It meant he'd read her reaction correctly; she wanted it too. Damn, he was nervous! He must calm himself. Don't ruin it by being anxious and awkward. He paused with his hand on the doorknob. He took a deep steadying breath then opened the door. She was standing there smiling at him. He saw it as a very willing smile.

❍

There was no doubt about it, Benjamin Wilson decided: his wife was getting ready to leave him. Her attitude had changed, especially in the last week, and at breakfast this morning it had become clear. He knew who was behind it. It wasn't just advice she'd been getting from that damned shrink! The thought enraged him. He couldn't live with the humiliation of losing her to another man.

❍

Hoss Davis the great American Hero. Bull Shit! More like white man's ass wipe. Hired goon. Hired to protect all of them and all they've stolen from us. "Stealing money from little girls." That was a good one, Hoss!

He poured a half-tumbler of Jim Beam and took a full swallow. Soon the big pig wouldn't be feeling so superior. He had something planned that would show up Hoss and his play police for the bumbling retards they were.

"You won't be calling this 'petty shit'," he said aloud to the empty trailer.

CHAPTER 2

"Oh, God" he gasped. "Breathe, damn it! Breathe! Don't die!"

It happened so quickly—so easily. He sank back, drained and sick. He looked down at her. Could it really be, so easily? Shit! He'd only wanted to stop her shouting. He had to get control of his feelings. CPR, that's what he had to do! He stretched her body out and knelt beside it, pinching her nose closed with his left hand and pulling down on her jaw to open her mouth with his right. He leaned over to blow into her mouth, then … he stopped.

What the hell was he thinking? He couldn't afford to revive her. She would tell everyone what had happened. He pictured himself on TV, being led to a patrol car by a cop. Not that!

He got up and looked down at her. He had to think. There was only one way now. He had to get rid of the body. He had to think this through.

"No mistakes," he said aloud.

She had stopped hearing.

❍

Hoss bit the bullet and called Wes Haldeck at his gas station. A few seconds of listening to Wes and he congratulated himself on being wise enough to avoid Wes's outrage in a public place. "It's not the money, it's the principle!" Wes shouted. He was going to fight for his principles. "If a man doesn't stand up for his principles, what is he worth?" Listening patiently, Hoss reflected that Wes had told him once that Braveheart was his favorite movie.

❍

At ten forty-five, Peter Dreisbach looked up from his desk at Hoss with the expression of a man who just reached a level of cognitive functioning to permit conversation with another human.

"I don't suppose," said Hoss, "anyone has told you yet about Harry Swifthawk's latest mooning of constitutional authority. No, of course they haven't or you wouldn't have that look of a babe just awakened."

"Hoss, I don't want to hear one word about that arm wrestling the two of you are addicted to. You always find some way of dragging me in to play referee." He wasn't just feigning irritation.

"The 'dragging in' you're referring to is also called acting as the County Prosecutor," Hoss retorted. "I know you'd rather have head lice than have to prosecute a Native American in an election year—not a correct image—but Wes Haldeck is reluctant to wait until after the election to be paid for the gas Swifthawk ripped off last night."

Dreisbach clasped his hands, wedged them between his knees and sighed. "Let's hear it."

Hoss began the tale and in the end Pete agreed to have a go at placating Haldeck. The issue could become a public opinion nightmare for him and he sure as hell didn't want to have to prosecute Harry Swifthawk, without an airtight case - not for seventeen bucks worth of gas.

An hour later, Hoss was allowing himself a beer with lunch on the bench behind the Riverside Inn. Duncan, the chef, had to bring it to him personally, because the teen-age waitress who'd taken his order wasn't old enough to serve alcohol. Dunc sat for a while and reviewed where he and his wife, Ariel, had wintered - Guaymas this year. A momentary wave of feeling very dull and very place-bound passed over Hoss.

This thought of the provincial nature of his life brought Marti Jensen to mind. What had she done and seen in those years she'd lived away? There had been a few reports from those who had chanced to come upon her - New York City, Boulder, Oaxaca. And, there had been plenty of rumors to fill in the gaps. Hoss had always been inordinately interested in both.

He suddenly smiled, thinking of Marti's performance on graduation day. She was all set to march into the auditorium barefoot. That, of course, had been quickly vetoed. It was 1979 and the authorities at Leland High had no doubt about what was acceptable and proper. She'd been forced to march in like the rest with her shoes on. But, when she climbed to the stage to deliver the valedictory speech, the shoes were draped around her neck, laces tied together. The speech had been a call to each graduate to "throw off the life-constricting lies learned at home, church and this Paleozoic school", and to force a change of "our corrupt so-called democratic government which presumes to crush the legitimate aspirations of the Nicaraguan people." Reverberations from that speech could still be detected in the school's old masonry. She was sure different from the rest of us kids. Different from her own family too.

So lost was he in this memory, that he walked a block past his office building. He managed to suppress further thoughts about Marti by promising himself they could be revived again when his workday was over.

Entering the building, Hoss heard a loud bass voice coming from the dispatcher's office. Shorty McQuade was holding forth. Barrel-chested, biceps stretching the short sleeves of his uniform shirt, Shorty looked as strong as he was. The slack seat of his pants betrayed him, however, as a post-sixty male. David Wicks, Russell Preva and Donna Roper—one of the department's two female deputies—made up his audience. Spotting his boss enter, Shorty included him.

"I was sayin, Hoss, that I coulda made the Department's budget for the month with the tickets I coulda handed out down at the 204-22 intersection. When you gonna let me start handin' out paper?"

"Give'em a few more days of seeing you there, Shorty. Let word get around we intend people to really stop at that intersection, then you can show them you've got more in that patrol car than paperbacks."

"I saw Shorty reading once." chimed in Russell Preva leaning his thin frame against a doorjamb. "Trouble was, the book was upside down."

"Now, everybody knows that's a damn lie," Shorty snapped back, "cause you don't know up from down."

The phone rang and Wick picked it up. "Leelanau County Sheriff's Department." As he listened, a sober look displaced his amusement at the banter. "What did you say your name was?" he asked after listening for half a minute, "Address?" He began making notes. "You say she saw her psychiatrist? And what is his name? Derek Marsh. What school was your daughter at? Pathfinder School." He listened again. "What kind of car was she driving? ... No sir, we haven't had an accident reported." Wick's voice was tense. "What number can we reach you at?" All those in the office had ceased talking and were listening. "We'll call you back, sir. Goodbye."

Dave Wick turned to face Hoss. "Guy named Benjamin Wilson is reporting his wife, Dr. Barbara Wilson, missing." He consulted his notes. "She was supposed to pick up their five year old daughter from the pre-school at Pathfinder at eleven-thirty. She never showed. Says this is completely unlike her. He was called by the school just after twelve and told his wife hadn't come, and the daughter was still at the school. He called his wife's office and was told she normally made rounds at the hospital in the morning and wasn't scheduled to come in to the office until two o'clock. He called the hospital, but she hadn't signed in there either. After that he went to the school and brought his daughter back home—that's in Elmwood Township—then he started calling friends to see if his wife was at one of their homes. No one had seen her. Seems she has an appointment every Tuesday morning with a psychiatrist—." He consulted his notes. "—Doctor Derek Marsh at eight forty-five and leaves his office at nine-thirty. Mr. Wilson called the doc, who said she had been there as scheduled, but he knew nothing that would explain her absence." Wick looked up at Hoss. "That's when Wilson decided to call here."

Hoss stood looking out the window, deep in thought. "I don't like the sound of it," he said finally. "Mothers don't forget to pick up five-year-olds."

"What if she got caught up shopping or maybe she had car trouble?" Preva argued.

"No, Hoss is right," put in Donna Roper. "The mother of a young child wouldn't let herself get that caught up, and if she'd had car trouble she would have called her husband or the school."

"OK, but what if she's a run-away wife and mother. She'd know the school would eventually call her husband to pick up the kid?"

"That's a point, Russ," allowed Hoss.

"I think I know this Dr. Wilson," said Shorty. "Pretty sure she's the neurologist who saw me when I had that dizzy spell last fall. Laboritis, she called it."

Preva looked puzzled. "Laboritis?"

"That's what she said I had. At first, I thought she meant that I was allergic to work."

"Right there's another argument against her being a run-away," put in Hoss. "Being a doctor, she has responsibilities to her patients and office staff. I feel strongly that we've got to treat this very seriously."

"Where's the psychiatrist's office?" asked Donna.

"Traverse City. Wilson didn't mention the address," Wick answered.

She slid off the desk where she'd been sitting and walked over to another desk and got the Yellow Pages.

"What kind of car was it?" asked Hoss.

"'03 Chrysler Town and Country, dark green."

"License number?"

Wick reddened. "I didn't get that."

Shorty sat at the computer. "What's their address? I'll get it."

Wick, relieved that he wouldn't have to call Benjamin Wilson back and ask for this elementary piece of information, read off the Wilson's street address.

"There should be no jurisdictional problem here," Hoss said. "Although the disappearance or its cause may have happened in Traverse City, Dr. Wilson is a resident of our county."

"Plus, he called us," put in Preva.

"The shrink's office is at 200 Bayside Parkway," said Donna Roper, closing the phone book. "I think that's the Peninsular Power Company's office building."

"It would take under ten minutes to get to Pathfinder School from there - plenty of time to get the kid." Hoss was talking aloud to himself.

"XGA 196," Shorty called out from the computer.

"Good. Dave, how many cars are out?" asked Hoss.

"Two."

"Call them with the description of the car, then call the Traverse City Police, Grand Traverse County Sheriff and the State Police with the information and request a BOLO for the car and Dr. Wilson. Donna, call Mr. Wilson and set up an interview. Tell him we need a recent photo. As soon as you get it, have copies faxed to the other agencies. And, when you talk to him, verify her regular schedule for this morning. Russ, check accident reports in Traverse City, then you and Shorty go down to the Elmwood area— divide it up and do a search. Donna, I've got to go to a Road Commission meeting at the Bingham Township Hall at three. Meet me there afterwards and fill me in on what we've learned." He paused, then said dead seriously, "Listen up guys, I have a dark hunch this is big time trouble, let's all have our heads up … big time."

CHAPTER 3

IF THERE WAS ONE THING Donna Roper did trust, it was her reading of a man. There was no doubt about this one. As a saleswoman for Kellogg she had endured his type many times—smiled and endured. Surely Benjamin Wilson must be deeply worried about his missing wife, but what was coming through loud and clear to Donna was his effort to impress her. Hell, he was hitting on her!

Much of her adult life, Donna had been an audience of one for similar performances, all aimed at persuading her that the man was a great guy who deserved her sympathy or admiration. A large percentage had but one motive. As with Mexican street vendors, there were times one was interested, but the constant pitch became tiring. She hadn't expected to run into it here, today, in these circumstances.

"Nothing like this has happened before. My wife is a very responsible person." He was trying to put sincerity in his voice, but he missed the mark. Donna had talked to others with missing loved ones. They'd sounded and acted very differently.

"How long have you known your wife, Mr. Wilson?"

"Nearly seven years. Seven great years." His look asked Donna to imagine how great seven years with him must have been. She managed a strained smile.

"And, you've been married for..."

"Six wonderful years."

Donna hurried on. "She's your only child?" she asked, glancing at the towheaded girl sitting on the porch steps out of range of their conversation. She was making bubbles that fascinated and excited her tan Labrador puppy.

"Yes, she's our treasure."

"What have you told her?"

"I said Barbara had to take care of a patient and that's why I came to pick her up from school. I've arranged for her to go to her best friend's house for dinner and a sleepover tonight. I'm afraid ... you know, phone calls and all.... "

"Yes, I understand," Donna, said. She came back to the marriage. "Has there been any recent disagreement between you and your wife?"

"No," he smiled, "You mean did we have a tiff this morning and she's off teaching me a lesson by making me worry? No, nothing like that."

Donna began to speak, but he waved this away, "You don't have to apologize for the suggestion that we were having trouble. I know it's the kind of thing you people have to do."

She forced another smile.

"Oh," he said, getting up suddenly, "You wanted a picture of Barbara."

Donna watched him leave. He looked to be in his mid-fifties and earlier in the interview he'd said his wife was thirty-four. She wondered where they'd met and why a woman physician would be attracted to him. He was below the line by Donna's standards: grimy complexion, forty pounds overweight and decidedly arrogant. On what was he basing this sure opinion of himself?

Whoa! She caught herself. This tendency of hers to delve beyond the limit of a specific assignment was out of control again. Hoss had sat her down just last month and given her an avuncular tutorial on this issue. She was here to get a photograph of the missing doctor and to prod Benjamin Wilson to search his memory for anything that would explain his wife's whereabouts—period.

Upon reaching his study, Wilson picked up the photo that was lying on top of his desk, one his wife's brother had taken when they'd visited him in Asheville last March. She was holding a paper plate of picnic fare, looking at the camera and saying something, laughing. Clearly, she was fond of her brother and her manner in the photo was free and joyful. When Wilson had received the call from this deputy, saying she wanted a recent photograph, he'd known immediately the one he wanted the police to have.

From his study he could look out onto the porch and examine Deputy Roper. She was not the sort of cop he'd thought he'd be talking to and it had him off balance. On her, the deputy's uniform was anything but masculine. She was tall and had the flowing sleekness and broad shoulders of a swimmer. Before this moment, the sight of a woman's hands had never turned him on. Hers were large with long tapering fingers that seemed to have an impatient life of their own, graceful and sensual. He'd stared at her hands, because he found her large, frank, brown eyes more than he could meet directly. As she talked to his daughter, Donna's quick, radiant smile and responsive laugh thrilled him. The light striking the side of her oval face modeled it, accenting the clean line of her jaw and determined chin. The only compromise she made to her professional identity was to wear her chestnut hair pulled back and gathered in a French braid. She excited him, all right. He was aware of it and cautioned himself. His behavior must look to be consistent with but one concern, his wife's whereabouts.

Wilson returned to the porch with the photograph. He held it out and watched one of her amazing hands receive it.

"It's the most recent; taken last spring."

Donna fought the impulse to look into the photograph for clues to answer the questions she'd already formed about this couple.

She reminded herself, the picture was for identification purposes only.

"Mr. Wilson, I know you've searched your mind for all the places your wife could have gone and you've drawn a blank. Many times, when a person is asked a question like this, they think of major destinations and overlook the small everyday thing, an appointment perhaps."

Wilson acted as if he were concentrating, searching his memory. "Yeah, I know the kind of thing you mean," he said, then threw in quickly, "That didn't happen, by the way. I mean she didn't mention an appointment other than with her psychiatrist." He shook his head, adding, "No, I'm sure nothing like that happened this morning. No unusual message from her that meant a break in routine."

"How about medical problems, something which would have required immediate attention, or could have even incapacitated her?"

"Like epilepsy? No, nothing. She was—that is, she is in perfect health."

"How much cash would you estimate she was carrying?"

"Not much. Everything she buys goes on her Visa. Airline miles, you know."

Donna weighed his responses. They were a bit breezy. Was it to cover anxiety, like a returning traveler facing a customs inspector, a box of Cuban cigars in his luggage?

"And this psychiatrist your wife was seeing, just how closely did you question him about what he knew of your wife's plans?"

Wilson thought a moment. "Not very closely. I only said that she hadn't picked up Trish and did he know anything about where Barbara might be. He said he knew nothing at all that could explain her absence. I thanked him and that was it."

"How long has she been seeing a psychiatrist?"

Wilson hesitated. "About six months," he answered tersely. He's touchy about the psychiatrist, Donna thought.

"As I suggested earlier, there may be some small thing you may remember which could help us," Donna began, "It would be valuable to get Dr.—Marsh isn't it? Yes, to get Dr. Marsh to search his memory, also."

"That's something of a reversal isn't it; getting a psychiatrist to search his memory? Did you have it in mind that I should call him? I don't think Barbara would like that."

"No, Mr. Wilson, I plan to call him."

Donna rose. "I'll go now, I want to get this picture distributed. The Grand Traverse County Sheriff and the Traverse City Police as well as the State Police have already been given a description of her car."

"Thank you. Please find her soon." The last word was choked by a sob.

The insincerity of it made Donna wince. "We'll do all we can. Finding your wife is our highest priority."

Donna turned, descended the steps and walked slowly down the front walk to her patrol car. Benjamin Wilson's gaze followed the rhythmic movement of her buttocks and she knew it.

❍

"It's open-ended, K.D. I don't know when or even if I can get away to get some dinner. —OK, if I'm in Leland, I'll call and we can meet at the Bluebird for a burger." He listened to his wife's question and then explained, "At first I thought it might be an accident or maybe a domestic quarrel—the odds, you know—but that's not likely now, so I went ahead and had a state-wide bulletin sent out with a special alert to the seven nearest counties. Carjacking, that's what I'm most worried about now. We've only had one case in the area, a retarded kid who'd been put up to it by some other teenagers. But it's become a way of life around Detroit and Flint and I'm always waiting for progress to spread north." He began nodding his head. "I do too, sweetheart. Right. Call you later."

Hoss put the phone down. He was still at the Bingham Township Hall where he'd sat impatiently through a 90-minute meeting about widening a road.

When he came out, Donna Roper was waiting in the lobby of the building and gave him an unadorned report of her conversation with Wilson, leaving out her thoughts about the Wilson marriage and Wilson's unusual response to her. "I had time to take the picture around to the other departments for copies to be made." She handed Hoss an 8 x 10 blow-up of the smiling Barbara Wilson. "Also, I stopped by the parking lot outside the psychiatrist's building just to make sure her van wasn't parked right there."

Hoss stared at the photograph intently. Donna came around beside him to look at the photo again.

"Who took the photo, do you know?" Hoss asked.

"I didn't ask, but it's a question that needs to be asked."

"Why do you say that?"

"Wilson's professed love for his wife seemed insincere. I guess I can't imagine her smiling at him like she is in this picture."

"What did you learn about her schedule this morning?"

"She usually goes to the hospital after her appointment with the shrink; she does rounds and so on, and then she picks up her daughter. After lunch at home she goes to her office for afternoon appointments. She didn't show at the hospital."

Hoss considered this for a moment, then said, "Sounds like something happened to her right after her appointment with the psychiatrist. Let's go talk to him. Just saying he didn't have an explanation for her disappearance isn't good enough. "

Donna was thinking that Benjamin Wilson didn't want Doctor Marsh to be interrogated. She felt sure the problem that had sent Barbara Wilson to see a psychiatrist involved her husband, but again she kept these thoughts to herself. It was only intuition, a woman's intuition, and voicing much of that wouldn't gain points in the department.

Donna called Marsh from Hoss's car. Marsh said he was very worried about his patient, but repeated that he'd already said all he could. He would, however, gladly talk to Hoss and his deputy at five fifteen, when he'd be free for half an hour.

"We've got forty minutes to kill," Hoss said. "I think we could spend some of that time productively showing her picture around that office building. Whaddaya think?"

"Good idea."

Hoss parked his car on the circular drive of the Peninsular Power Company's new building. Overlooking Grand Traverse Bay on one side and downtown Traverse City on the other, the Peninsular Power Company's new building was an investment in public image. The Power Company occupied the lower two floors; the offices on the upper three floors were now the most prestigious addresses for the city's professionals.

The front and back walls of the lobby were floor-to-ceiling glass. Behind the rear glass wall was the reception area of the Power Company. A young woman was sitting at a desk in front of a low partition behind which could be seen the office personnel at work and beyond them, through large windows, the blue-green water of the bay.

Entering the lobby, Hoss nodded toward the receptionist. "She's got a great view of the traffic in the lobby. Let's start with her."

The young woman looked up, startled. Hoss's massive bulk walking up to your desk produced the immediate impression that a truck has missed a turn and is about to sweep right over you.

He attempted to neutralize the effect with a disarming smile. "Afternoon, I'm Sheriff Davis of Leelanau County and this is Deputy Roper."

"Oh, yes," the receptionist replied, recovering her composure, "I've seen your picture in the paper. I live in Suttons Bay."

"Ah yes, well, we're inquiring about a missing person." He took one of the copies of the photograph of Barbara Wilson from Donna and showed it to the receptionist. "Have you ever seen this woman before?"

The young woman studied the picture with serious attention. Nodding, she looked up at Hoss and Donna. "Yes, I've seen her, I wasn't sure at first. She looks different somehow, but I have seen her waiting for the elevator. She doesn't work for the Power Company, so she must go to one of the offices upstairs."

"Today? Did you see her today?"

She thought a few seconds then shook her head. "I don't think so." Her expression was apologetic. "You have to understand, I don't really look out into the lobby much, but I am sure I've seen her here before. Is she the missing person?"

"Yes, she is. Apparently she was in this building this morning, and, as far as we know, hasn't been seen since. If you remember something, or hear anything that would be useful to us, please call me at the Leelanau County Sheriff's office."

Having a second thought, Hoss handed the photo to the woman. "I'll leave this copy with you. Please show it around to the people you work with."

"I sure will," she replied eagerly.

Donna consulted the directory next to the two elevators. Dr. Derek Marsh was in 504.

The elevator doors opened at the fifth floor, and Hoss and Donna stepped into a wide hallway, at each end of which was a full window. A quick appraisal told them there were half a dozen offices on the floor; three had glass walled reception areas open to the hall. The rest had only solid doors—number 504 was one of these.

Donna moved toward the law office of Herbert, Coburn and Silver, which was located between the elevators and suite 504. The reception area was a walnut-paneled foil for the chrome and rosewood desk of the receptionist. A prospective client would know in advance to expect high legal fees.

Donna made the introduction to the receptionist, an intelligent looking middle-aged woman, showed her a copy of the picture and asked the question. The woman took the photo from Donna and examined it.

"I'm so glad to see she can smile. You say she's missing? What do you mean?"

"We're not sure what it means at this point," Donna replied calmly. "What did you mean about her smiling?"

"I'm sorry, that was inappropriate, I mean with her being missing. It's just that she has been coming to see Dr. Marsh for several months and I haven't seen her smile yet. I can tell when they're getting better. At first they hurry by without looking at me. Then, they nod, then nod and smile. When they stop and say hello and talk about the weather and ask about my family, I know it's about time they'll stop coming."

"How did you know she was seeing Dr. Marsh?" Donna asked.

"I've seen her going into his office."

Donna turned and looked out of the glass wall in the direction of the psychiatrist's office. She couldn't see the door from the woman's desk.

The secretary, guessing Donna's thoughts added, "When I was out in the hall going to the restroom or to the office down the hall."

"Did you see her today?" Donna asked.

"Yes, this morning, right after I got in—about quarter to nine. She was going to his office."

"You're sure of the time?"

"Yes, I had opened our office and was on my way to get water for the coffee maker. Our office opens at nine."

"Did you see her leave?" Hoss asked.

She considered the question. "No, I'm pretty sure I didn't, but that wouldn't mean anything, because I'm not out here at this desk all the time."

They thanked her and crossed the hall to the attorneys' office on the other side of the elevators. Hoss noticed that this secretary's seat was positioned so that a partition blocked much of her view of the hallway.

This woman looked at the picture and quickly shook her head. "I don't think I've ever seen her before." She was positive she hadn't seen her that day.

The same negative answer came from an architect's receptionist.

One office door, Clinton Woodley, Patent Attorney, was locked. Past Dr. Marsh's office and at the end of the hall was 506, the remaining solid door. The lettering said, Ferris Tull & Associates, P.C. Hoss glanced at his watch, saw that five minutes remained before the time of their appointment with Dr. Marsh, so he knocked on the door, then tried the handle. He and Donna stepped into a small room with red leather chairs and quiet background music. The door to an inner office opened and a dark haired, energetic looking man in his late thirties stood facing them with an inquiring expression.

"Ah, the gendarmes. Did I forget to pay a parking ticket? Ah no, Leelanau County. You people don't have parking meters. I'm Ferris Tull," he said holding out a hand, which Hoss knew would have a very firm grip.

"Pleased to meet you Mr. Tull. I'm Sheriff Davis and this is Deputy Roper. We hope you wouldn't mind taking a moment to look at a photo to see if you have seen this woman before."

Tull studied the picture, and as he did, Donna studied him. He was sure of himself, had an easy manner, was a man who could sell bottled water to someone living beside a mountain spring.

"She certainly looks different when she's smiling. This is Dr. Wilson—Barbara if I remember correctly. I was on the same program with her at Munson Hospital last winter—a program on stress management on the job. She handled the medical side of the issue, and I the business perspective. Why are you inquiring about her, if you don't mind my asking?"

"She's missing. Last seen this morning in this building. Did you happen to see her today?"

Ferris Tull shook his head. "No. I don't believe I've ever seen her except at that meeting."

"Her not smiling must have made a big impression?" Donna ventured.

"I don't know that I'd put it that way. It's just that she looked so different it was difficult, at first, to identify her from this picture. Now that you've said it, however, I guess I was wondering what was making her so unhappy that night at the meeting."

Hoss looked at his watch again. He took the picture from Tull and thanked him for his time.

"The two faces of Dr. Wilson," said Donna when they were out in the hall.

"Yeah, the difference certainly impressed these people. Maybe this psychiatrist can explain it to us."

Dr. Derek Marsh opened the door between his consulting and waiting room at the precise time of their appointment. He stood aside and asked them to come in. The view over the bay from his office was breathtaking. Hoss figured the room contained more oriental rugs than a Sultan's harem; even the couch had one spread across it.

A new patient would certainly be impressed the first time he or she walked into this room, thought Donna. The man himself was pretty impressive too.

"Let me state at the outset, that I will be unable, because of patient confidentiality, to tell you anything about my work with Dr. Wilson." He said this in a friendly but firm tone.

He is a very handsome man, thought Donna. Must be difficult for his female patients not to fall in love. His manner was as smooth as that of Ferris Tull, but a professional distance replaced Tull's informality. Finally, Donna noted that he was very well dressed—his suit bought on a shopping trip to Chicago, she speculated.

"I told Mr. Wilson that I know of nothing that would explain her absence and that is about all I can say." Marsh added with an understanding smile, folding his hands and laying them on his finely clad lap.

"Doctor, I understand there's a need to preserve confidentiality about things that invade your patient's privacy, but surely there are many things Dr. Wilson herself would quickly reveal if she were here with us right now." Hoss paused and saw that his logic had failed to convince the man. "We're not nosey busybodies. Whatever we learn is kept confidential unless it has to come out in court. Surely you can tell us something about Dr. Wilson's life that would help us start a line of investigation."

Well said, Donna thought, and she looked at Marsh, expecting him to agree.

"I appreciate your position, Sheriff Davis, but when I told Dr. Wilson that what was said here would remain confidential, I did not amend that statement by adding I would, of course, tell the police what they might want to know about her." He held his well-tended hands palm upward, the universal sign of one's inability to act. He saw the frustration on Hoss's face and added, "I'm as baffled as anyone about her disappearance."

"You know Doctor, we *do* have different expertise than you. I'm sure you know better what to look for in diagnosing a mental illness than we do. You should extend the same respect to us. We just might know better what is relevant in a case like this."

Dr. Marsh gave Hoss a tolerant smile that he spread around to include Donna. "The reasons why a person might disappear are the kinds of motives I work with all the time. I think I'm well-qualified to make a judgment on this subject."

The doctor's calmness heightened the tension in the room.

Donna glanced at Hoss to see his reaction. She knew him well enough to know he was very irritated with the good doctor. But, just as she expected, he wouldn't show his irritation to Marsh.

Donna hoped to steer the two men away from locking horns. "We have shown this picture," she said, handing it to Marsh, "of Dr. Wilson to a couple of people who have remarked with surprise on the fact that she is smiling in the picture." Donna noticed the interest the picture held for Marsh. He only half-listened to her. "Could you help us understand their surprise?"

Marsh handed the picture back to Donna. His expression showed what she took to be conflict. Perhaps he wanted to explain, but if this were so, the inclination was overridden by a professional rule.

He shook his head. "I can't comment on that."

Hoss stood up abruptly. "Thank you for your time, Doctor Marsh. If you remember anything which in your judgment does bear on the problem, and you can talk about, let us know right away, OK?"

Hoss didn't wait for Donna to leave first, as he usually would have done, but preceded her to the outer door. She looked back at Derek Marsh, who was standing at his consulting room door watching them leave. His professional façade had been replaced with something else; was it relief?

Donna had difficulty keeping up with Hoss so great was his haste to leave the building. They were ten minutes into their drive back to the Bingham Township Hall and Donna's patrol car, before Hoss spoke. "Some people sure make it hard for a person to earn a day's pay."

Donna smiled. "Want a LifeSaver?"

"What flavor?"

❍

K.D. took the kettle off the stove and poured the boiling water into the glass cylinder containing the freshly ground coffee and pushed the plunger part way down. She stood at the counter in her small kitchen looking into the backyard while she waited for the water to leach out the coffee's essence. She was a trim, attractive woman. Her lean muscular body said she was physically active. Her quick eyes and the set of her mouth said she was the family's designated worrier. Long ago she had learned to restrain herself from sharing all of her concerns with Hoss. He usually breezed along content to do what he could each day. She envied him this simplicity, because her own mind couldn't avoid concerns such as "global warming", radioactive waste and human rights. Life with Hoss had been uncomplicated. Emotionally, he was a low maintenance person. So was her daughter, Kristen, who always solved all her own problems, only reporting her well-thought-out solutions.

K.D.'s latest worry was the upcoming primary election. Only one party had any hope of winning office in the county, so the primary was the election. Hoss had been re-elected four times.

Those past campaigns had produced no anxiety. He had run unopposed each time. The campaign and the voting had been more like a celebration of his popularity. This year it would be very different.

A slate of candidates had been put together to challenge all the present office holders. There were rumors that the group was selected and backed by a syndicate of outside investors personally worth a billion. Jason Ackerman was its kingpin. If the rumor was true, and K.D. was sure it was, then it followed that the candidates had accepted the syndicate's financial backing in return for promising to clear the way, once elected, for the syndicate's ambitious land development plans for the county—plans that had been stymied by the current, conservation-conscious administration.

Kip Springer was the person Ackerman had selected to run against Hoss in the primary. Kip was a very popular personality and probably the only person in the county who could give Hoss real competition. K.D. had been following this political development over the past six months, gathering her information from the remarks of friends.

"They're out to rape the county!" K.D. thought, as she fairly smashed the coffee plunger to the bottom of the cylinder. Ackerman was sure to use anything that would serve his purpose. He was working hard to discredit the present county government. Could there be anything in this doctor's disappearance they could use against Hoss? Probably not, but it made one more thing she could worry about.

K.D. poured some of the coffee, still angry. She was happy that their daughter had already moved down to East Lansing where she'd snagged a summer job to earn spending money for her freshman year at State. Kristen would have enough on her own mind without the tension she'd surely pick up from her mother. K.D. hadn't shared any of her concerns with Hoss. He didn't like this negative, cynical side of her. She suspected, though, he must be feeling the pressure, too. He certainly hadn't been himself at breakfast.

❍

Hoss *was* anxious. Driving back to Leland, after dropping Donna off at her patrol car, he concluded that the uneventful life of the Leelanau County Sheriff had lulled him into a kind of torpor. Truth be told, if it turned out that they were, in fact, dealing with the abduction of this doctor, he was about as prepared as he'd be for a terrorist attack. From time to time, in theory, he had drilled his small force for a big crisis. He'd gone with them to workshops on special problems and had made current publications on police procedure available, but the reality of the gentle life in the county blunted one's edge.

The challenge that this doctor's disappearance presented was like that of the "tackle eligible" pass play they'd used in college. It might be used only once in an entire football season - you sure as hell didn't want to drop that one pass.

Unavoidable, also, was his concern about the primary election. He had made a life for himself in his role as sheriff in the community and had been planning to see it all the way to retirement. He could probably get another job, but would it hold the same interest for him, and pay as well? K.D. and Kristen depended on him. He pictured his daughter's smiling, trusting face. Beginning one's freshman year was hard enough without your father losing his job.

Toward evening, he had settled on the discouraging conclusion that they were faced with a carjacking. It was the simplest explanation for the disappearance now that the likelihood of an innocuous cause was fading. He'd learned long ago to pursue a hierarchy of simplest causes until he came to the right answer. Most of the time you didn't have to go beyond the second item on the list.

Another idea nagged him; it had since the morning when he'd taken that verbal swing at Harry Swifthawk by suggesting he picked on little girls. He'd wondered then if Harry would feel obligated to retaliate. Abducting this doctor was way beyond any of the stunts Harry usually pulled, but the idea nagged Hoss just the same. It nagged, because if true, then he, Hoss, was partly to blame. This twinge of guilt made his hand go to the intercom and he spoke to David Wick.

"Dave, is anyone up near the reservation?"

"Shorty's at an accident on 22 just south of there."

"Patch me through, please."

He waited as David tried to raise Shorty, who was no doubt out of his vehicle.

"Deputy McQuade." said Shorty, out of breath, but with as much of his official on-the-air voice as he could manage.

"Hoss here. What have you got up there?"

"Deer jumped in front of a car. The herd's too damn big, deer everywhere."

"Have you got more to do?"

"No. Wrecker just pulled away. Took the animal too."

"I've got a little job for you. You have to do it carefully—an interrogation on the reservation. I want you to find Harry Swifthawk and question him about his whereabouts from the time I left him this morning at six thirty, until, say, one o'clock, and check out whatever he tells you. I had a talk with Will Blackbird and Charlie McNab this morning telling them I was going to talk to Harry. They implied it was OK with them. We'll just stretch the invitation a few hours."

Shorty didn't answer, and Hoss wondered if the connection had been lost.

"Hoss," Shorty said at last, "he'll find a way to go shouting all over the reservation that we're trespassing and abusing him. You know what he does." Shorty didn't say it, but he was also thinking, why are you doing this to me?

"That's why I said you have to be careful. Don't give him anything he can use, but do the job."

"You're the boss. Promise not to fire me if it all goes to hell."

"I'd never fire you. How else could I keep an eye on you if you weren't at work every day?"

Shorty, too, had been down the sandy road to Harry's trailer many times in the last few years, sometimes with Hoss and other times on his own. He wondered why Hoss was in such a rush to question Swifthawk. If he hadn't been in a hurry, Shorty knew that Hoss would never have given him the job. Shorty wasn't a popular man on the reservation. In the past, he'd been pretty rough on members of the Band, and although his views had mellowed somewhat in recent years, deep down he believed the whole reservation idea was outdated nonsense that should be junked, along with the Band's right to have gambling. "Shit! They're no better than the rest of us and should obey the same laws and take their lumps in life like everyone else."

Shorty had given Swifthawk a few of those lumps over the years, and Shorty knew that if Harry could stick it to anyone in the Department, he'd be the one.

He parked his car at the same spot Hoss had in the morning and endured the onslaught of Yellow's attack and retreat. Buddy's pick-up truck was the only vehicle in the yard.

To appease Yellow, Shorty moved up to the trailer very slowly and knocked. There was no answer, but he could hear the muffled sound of a television commercial.

"I know you're in there, Buddy," Shorty said in a tired voice, which implied he wasn't going to tolerate any shit.

There was still no answer. He was looking in the direction of the pick-up and had an idea. He walked over to it and looked at the license plate. Smiling, he returned to the trailer's door.

"If you decide to talk to me, I'll be out in the patrol car writing you a ticket for an expired plate and calling for a hook to tow your truck away," he bluffed.

The door opened. "Oh, I thought I heard a noise," said the broad, burly man. He was wearing jeans and a t-shirt, his long black hair combed straight back.

"I need to talk to Harry."

"He ain't here."

"Where is he?"

"No idea."

"That right? You sit and think. I'll be out in the car making that call. And, please don't bother saying something smart to me that would make me mad, cause I'd have to go and call that wrecker regardless of what you remember."

"Bullshit! I don't have to have a plate on a car sitting on my own property."

"How about if I say I just followed you here?"

Buddy stared at the older man. The look said that if this meeting were in a lonely wood, Shorty would never tow anyone's truck again. "He's working with Pierce Groves up at the Casino." He slammed the door in Shorty's face.

There had been nothing about this encounter that presented a problem for Shorty. Was there another way to handle a hard-ass like Buddy?

As Shorty drove slowly back out the sandy road toward the pavement of Highway 22, he saw a familiar figure walking his way. He stopped the patrol car in the middle of the road and waited.

Harry Swifthawk walked up to Shorty's window smiling, acting unnaturally friendly. Shorty, surprised by the absence of the usual cockiness, became wary.

"I have some questions, Harry."

"Sure, Shorty. What's on your mind?"

Harry was obviously nervous. Shorty had never seen this before. It sure as hell wasn't he who was unnerving this chronic troublemaker.

"Hoss sent me with some questions. Answer them quickly and I'll be on my way. Give me a hard time and we'll put in a long hard night."

"No need to get on the muscle, Shorty. What does Hoss want to know?"

McQuade studied the man. He'd seen a lot of people trying to hide something and Harry at that moment could have been the model.

"Where's your car? Why are you walking?"

"I loaned it to a friend—wanted to take his girl to a movie."

Could be, Shorty thought, these guys are always swapping cars around. "Hoss wants to know your whereabouts for every minute since he left you this morning."

"OK, sure."

"Just a minute," Shorty picked up his notebook from the seat next to him. "Go ahead."

"I had some breakfast, then went to work. I've got a job with Pierce Groves. He's got the contract for the landscaping of the casino's new restaurant."

Shorty waited. "And?"

"Well, that's it. Oh, I stopped with a couple of the guys after work for a beer at the Running Deer. I'm just coming from there." He'd recited this like a kid who, having played hooky, spiels out a prepared account of his school day to his old man.

Shorty began writing, asking at the same time, "Who is on that crew with you?"

"Jerry Crow."

"And?"

Harry hesitated a millisecond, but the delay didn't go unnoticed. "Law Henderson and his brother, Jimmy."

"What about Groves, wasn't he there?"

"Early in the morning, but he left, so there's no use asking him anything."

Shorty stared at Harry. The man was so nervous he was coming apart. He'd never witnessed Swifthawk make such an obvious blunder. What Harry had just said was that he had an alibi worked out with Jerry Crow. Also, he either hadn't talked to the Henderson boys yet, or they'd said no dice. And, it was clear that he didn't want Groves to be asked about the morning.

"What's this all about, Shorty?" Harry asked politely.

"Damned if I know. Hoss didn't say. What do you think it could be?"

"Well, how would I know, Shorty? It must be important sending you all the way out here."

Shorty shrugged. "I'll go now and pass this on to Hoss."

"Are you going to talk to Crow and the Hendersons?"

Jesus, Shorty thought, this guy's unraveling.

Pierce Groves was the man Shorty wanted to talk to first. He called his home and was told Pierce was at a meeting of the Northport Festival Committee going over plans for the annual Fourth of July Whitefish Boil. Northport was ten miles farther north toward the tip of the peninsula. Shorty wanted to read Groves's face as he was asked about Harry, so he decided to make the drive.

Shorty guessed that the meeting would be held in the back room at the Library. All meetings of this sort in Northport were held there. There was also a suitable room at the Fire Station, but experience had shown that for some reason gatherings held there tended to get out of hand and little was accomplished. Shorty parked his car, walked through the main reading room of the library and opened the door to the back room. All five committee members looked around. He knew them all. He'd gone to school with two of them. A volley of quips about a "foreigner" being sent to spy on them had to be returned in kind before he managed to get Pierce Groves aside to ask about Harry.

"As far as I know, Shorty, Harry was working all morning. We started at seven. I had to leave about half an hour later to drive to Traverse City for an appointment and to get some supplies. But he was on the job when I returned at twelve-thirty. Why?"

"Don't really know why Hoss wants to know. Was Harry there the rest of the day?"

"Yeah."

This covered the time period Hoss was interested in—as far as Pierce knew, at least. Shorty started to thank him and then had a thought.

"Did he seem his usual self this morning?"

"Well, now that you ask, I noticed that he was very preoccupied. I was telling him what I wanted him to do while I was away and he was doing the 'uh-huh' thing. Not really listening."

"Anything else?"

"Yeah. Again, I didn't think about it much at the time, but I was irritated when I got back, because he hadn't done half of what I'd told him to do. It's not like him. True, he can't be relied on to show up for work, but once he's there, he's a good worker."

"Is it possible that he wasn't there part of the time you were away?"

"I suppose.... It could account for the little he'd accomplished."

Shorty thanked Pierce and left. He figured he didn't have enough to call Hoss, so he decided to confront Jerry Crow. Shorty would attempt to trick Crow into a contradiction. After that, he'd call Hoss and let him decide the next move. Shorty didn't want to do anything on his own that might end in a screw-up. He had only seven months until retirement. A screw-up would be no way to end thirty years on the force.

Instead of going to Crow's home, he followed a hunch and drove to the Running Deer. The bar was a relic from pre-casino days, a board and batten shack whose rear deck overhung the water of Grand Traverse Bay. It was easy to believe that birch bark canoes once tied up to it.

Rock and roll pulsated into the gravel parking lot. Shorty took in a deep breath of the clean evening air, pushed open the door and walked in. Immediately he thought of the movie, *Beverly Hills Cop.* Every Indian eye turned on him like he was George Armstrong Custer, and like Custer he was surrounded. Slowly, the patrons began to return to their conversations, but the electric charge in the room had increased several thousand volts. Indeed, Shorty was not popular on the reservation.

He went to the end of the bar and shouted his order to one of the two young women bartenders. "A coke, please, Ma'am."

He hadn't waited to be asked for his order, because he knew he'd be standing a long time before that ever happened. Begrudgingly, the bartender thumped down a can on the bar in front of him. Just then, Jack Moses, the stern-faced manager of the Deer came out of a back room. He looked first at Shorty and then at the Coke.

"Five dollars," he said.

Shorty gave Moses a blank look that said, "You gotta be kidding!" then dug into his pocket and produced what amounted to an entrance fee. He turned his back to the bar and surveyed the room. Jerry Crow was looking at him through the heavy smoke. He sat at a table with two other men near the door to the deck. Although he knew Crow by sight, Shorty had never talked to him. The other two could be the Hendersons. The only place to talk would be outside on the deck. Shorty walked past the table and motioned to Crow with the Coke can to follow him.

A man and woman were out on the deck, but they were deeply occupied. Shorty put one foot up on a bench at the deck's edge and lit a cigarette. The June moon, the Strawberry Moon, was just rising above the trees across the bay, making its way into a clear and still night.

A few minutes later, the door opened and loud music poured onto the deck until the door closed again. Jerry Crow now stood with his back against the building.

Without looking at Crow, Shorty said over his shoulder. "I know Harry left the job this morning. What I don't know is where he went."

Shorty took a quick look at Jerry Crow, then turned back to look at the moon's track across the bay.

"What we're talking about here is some heavy shit, Jerry. It isn't at all like you'd be covering for him so he could sneak off to go fishing. If he takes a fall on this one and you're with him, you'd be an accessory and looking at ten years in Jackson Prison."

Shorty was blowing smoke. He didn't know what Hoss wanted with Harry. It certainly hadn't occurred to him that Hoss was thinking of Swifthawk as a possible abductor of Barbara Wilson. Bullshitting was just Shorty's style.

There was no reply from Crow, so he repeated, "You gonna tell me where he went?"

"I ain't sayin' a fuckin' thing to you, man." A blast of music said Crow had gone back inside.

What this meant to Shorty was that Harry Swifthawk was now alone. No one was going to give him an alibi for that time period. The bluff had worked. He'd gotten Crow thinking the question was *where* Harry had gone and not *if* he had gone. If Harry had been on the job, Crow would have said so loud and clear. Shorty was pleased with his success. He could now pass the ball back to Hoss. He put the unfinished five-dollar Coke on the bench, then gave it a second thought and picked it up again. He glanced at the couple who remained oblivious to what had just passed between him and Crow and made his way back to the parking lot the long way around the outside of the building.

❍

Through the window he saw the moon rising. The sky was cloudless—just what he needed for what he planned to do. It had been agony waiting and wondering if the police would think to check the garage. It would have ended for him right then and there, but they'd overlooked it. He'd need just as much luck tonight, when he took the van from the garage to get rid of it and its passenger. Just keep your head! Think everything through carefully. Overlook nothing. No mistakes!

CHAPTER 4

FOUR UNFINISHED CANVASES LEANED AGAINST the inner porch wall. The point of view of each was from the hilltop above the house looking down into a narrow valley and back to a distant orchard. The palette of colors she'd used was slightly different for each painting, but all four had been painted in the late afternoon just before the light faded at dusk.

Marti had been forced to abandon these canvases until the leg cast was removed and she could climb the hill again. The day after the cast was applied, she attempted to get to the hilltop, but failed. She drove her Civic hatchback up the unused farm road that ran next to her house and parked about one hundred yards below the top of the hill where the old road turned away toward a distant cherry orchard. She unloaded her painting materials: easel, paint box, one of the canvases and a folding stool. She then discovered how daunting a task it was to climb a steep hill on crutches. It demanded all her strength to swing her body up and regain her balance. There was no way she could do it while also clutching painting paraphernalia. Crestfallen, she abandoned the attempt and backed her car down the hill, fearing she'd get stuck in the soft sand if she attempted to turn the car around.

Marti sat now on a chair in the field outside her house, looking up at the hill. Since she couldn't get to the top, she'd paint a view of the hill from the bottom. Sunset approached. The colors just mixed on her palette were several deep hues: green, plum and golden ochre. She worked quickly with her brush for a few minutes, then leaned back and appraised the effect. Her hand reached for the cadmium orange and squeezed a dab onto the palette. She swished the brush through paint thinner and wiped it out on a rag, then dipped the tip in the strong color and added several careful touches to the picture. She laid the brush aside and looked from her work to the field in front of her, then back again. She was frustrated. Her paints had not captured what she felt. Her creative urge, she decided, was held captive by the unfinished canvases that waited on the porch for her bone to knit.

Lacking sufficient light now, she cleaned all her brushes and, since there seemed to be no threat of rain, left the easel and canvas there after slipping a garbage bag over them against the dew. She climbed up one of the crutches and stood. The three-quarter-length cast was not heavy, and she was able to bear her weight and walk with it, but it was cumbersome. She had a sense that she was engaged in some childhood game that required her to perform a common task in an unusual way, like running in a burlap sack.

She swung on the crutches to the corner of the house. From there she could watch the sun set into Lake Michigan. The water was uncommonly calm. A fiery red carpet lay rolled out across its surface. Marti made a point of watching the sun set each day. She'd watch and utter a soft salute of thanks to the departing day, "Thanks, June seventeenth, you were a good one." She waited until the color began to fade from the clouds then went inside to make supper.

Taking care of herself was something she had learned to do well and happily. Still, from time to time she yearned for the company of others, especially of a man—fiercely. This had led her to call Hoss last night. She'd liked him in grade school and desired him in high school. He was very shy back then and not one to seize the kind of opportunity she'd offered. Well, she smiled, he was a big boy now. Her message last night was clear. She knew he wanted to, but would he?

❍

Someone looking in through the window of Jason Ackerman's study (a window out of which one would see a sweeping view of Lake Michigan in the last light of the long June day) would see what appeared to be a stern father lecturing his handsome but profligate son on the fundamentals of social and family responsibility. The impression gained from that vantage point would be much closer to the truth than what would be concluded by listening to the conversation inside the room. There, Ackerman's words conveyed only a mild rebuke of Kip Springer's campaign efforts cast in the form of friendly advice about strategy.

Earlier in the day, Ackerman had learned from a source inside the Traverse City Police Department about Dr. Wilson's disappearance. When the same person called to tell him that the disappearance was being treated as foul play, he'd called Kip and instructed him to come to his home.

Ackerman and his partners had concluded they would only be free to pursue their land development goals if those in the county government who opposed those plans were removed from office. A sheriff did not make zoning policy, but Ackerman had two reasons to discredit Hoss Davis. First, he was a good friend and supporter of the obstructive county officials and made no secret that he opposed Ackerman's plans. Second, Hoss was a very active leader in a non-profit organization called the Conservancy whose name summarized its purpose.

"It's a gift," Ackerman was saying, "I had considered your contest with Hoss Davis to be the one we were least likely to win. Not that you aren't a better candidate," he quickly threw in, "but it's difficult to attack him, like picking on his namesake from Bonanza. We've got an ideal opening here. We mustn't waste it." Ackerman's tone was collegial. What Kip Springer didn't know was that Jason Ackerman never treated anyone as a colleague unless it was to achieve his own ends.

"This is politics, Kip. Politics is like war; if you have an opponent in your sights and you delay pulling the trigger just because he might be a good guy, or you'll make his mother weep, he'll pull the trigger first and you'll be history." Ackerman's tone became avuncular. "You're not ready to be history at this time in your life are you, Kip?"

A conspiratorial smile appeared on the handsome young face, tanned by golf outings to Doral in March and Pinehurst a month ago. "I never cared for history, Mr. Ackerman." Kip usually called everyone by their first name … almost everyone.

Kip Springer's problem was that he didn't know for sure just what he wanted, other than to go on doing just what he had been doing—playing at working in the family's lumber business and indulging his natural inclinations: golfing, crewing, schmoozing and relieving the lonely pain of widows and divorcees. The problem was, this option had played itself out. His father, Jess, decided to retire and it was his judgment and that of other family members who had personal financial interests in the continued success of the business, that Kip would not make the reliable manager that the business demanded. Consequently, a real businessman had been installed.

Kip didn't blame them (he knew they were right), but it meant he would have to find some other respectable base from which to sally forth. The new manager of Springer Lumber had let Kip know that while he would always be welcome—everyone liked and enjoyed Kip—shooting the breeze with the boys at the lumber yard would no longer carry a salary.

When Ackerman had first summoned Kip to this same room two months ago and offered him the sheriff's spot on the new slate he was putting together, Kip thought it was surely the work of divine providence.

Now Ackerman got up and took a cigar from a humidor cabinet. He offered one to Kip, who accepted it gladely. The older man lit his own first, creating a grand cloud of smoke, then handed over the lighter. Kip, busy lighting his cigar, was unaware of the contempt with which his host now studied him.

Ackerman, in his mid-sixties, had the physique of an athletic man twenty years younger. It wasn't athletics, however, one thought of when Jason Ackerman stood over you as he now stood over Kip. It was raw power. He was only a little over average height, but his presence was that of the eight hundred-pound gorilla of the joke. You knew he'd sleep wherever he wanted to.

Ackerman smiled through the smoke, at the same time rolling between the fingers of his left hand the gold tennis ball pendant he always wore around his neck.

"Good, Kip. I don't give a shit for history, either."

He had spent as much time on these preliminaries as his personality allowed. Deliver the message, get this lightweight on the road and get on to more serious matters!

"This woman disappearing is the kind of situation which stirs up a lot of insecurity in people. Wife goes off to work and never comes home—probably raped and tortured. It could happen to my wife, the men all think. It could happen to me, think all the women. It takes something like this to reveal just how unprepared our police force really is. What's Sheriff Davis doing to catch the guy before it's too late to save Dr. Wilson? Nothing! And, please, Sheriff, don't insult our intelligence with crap like, 'Everything is being done,' or 'Promising leads are being pursued.' Tell us what's being done. We're not children whom you can satisfy with a trivial promise. If you can't handle a serious situation like this, then move over and let someone do it who can!"

Ackerman's aggressiveness startled Kip, who stared at him and blinked.

Ackerman continued, "If there is no break in the case by tomorrow, I've arranged for a reporter from Channel 8 to come to your campaign headquarters at two in the afternoon. He'll catch you hustling out of the building as if you were on your way to a White House conference. He'll ask you for your impression of how the investigation is being conducted by Sheriff Davis. You'll know what to say, right, Sheriff Springer?"

After being dismissed, Kip got in his LeBaron convertible and drove slowly out the long meandering drive. He was troubled—shaken. The performance Ackerman had outlined was not his style. Kip was a good friend to everyone. Hell, he liked Hoss a lot. He'd looked upon the election like a golf match: no hard feelings, loser buys the beer. It would also be dishonest to make the statements Ackerman wanted him to make. He believed Hoss was probably doing a good job with the available resources. Kip's idea of campaigning was to make use of his popularity, his social presence; get around to all the social events he could, laugh it up at Rotary lunches, press flesh, kiss babies. His notion of what it meant to be sheriff was similarly naïve—a kind of prolonged costume party. The department should be able to run itself. Nothing ever happened in the county, anyway. This Wilson business was the first thing of its kind in his memory.

For a moment, Kip was sorry he had ever agreed to run. He had agreed, however. He had joined up. He had given his word. There were many ways in which he was not a strong person, but he was loyal to a fault.

❍

At 11 p.m. Hoss sat alone in his office. The only light in the room came in from the hallway. He leaned back in his desk chair, hands behind his head, looking at the lights from Flint's Marina reflecting in the Carp River as it flowed past the County Courthouse and into downtown Leland. For over an hour he'd overheard Kate, the night dispatcher, answering calls in the outer office. About every other call came from the news media. All wanted information about the missing doctor and Kate repeated the standard, polite but deflecting response they had decided upon at the earlier staff meeting.

There had been no break in the Wilson disappearance. All afternoon Hoss had reviewed the possibilities and shifted his small force to focus on new objectives, as the passing hours made another theory seem more likely than the last. First he'd concentrated on a search for the van along local roads, paying special attention to places where a vehicle could leave the road accidentally and not be readily noticed: deep ditches, creek beds, banks running down to lakes and the like. He'd kept his deputies at it until dark. They and the Traverse City police had managed to cover all the roads Dr. Wilson could have taken in a fifteen-mile radius from the Peninsular Power Building.

Whatever happened to Barbara Wilson occurred right after her appointment with the psychiatrist. Hoss could picture it in his mind: she came out of the building, got in her car and someone opened the door and got in, too. Carjacking! Unfortunately, this was now the most likely explanation. If so, was it possible that Barbara Wilson was still alive? Hoss thought it unlikely. Too much time had passed. There was a slim chance, however, that the carjacker still held her, uncertain of what to do next. A house-to-house search was an impossible task, but Hoss had another idea that might flush the abductor. He'd asked the local news media to include in their news broadcasts the fact of Dr. Wilson's abduction and a description of the green Chrysler van. Viewers and listeners were asked to be on the look out for the vehicle and to immediately call their local police. Since the van hadn't been discovered along any of the roads, it meant it had either been driven far beyond the area of search, or that the abductor had hidden it. Hoss hoped it was hidden in a place that could be easily linked to the abductor, so that after hearing the broadcasted alert the guy would decide it was crucial to move it. To catch him when he did this, Hoss believed, was their only hope of rescuing Barbara Wilson. Hoss didn't think the abductor would attempt this while he knew the police had a full shift on the road. He'd wait until late at night when he expected to be dealing with a skeleton crew. That would be the wrong strategy, of course. Rush hour would be the best time, but normal psychology and a hundred movies the guy had seen throughout his life would tell him to move the van at night, probably around 3 a.m.

The huge problem, of course, was that there were so many roads on which surveillance must be mounted. Two hours ago he'd made the decision to put all ten deputies on duty from ten o'clock until seven in the morning. He asked for and received the participation of every volunteer fire department in the county. They would station themselves, all night, along the roads within the borders of their fire fighting responsibilities. He also succeeded in getting the same plan implemented in Grand Traverse County. One hundred and fifty people, give or take, in his county alone, would be stationed out of sight along the county's roads, concentrating on those in the southern end of the peninsula bordering Traverse City. No one would be able to drive a green Chrysler van unseen in Leelanau County.

❍

He'd made a bad mistake. He'd acted impulsively when she began to scream. He had to put that behind him, now. A critical moment lay ahead. Once it was past, he would be home free, but what he had to do involved risk—a fatal risk—if he blew it. He had to take that chance and it had to be tonight. It would be better if he'd been able to wait days before getting rid of the body and the van, but that was impossible. He couldn't leave the van in the garage any longer. He believed he knew what the police would do. They'd have everyone and his cousin working overtime tonight. The roads would be covered like a Snickers bar on an anthill. They'd be off the road, out of sight, waiting for a green Chrysler van to pass. And what was he going to do? He was going to drive right by them on a road they'd never think of.

❍

Through his open office door, Hoss could see the large clock above the dispatcher's desk across the hall. Twelve o'clock. Everyone would be in place, observing radio silence until a positive sighting. Two cars, McQuade and Preva, were to check in at the normal intervals so that anyone listening to the police frequency would believe it was business as usual. Nothing to do now but wait.

He'd gone far out on a limb setting up this extensive trap; the stakeout seemed the logical step to take, and he'd acted. Dr. Wilson's life had been his only concern. There would be a lot of people losing a lot of sleep tonight. No problem if things went as he hoped and they caught the guy. As Gus Reynaud, the Grand Traverse County Sheriff, remarked, everyone would be proud they took part and would tell the story for years to come. But if they came up empty-handed—. Hoss didn't continue the thought.

He picked up the phone and dialed home, conveniently reminding himself that he'd promised to call K.D.

"It's a gamble, all right. I'm putting all my chips on this number. Gus Reynaud cautioned me that there'd be plenty of criticism if I put together this big operation and we don't catch the guy." He was spilling out his worries to a woman who'd fallen asleep sitting by the phone. She knew he was expecting her to absorb his worries and restore his confidence in the end. "I sure as hell can't repeat it tomorrow, the combined police force of two counties will be wiped out with lack of sleep."

"If it works, Hoss, it'll be very big. After all, a woman's life is at stake, and you have a good record with your hunches," she said.

"That's right, but that's what the guy thought who designed the Edsel. Hey, I'm not really as gloomy as this sounds. I'm confident we'll catch him tonight."

"That's my boy."

"Either way, I'll be here all night. I'll give you a call in the morning before I head home for some pancakes."

"As long as it's before ten. I'm leading the aerobic dance workout at the Old Art Building tomorrow."

"I'll make it."

❍

He went into the garage and stood quietly for a few moments beside the van like an Olympic gymnast preparing himself mentally. He brought his head up. He was ready. Climbing into the car, he couldn't resist a glance into the back to see if she was still there wrapped in the plastic sheet. He eased out of the garage and onto the driveway. The next few minutes were the bad ones. He needed a little luck. He would only be driving on Highway 22 for half a dozen blocks before he turned off onto a side street and there was no good place to conceal a police car on that particular stretch of highway. He had to drive slowly and look like anyone going home after making a special trip to get milk for the next morning. Here's 22, so far so good. Just—. Shit! Where did all that traffic come from? Must be from the casino—limping home broke. No cops, though. OK, now, easy does it, a left turn up the hill to the railway crossing. Now, onto the old rail bed.

He began to breathe easily. He wiped sweat from his face with his gloved hand and laughed out loud. He had a private highway. The old railroad tracks that ran the entire length of the peninsula had recently been torn up and removed in order to build a bike trail. Rails to Trails! The old gravel bed made a satisfactory road for the four-wheel drive of the van and the gravel was bright enough in the light of the full moon for him to follow the track without headlights. The Sheriff and his deputies will be spending a long, boring night.

❍

Donna munched a carrot and listened to Shorty report that he'd stopped a truck with a burned out tail light. Donna smiled. Bullshit came naturally to Shorty. It was a quarter past twelve. She was parked on the entrance road into the Delft Hills subdivision. The lights on the ostentatious entrance columns played out across Highway 22 illuminating each vehicle that passed. Traffic had thinned out to the constant trickle driving south from the Leelanau Sands Casino.

A dark-colored Chrysler Town and Country passed, going south. Donna accelerated out onto the highway into a side-drifting turn. She charged up to within ten yards of the van, saw that it was dark blue, hit the brakes and backed off. She could see the driver look with alarm into his rear mirror.

"Poor guy," she thought, "he's probably had cars popping out onto the highway and rushing up behind him all the way down from the casino. If he's a winner, he'll think the Indians want their money back."

One nagging thought had been bothering Donna all night. It had come to her earlier when she was at the Wilson home: she hadn't thought to check the garage to see if the van was right there. And why had this thought bothered her? Because in a suspicious disappearance you should look to the spouse first. That was elementary. But at the time she'd questioned Wilson they hadn't yet settled on foul play. These thoughts had been going through her mind as she sat watching the passing traffic from her lookout post.

She thought about Wilson, his behavior and her instinctive distrust of him. He had no alibi that they knew of for the critical time after his wife had left the psychiatrist's office until the time he picked up their daughter at school. Why had they neglected to check him out further? Hoss had hit upon the idea of a carjacker and they had all ridden off in that direction.

Delft Hills was only three miles from the Wilson home, and Donna's pursuit of the van had already taken her one mile in that direction. Why not check out the garage right now? There were volunteer firemen watching 22 just north and south of her post, and since it was only midnight it was reasonable to assume they were wide awake. But still, a good soldier doesn't leave her post. "Face it," she said aloud, "you're not a good soldier."

Donna turned right on Crain Hill Road and climbed the long bluff overlooking Grand Traverse Bay. There were half a dozen houses on the Wilsons' street. The Wilson house was dark. She parked and got out.

So bright was the moon that her presence and her mission would be clearly seen by anyone caring to look outdoors. Donna walked directly to the side of the Wilson's two-car garage. Her heart beat faster as she raised her flashlight to the window. Would the beam of the light fall on a dark green van? … No, and the excitement of the previous moment was replaced by cold disappointment. The space nearest the window was empty. Parked in the other space was a white Taurus sedan.

She walked back to her cruiser, then stopped with her hand on the door handle. She walked back to the house and climbed the porch steps. Was Benjamin Wilson at home? She had to know. She rang, waited, rang again, and then knocked. Donna stood and stared a long moment at the dark house. Turning abruptly, she returned to her car and opened her notebook and looked up the phone number that she'd written earlier that day. She dialed it on her cell phone. The Wilson's phone rang four times and the answering machine kicked in with his voice inviting her to leave a message. She decided against it.

Benjamin Wilson was not home, but his car was! Was he out driving in the van? "Damn!" she cursed herself aloud. "If I had only thought to look in the garage the first time!"

She should wait here for Wilson to return home, but she also had to call Hoss and tell him what she'd done and what she'd discovered. She dialed headquarters' number. She knew Hoss would be angry with her. Well, he would get over it.

Hoss wasn't angry, but he made a mental note that he'd need to have another talk with her about following procedure. He told her now, however, that she'd had a good idea but should have called before leaving her post. He agreed she should wait there for Wilson to return.

Hoss hung up. Donna's idea about the Wilson's garage caused him to think of another garage, the tenant's' private garage in the basement of the Peninsular Power Building. There had been no reason to look there in the afternoon when they interviewed the psychiatrist. Now, however, any place the van could be hidden which also had some connection with Barbara Wilson should be searched. He picked up the phone again and dialed the Traverse City Police.

❍

It was harder going than he'd expected. In some places where the crossties had been lifted, there remained trenches that tossed the van like a dinghy on a rough sea. Another complication he hadn't anticipated was the storm moving in from the west. The sky in that quarter lit up regularly with lightning, and a sharp line of cloud slid eastward like the roof over a domed stadium, closing out the moonlit sky. He was afraid the rain would come before he could get to the isolated road where he planned to leave the body. If it did, would he be able to see well enough to find the narrow dirt track that he'd been to only once before? One sure thing: by the time he got home safely he'd be damned wet.

CHAPTER 5

DONNA'S CALL HAD SHAKEN HIM. Realizing they had overlooked the husband carried for him the same embarrassment as being told in public that his fly was unzipped. She'd been right, of course. Why had he settled so readily on the carjacker theory? Because, he reminded himself, it held out the remote chance of finding Dr. Wilson alive. If he'd begun by investigating her husband, it would have meant delaying the most critical action to preserve her life. If her husband was behind her disappearance, she was almost certainly dead already. So, he assured himself, he'd been right to proceed as he had.

"Hold on there, Hoss, ol' buddy, not so fast," he muttered to himself. "That's all true, but you didn't reason it this way beforehand. The truth is, you overlooked the fucking husband!" He smiled. "And, thank you, Donna Roper and that pretty, brainy head of yours."

Her call had made him think of another garage. The image of a decaying shack attended by the sound of a barking dog. Swifthawk's garage. He'd been so occupied directing the stakeout that he'd forgotten Shorty's report that Harry had tried to set up a cover for those critical hours this morning. There might be any number of reasons why Harry had skipped off the job, but now that he'd thought of Harry's garage he couldn't put the thought aside, and it brought him reflexively out of his chair. With everyone else involved in the stakeout, he was the only one available to check it out.

Hoss yelled to tell Kate Schott where he was going, as he hurried out of the building to his patrol car. Once he got past downtown Leland, he put his foot to the floor along the winding back roads between Leland and the reservation. At the crest of one hill he caught sight of a line of lightning moving toward him like an electric curtain across Lake Michigan. He glanced again toward the charging storm and tried to calculate when it would hit. He thought he'd be able to get to Harry's place ahead of it.

Speeding past a farm, he noticed a pickup truck parked, with its lights off, in the center of the farmer's driveway. Two men in the dark cab watched him flash past. Northport firemen. They'd be wondering if the speeding patrol car meant the van had been spotted and were probably itching to follow. He glanced in the rearview mirror. They were staying put. Good. He raced on, making a normal twenty-minute drive in twelve.

A light shone dimly through the closed curtains of the trailer's windows. Both Harry's car and Buddy's truck were outside. Hoss parked so that his headlights threw their light on the decrepit garage. He got out of the patrol car slowly and braced himself for Yellow's angry reception. It came before he had time to close the door. This time, almost immediately, Buddy appeared behind the screen door.

"Who's there?" he demanded.

"Hoss Davis. Call off your hound."

Scowling, the stocky man stepped outside and yelled at the dog. Yellow looked back toward Buddy, but kept barking. Buddy took a final pull on his beer can, then threw it at the dog. It was a near miss, but Yellow got the message and sidled off into the darkness.

"I want to talk to Harry."

"He ain't here."

"Go somewhere without his car?"

"Looks like it."

The sky lit up and thunder crackled and boomed. Hoss glanced up. In five minutes it would be raining. He reached inside the patrol car and grabbed his flashlight.

"I want to look in the garage. You come with me."

"You got a warrant?"

"I can get one. You want to cooperate or not?"

"Not."

Hoss pointed the powerful beam of the flashlight at the garage door. There was no lock, only a simple latch.

"If that's the way you want it," he threw back over his shoulder at Buddy.

Walking up to the garage door he noticed, in the packed sand, fresh tire tracks leading into the building—new tires with wide treads. Hoss turned and trained the flashlight's beam onto Harry's car—narrower treads, nearly bald. He turned back to the door, unfastened the latch and pulled. The door didn't budge. Its old hinges no longer supporting it, let it lie heavily on the ground.

He put the flashlight down and lifted the door with both hands and swung it open. He picked up the light and shined it where he expected to see Barbara Wilson's van. The garage was empty. He played the beam on the floor. No tracks. The sand floor had been swept with a broom—recently.

Swinging around, intending to order Buddy to account for the tire tracks and their recent obliteration in the garage, Hoss found himself alone. He drew his gun and walked quickly to the door of the trailer and threw it open. No one was inside. He stepped into the narrow room and looked along its cluttered length. A quick survey convinced him Barbara Wilson wasn't there. He wanted to search it for any evidence of her having been there, but he had no warrant. Whatever he found in an illegal search would be inadmissible in court. There were the tire tracks, however. He had to cover them in some way or the rain would wash them away.

Hoss banged out of the trailer and sprinted to his car. The emergency blanket he carried was waterproof and stiff enough to withstand a downpour. He holstered his gun, opened the trunk, grabbed the blanket and jogged back to the garage, where he spread it out over as much of the tracks as it would cover. The wind was picking up. Something was needed to hold the damn blanket down. His searching flashlight beam fell on the woodpile. He ran to it and gathering up four logs in his long arms he hurried back and placed one at each corner of the blanket. Even then, the wind was filling it like a parachute. He brought more logs to place along the edges until he was satisfied that it was proof against the storm's best effort.

❍

A loud clap of thunder awakened Marti. She lay listening to the rain beating steadily and heavily on the roof over her bedroom.

She'd awakened from a dream in which a van had been backing down the dirt road that ran next to her house. The car's interior lights were on and the driver was leaning out and looking backward.

She remembered vaguely having gotten out of bed. Had she responded to the dream by actually going to the window to look … or had that been part of the dream, too? She couldn't remember. She stared at the dark rectangle of the window, lit repeatedly by the lightning, until her thoughts became ragged and she drifted back asleep.

❍

As if a gigantic strobe light had flashed, lightning lit the yard. The picture imprinted on Hoss's retina at that moment was of Yellow standing near the end of the trailer watching him, small trees bowed down by the force of the arriving wind, and a figure … standing twenty yards behind the trailer at the edge of the woods. Broad, dark lines ran vertically down the person's face.

"What the hell?" Hoss exclaimed.

Then, complete darkness. Another bolt hit, the scene lit again, the figure gone. This time the rain crashed down with the thunder.

He was soaked by the time he got to his car. He drew his weapon again and sat as a waterfall, backlit by his car's headlights, cascaded over the windshield. What had he seen? Was that Swifthawk? Wearing war paint? Had he imagined it? Was it a residue of old images and prejudices called up from the John Wayne westerns of his childhood?

The tire tracks had changed everything. Not so much the tracks themselves as the fact that Harry had taken the trouble to erase them in the garage. He probably backed the Wilson van out of the garage and got out to sweep the floor inside, then, afraid someone would see the van parked there, hurried away, planning to take care of the tracks outside the garage when he returned from getting rid of the van.

If Dr. Wilson was still alive, where on the reservation could Swifthawk be holding her?

Hoss badly wanted to get his hands on the bastard at that moment and force him to talk. Immediately he remembered all the times he had interrogated Harry and how he'd never succeeded in getting one straight answer. Always a cock-and-bull story and always someone to back up the lies. The important thing at the moment was to protect the evidence of the tire tracks. He had to stay until he could get someone to relieve him. He picked up the cell-phone and dialed headquarters.

"Kate, get Shorty McQuade on the phone, not the radio, and have him come to Harry Swifthawk's place, right now." Hoss waited on the line, until Kate confirmed that Shorty, ten minutes away, was coming.

❍

He hadn't been able to drive as far back into the old orchard as he'd intended. The rain had turned the dirt track to mire and he was afraid the van would get stuck. He didn't think it mattered.

Not many people knew what he knew, that the casino stood at a point where an old logging road once joined Highway 22. Probably only those who roamed through the woods above the casino, searching for morel mushrooms in the spring as he had, still knew about it. The abandoned roadway was choked with brambles, but was otherwise passable with the four-wheel drive. He used the headlights through the woods, but switched them off as he approached the casino, its bright lights visible through the heavy downpour.

Day and night, the casino's parking lot was at least half filled. The police certainly wouldn't expect him to take the van out for a night of gambling, so no one would be watching the lot. One more van among dozens of others. He would run a last check on the interior, now emptied of its recent, silent passenger, to be sure he'd left no evidence and be on his way.

❍

Shorty's voice came over the police radio, "Russ, I'm going back to headquarters to get a coffee and take a dump."

Hoss smiled to himself hearing Shorty's version of "business as usual". Ten minutes later Shorty's headlights lit up the interior of Hoss's car. Flashlight in hand and clad in a yellow slicker, he appeared at Hoss's window.

"Get in, Shorty," Hoss yelled over the steady drumming of the rain.

Shorty slammed the passenger door after him and sat dripping. "For a man's got such a pretty wife, you sure can find some weird places to spend an evening."

❍

"It looks to me as if the guy is just shooting in the dark. Doesn't know what else to do," Jason Ackerman said into the phone, affecting a tone of civic concern. "Sure as hell glad it's not one of our wives whose life is in the hands of this clown." Ackerman was sitting in a deep leather chair watching the rain bounce off the newly waterproofed wood deck outside his study while rolling a handmade Havana back and forth between his thumb and fingers.

He was talking to Eugene Lessum, the party's former State Chairman and now Administrative Assistant to the Governor. Lessum was a political animal, and as most did in his position, employed a mental filter that separated out that which had political meaning to his future. He needed to listen carefully, because, apart from large corporations, Jason Ackerman was his party's largest individual donor in the state.

"I shudder to think of it, Jason." Lessum tried to match the other man's tone of civic concern.

"Can we stand by, with good conscience, and watch this fool bungle a woman's chance to live?" Ackerman's tone was moving toward moral outrage.

"I've only heard a little about the case at this point, Jason. You seem to be on top of it, so why don't you tell me your thoughts." He believed he knew the direction Ackerman was heading. For some reason, Ackerman wanted to discredit the Leelanau County Sheriff. These situations could become political quagmires and Eugene Lessum wasn't inclined to wade in.

"Reluctantly," Ackerman's tone expressed pained resignation, "we here in this area have concluded that this matter must be put into competent hands. This case must be placed under the jurisdiction of the State Police."

Ackerman had turned some of his cards up on the table. There was one card still down: he still hadn't revealed his motive for this request, and Lessum was sure the motive had nothing to do with saving the woman in question.

"Who shares this view?" Lessum asked.

"Mayor Barbour of Traverse City and Jerry Beasley, the Grand Traverse County Administrator, both good men."

"Good men" provided a pointed reminder that they were good soldiers in the party. Lessum thought quickly.

"What did you say this sheriff's name is?"

"Davis. Hilyard Davis. The lout is as big as a billboard, so he picked up the name of Hoss. That's the way most people up here know him."

"Help me out here, Jason. I'd appreciate it if you'd send me some material about the way he's mishandling the case. I'll contact the Attorney General and the Governor if necessary. I'll move on this right now, but get that material to me, because I'll need it."

Jason Ackerman blew a plume of cigar smoke. He knew Lessum didn't need material from him. A phone call was all he had to make. Lessum was stalling for time so he could check this out up the line of command and cover his ass.

"I'll do that, Eugene, and you talk to the Attorney General. I'm sure he'll make a quick decision for this woman's sake. That's what's needed in an Attorney General, someone who'll make a quick move when justice and his friends are in need."

Lessum heard the threat. Ackerman obviously knew he, Lessum, had his eye on the party's candidacy for Attorney General in the next election, now that Boyd Steward had declared he was stepping down after twelve years.

“You have a friend in this department, Jason, rest assured.”

Ackerman pressed the off button on his phone, then dialed again. A rain-soaked squirrel running along the railing of the deck paused and looked in at the man who sat comfortably in the dry, soft chair. Eyes met for a moment, a chasm separating their circumstances. The animal dashed on and Ackerman spoke into the phone.

“Jerry. Jason Ackerman. I just talked to Eugene Lessum. He’s ready to move. It would be good if your sheriff, Reynaud isn’t it, made some statement about Davis’s poor handling of the case, wasting precious time and so on. Whaddya think?”

“Good idea, Jason, but if we can coordinate the statements, Reynaud’s and a statement from the Governor’s Office, so they follow one after the other, it would have more impact,” Jerry Beasley replied with faked enthusiasm.

Another wimp covering his ass, Ackerman thought. He doesn’t want to be the first to act. “Good idea, Jerry. I’ll call you when I get the word from Lansing. You can get your man ready in the meantime. You, yourself, will be able to make a statement then, too, of course.”

“Of course.”

Jason Ackerman hung up. He sat thoughtfully smoking for several minutes, then he got up and walked to the window and watched the rain, his fingers automatically beginning to rotate the gold ball that hung from his neck. “Nicely, nicely,” he murmured.

❍

Donna moved her patrol car into the Wilson driveway. She had the wipers on, but still couldn’t see through the windshield, so she lowered her window a crack, the rain spraying her shoulder. After a few minutes, quieted by the drumming of the rain on the roof of the car, her thoughts drifted. What would it have been like to be Barbara Wilson? Not a happy lady—very unhappy, in fact. Her husband was a lech, all right, but was there something else? Dr. Marsh could tell them so much, if only he would. Maybe she should have a go at him without Hoss there. Men talked to her. After all, Marsh, while he pretended not to be, was an ordinary man.

If she were free to act on her own, she continued to muse, how would she proceed? She'd start a background check on Wilson, talk to the neighbors, check on bank transactions, especially large or atypical withdrawals or expenditures and talk to Dr. Wilson's office staff and to her colleagues.

Hoss was right to concentrate the department's effort on the chance the abductor moved the vehicle tonight. Good try—but so far, no luck. If morning found them with an empty net, they should concentrate on Benjamin Wilson. That's where she'd put her money.

❍

Ten minutes after Shorty arrived, the rain diminished from a cloudburst to a steady downpour. Hoss decided it was time to leave the job of guarding the tire tracks to Shorty and return to his office, in position to coordinate the chase if the van was spotted.

"Come with me and I'll show you where the blanket and the tracks are." Saying this he got out of the car's shelter and led Shorty out across the flooded yard.

They came to the place where the blanket should have been spread out, secured with many logs. Instead, they stood looking down into water filled ruts, the blanket thrown to the side.

"Holy shit!" Hoss exclaimed. He stood stunned, shining his light first on the sandy soup where the tire tracks had been, and then over to where the blanket lay in a crumpled heap.

"Wind must have blown the cover off," Shorty observed.

"Wind, hell! Look at those logs. They've been thrown aside. Someone sabotaged the evidence. Did it while the rain was coming down so hard I couldn't see out the windshield, and we don't have to look very far for that person." Staring at the flooded ruts, he grunted a self-chastising, "Should have parked my car right up over one of the tracks."

Hoss flashed his light across the garage floor. "See where the floor has been swept? We can at least preserve that and whatever else the garage can tell us. Drive your car right up here to the doorway and leave your headlights on and have your weapon ready.

❍

He slipped through the door and locked it. He was tired enough to sleep a week, but safely home. "I got away with it," he boasted into the dark room.

❍

Four A.M., Donna was bored. She'd gone over the case in her mind several times, but planning had its limits. The chase excited her. She'd never felt anything like it in any other job, but three hours sitting in a closed car in the rain wasn't her idea of excitement. The absence of stimulus caused her thoughts to flow along personal memory channels, the ones she normally kept dammed off—unpleasant channels of regret and self-reproach, memories of bad times with people, family and others, unintended hurts and frank revenge, chances missed, longing, disappointment. The thoughts led to the name of a man.

She threw open the car door and stood outside in the rain. She had to walk! From the trunk, she retrieved her yellow slicker and put it on.

Starting out along the road, she glanced back toward the house. From this new angle she was able to see deeper into the interior than she had from the car, and she saw a dim light through one window. Abruptly, she returned to the house and climbed onto the front porch. Through a living room window she could make out that the light was coming into a hallway from a room at the rear. She was sure it had not been on earlier, when she'd looked through the same window.

She leaned on the doorbell. When there was no immediate response, she began pounding on the door. Finally, the porch light went on and Benjamin Wilson, wearing a bathrobe opened the door. He was surprised and apprehensive.

"Officer Roper, what's going on?"

He was startled and anxious about seeing her here, of that, Donna was sure.

"Is there … news about Barbara?" he asked.

"No, Mr. Wilson, no news. Do you mind telling me where you've been tonight?"

He stared. "I don't know what you mean. I've been here all evening."

"I came here at midnight. There were no lights on and no one answered the door. I've been parked in your driveway since then."

"I had some things in the washing machine in the basement. I probably didn't hear you."

"You do washing in the middle of the night?"

"Not usually. Too bad you didn't call to let me know you were coming."

"But you wouldn't have heard the phone, washing away like you were."

"That wouldn't have been a problem. There's an extension in the laundry."

"You should have quit after claiming you couldn't hear the door. I did call you. It rang until your machine came on."

He was speechless. Donna's vision had adjusted after the sudden brightness of the porch light, and she could now see more detail in the semi-darkness where Wilson stood inside the doorway.

Her gaze traveled downward to his soaked and muddy shoes. Wilson looked down, also, staring at the soggy, running shoes as if they belonged to someone else.

Reflexively, Donna took two steps backward. Her training and her common sense said this situation required backup.

"Where have you been?" she demanded.

"Uh, I went for a walk."

Donna was sure she was faced with a chance to force a confession, and she didn't want interference from one of the other deputies. She made a decision and took her cell phone from its holder and dialed Headquarters. When Kate Schott answered she told her she was now entering Benjamin Wilson's house to question him.

Wilson stood and listened to her.

"Go on inside," she said. "We're going to talk."

CHAPTER 6

DAWN BROKE. THROUGHOUT TWO COUNTIES lawmen and firemen got out of their cars, stretched and relieved themselves. Some took in and enjoyed what they saw around them.

Two Grand Traverse County deputies watched the soft, pink, eastern light slip under patches of fog on the bay. A couple of Northport firemen walked down to the harbor to limber their stiffened legs and watch the tall ship Manitou set out on a cruise. Deputy Becky McConnell, the only other woman on the Leelanau force, had spent the night parked at a roadside picnic area where County Road 616 rises above the southern end of Glen Lake. She stood now at the edge of the mowed space and looked down on the misty water, its rim of dark pines outlining the lake like mascara around a captivating eye.

These experiences were the few exceptions. Most of those involved in the stakeout had different feelings. Next to many of their vehicles lay the rain-soaked butts of enough cigarettes to cause the kind of raw throats and hacking coughs that led to vows of abstinence. Inside their cars and trucks lay empty Styrofoam cups and donut bags. Most felt slightly sick and disgruntled. "Whose stupid idea was this, anyway?"

At seven, Hoss was seated across from K.D. eating a stack of pancakes with scrambled eggs. He was animated, in spite of the failure of last night's two-county surveillance effort, because he believed the discovery of the tire tracks in front of Harry's garage was sure evidence of his guilt. He was outlining his plans to K.D. for gathering further evidence when the phone rang.

K.D. spoke for a minute to Pete Dreisbach, then, holding her hand over the receiver, she held it out toward Hoss. "Pete's saying he must be abnormally dedicated to public service to get up so early."

"I just left Judge Burdick's house," the County Prosecutor went on in a gravelly voice when Hoss came on the line. "Standing there in his pajamas, he signed the search warrant for Swifthawk's property. That's for our own court. I'm basing it on the stolen gasoline. I've talked to the Tribal Police, and they've agreed to meet you at Harry's trailer to aid in the search. They aren't going to go out on a limb for our friend Harry. He's been nothing but trouble to them as well."

Hoss agreed, "If it turns out he's the abductor, I don't imagine they want to be seen as his protectors."

"At this time, I'd say you're right. A few years ago, before the casino was built, they didn't give much of a diddly what anyone outside the reservation thought. But things are different now."

Dreisbach was referring to his belief that the tribe had become more involved in the life of the whole peninsula since gambling profits had made it a factor in the area's economy.

"Did Judge Burdick give us a warrant for the Wilson house?"

"Oh, yeah. No problem there. He said, 'Cherchez le spouse, I always say.' I've got to get in touch with the federal judge, I'll call you later."

Hoss got back to his breakfast, smiling. Things were going his way.

"What's that about a warrant for the Wilson house?" K.D. asked, pouring more coffee for them both.

"Donna Roper caught him lying last night. He wasn't at home at midnight, but his car was, so she waited for him to come back.

Apparently, she caught him sneaking in the back door at four." Hoss laughed out loud.

"What's so funny?"

"She found him in his bathrobe, claiming he'd been home all the time, except he hadn't counted on Donna noticing the wet shoes he was wearing. After that, he admitted that he'd been out 'walking.' He wouldn't say more."

K.D watched Hoss eat. She loved this big man. He was gentle and good, but, while he was smart, he possessed a fundamental naiveté that sometimes caused her to feel as uneasy as a mother whose small child is out in the world alone. At times he could become instantly enthusiastic, as now, and be blind to complications. In her wish to provide a counterweight to his blind momentum, she knew she came across as a jaded, world-weary cynic. She certainly didn't want him to see her as a controlling and deflating parent, but she hadn't been able to prevent a reflex reaction when she thought he was about to step into a hole. Now she felt a measure of reassurance. She didn't know Donna Roper well, but she was beginning to see her as an ally in her own effort to protect Hoss from himself.

❍

Dr. Derek Marsh had come to the office early. Entering the garage beneath the Peninsular Power Building he noticed the Traverse City Police car. The cop noticed him, too, and got out and came over to Marsh as he parked.

After introducing himself and asking Marsh to identify himself, the cop said, "As part of an investigation we're asking all the tenants who use this garage if they have seen a dark green, 2003 Chrysler Town and Country van parked here at any time and especially in the last two days." He looked up at Marsh from the clipboard where he'd written the doctor's name.

"No I haven't, but then I can't say I really pay much attention to what cars are down here."

The cop began making a notation.

"Is this in regard to the disappearance of Dr. Wilson?"

The man looked him in the eye. "Yes, it is."

"Any leads, yet?"

"We can't comment on that," he returned. Another car had entered the garage. "Please excuse me, sir."

Derek Marsh got in the elevator and pushed the button for the fifth floor. What did this mean? Had the police narrowed their search to this building, or did it mean they had nothing and were asking everybody questions in the hope of turning up a lead?

He unlocked his office door and went inside. He paused, remembering the interview with the Leelanau County Sheriff and his deputy. Again, he reviewed yesterday's conversation. Had he said anything that would have caused them to suspect him? He relaxed. No, there had been nothing.

He looked out over the bay as he did every morning. Several boats were anchored in the same area, their sonar having picked out a school of salmon. The electronic fish locator made the problem of finding fish a snap. Wouldn't the police be happy, thought Marsh, if they had a similar device?

Marsh's memory returned to something else about the previous interview—his immediate attraction to the tall, shapely deputy. Deputy Roper, the Sheriff had said. There was the potential for a chemical reaction there—an explosion! She wasn't your average cop. What was her story? He recognized something familiar taking place within him. Was it happening again? Was his will locking onto this woman like a homing missile? Yes, he decided, he must get to know her better.

❍

Jerry Beasley had acid indigestion—more than that, perhaps. Being the Grand Traverse County Administrator was, he had grumbled to his wife, "like trying to empty a sewer with a bucket—no end to it, it keeps coming down the pipe." He had gone over to the Sheriff's office to tell Gus Reynaud what the party organization required from him, and Reynaud had heard him out calmly like a soldier hearing his marching orders. Beasley was encouraged.

"Why all this attention to Hoss Davis?" Gus asked when he'd finished.

Beasley considered spewing forth the official line about the danger to Dr. Wilson and the need for competent action, but he didn't believe Gus would buy it. He knew Gus had cooperated with Davis on the stakeout operation last night and wouldn't likely consider Davis's actions to be incompetent. He decided on the direct approach. "As you know, Gus, the leaders in the party have had no success getting our choices past the primary in Leelanau County for some time, the incumbents have been too popular. There is an aggressive campaign this year to unseat them. Hoss Davis is getting a lot of press out of this missing Wilson woman. From our point of view, this is not good, especially if Davis solves the case. Not good at all. It would be better if the publicity hurt the cause of all of the incumbents. The public needs to be convinced Davis has bungled. We want the citizenry to come to demand another enforcement agency take over the investigation."

Beasley was pleased with his succinct encapsulation of what he considered to be complex Machiavellian strategy.

"Why are you telling me?"

"The plan is for the State Police to start a parallel investigation. They can't legally take the case over, but the voters will see it as the same thing. Before they do, The Mayor and I will make a statement about the community deserving more competent police action than we're getting. We want you to back-up our statements."

Reynaud had been studying Beasley with the fascination of a person watching a snake cross the road. Finally, he allowed, "I think it stinks. I won't have any part of it."

The response stung Beasley. He blurted out angrily, "It doesn't matter what you think! you'll do what—."

"Or else what?" Reynaud's tone was icy.

Realizing his anger and threat had been a mistake, Jerry Beasley backed off. "I'm sorry, Gus, I didn't mean that. It's just that there's pressure on me."

Gus Reynaud was wary. He didn't trust Beasley or any of the other politicians. Reynaud had needed the party's backing to gain his first term as sheriff, but he'd been re-elected twice since then, because he ran a good department and the voters knew it. If anything, the party needed him more than the other way around. Even if that weren't the case, he wasn't going to stoop to this dirty work.

"Hoss Davis is a good lawman. He's helped us in this county on numerous occasions," Gus said. "I don't think he's handling this case badly, either. He took a chance last night that didn't pay off. So what? I think it was the right move."

Beasley knew better than to push Reynaud. This was apparently one of those fraternal lawmen things—loyalty to the club. He'd talk to the Mayor, who was a hunting buddy of Gus's. If they couldn't get Reynaud's cooperation, they at least needed his silence. Beasley knew Ackerman would not be pleased with his inability to get Reynaud in line, and Beasley had never known a man who demanded to have his way more forcefully than Jason Ackerman. Once again, he could see it coming down the pipe, just like he'd told his wife.

❍

The unexpected thing that Hoss and his deputies found when they got Buddy to unlock the trailer door was Harry Swifthawk in a deep sleep. The two deputies began the search, while Hoss questioned the sleepy-eyed Chippewa.

"You oughta go to Hollywood, Harry. Your acting talent is wasted on us Leelanau County yokels. You'd be the pet of the great directors. Know why? 'Cause you learn your lines so well. Hell, I bet you write 'em, too. A regular one-man film crew."

"Thanks Hoss," Harry said with mock gratitude. "I don't suppose you'd give me a letter of recommendation?"

Hoss became angry with himself for getting into this banter. "So, your story is that you spent most of the night with a 'little girl down the road.' You got up out of her warm bed and decided to walk home in the rain. Because it was difficult to see in the rain, you never saw a patrol car parked in your driveway with its headlights on. You know nothing of tracks outside your garage, and you swept the garage recently because 'it was due for a good cleaning.'"

Harry smiled in apparent admiration. "Hoss, we could go to Hollywood together. You're a damn quick study, too."

Hoss turned away abruptly from Harry and joined the others in their search. They had found nothing so far. Hoss was surprised they hadn't turned up any drugs, not even a joint. A bigger surprise was the painting that hung over the worn couch. It was one of Marti's paintings. The style was unmistakable. Hoss leaned over to get a good look at the signature. Sure enough, Jensen.

"Where'd you get this picture, Harry?"

"Why?"

"Because I want to know."

"Because you don't think a dumb Indian should have a piece of art?"

"Have it your way—where did you get it?"

"I bought it at an auction."

"Suttons Bay?"

"Yeah, how'd you know?"

"Why did you buy it?"

"Why would you buy a picture?"

Hoss looked away to end the fencing, but he didn't think for a minute Harry's reason for having the picture sprang from art appreciation. His gaze lit on the bookshelf over Harry's bed. Again, he was surprised to see several Hillerman novels and a three-volume set of *The Birds, Trees and Wildflowers of North America*. Russ Preva had opened the door of the small refrigerator and Hoss could see that it was devoted to beer, Bud and Heineken. No surprise there. Hoss thought he remembered seeing Harry with a can of Bud, so Buddy's was the Dutch beer. Over the stove, they had an unusual collection of cookbooks for a couple of seldom-employed boozers: *The Joy of Cooking, The Wok* and *The Culinary Art of the Ojibwa Nation.* Hoss started to reach for this last volume, when Harry shouted in protest as Russ Preva started to pull a box out from under his bed.

"That's personal stuff. You can't look in there."

"Ease back there," warned Hoss, "We have a legal right to look at anything we want to." He watched over Russ's shoulder as he removed the contents of the box: high-school diploma, divorce decree, automobile title and a birth certificate in the name of Harry Stillwater. Hoss quickly looked at Harry, who met his glance defiantly. When he looked back at the box, Russ was holding a sheet of paper. On it was a list of names.

"Let me see that, please," Hoss said and took the paper from Russ. He knew all the names on the list. They had gone to school with him, had even been in his class. There were about a dozen names on the list and each had been crossed out except one, Marti Jensen. Next to her name Harry had penciled a star.

"What's this list for?" demanded Hoss in a tone which was half command and half puzzlement.

"Nothing particular."

"Don't give me that. You've got it in here with your important papers."

"It must've got in there by mistake. Let me see it."

Hoss handed over the list.

"Oh yeah, this is a list of people I was assigned to contact for donations for our library. That was way before the casino was built. Don't need no damn donations no more."

"And this one, the painter of that picture, why isn't her name crossed off, and what's this star mean?"

"I guess I didn't get around to callin' her.

"What's this star mean by her name?"

"Beats me."

"She only moved back here a few months ago. The casino is ten years old, and you said this was from a time before it was operating."

Harry shrugged. "You'd have to ask the person who gave me the list."

"Who would that be?"

"Damned if I can remember."

Here was the familiar runaround. Hoss felt the familiar anger Harry Swifthawk always brought out in him. One thing was certain: the reason for the list wasn't what Harry claimed. He'd been crossing people off the list, all right and hadn't eliminated Marti, but it had nothing to do with any damned library.

"OK, I want a straight answer about this. I want the name of the girl you were with last night. I want it—now—or I'll turn this over to the Council. You know we wouldn't be here if they hadn't wanted you searched and questioned. You'd have to go before them and tell them your lies. You wouldn't like that, would you? So, what's her name?"

"Jeeze, Hoss, you're great. That was Gary Cooper wasn't it? 'Tell us where you hid the money, or I'll turn you over to your own people.' And then the music would go, tum tum tum – tum tum tum."

Hoss made a move toward Harry.

"OK, OK. I was with Mary McNab."

"Charlie McNab's daughter? Does he know?"

Harry became uncomfortable. "I never asked him."

"Where does she live?"

"With her aunt."

Make that her great-aunt, Hoss thought. He'd met her but couldn't remember her first name. She must be in her mid-eighties.

"Did her aunt know you were there last night?"

Harry surrendered. "No."

"You left in the middle of the night because Mary made you go before her aunt got up."

Harry didn't bother to respond.

Hoss went outside and told the deputies that Harry was free to go but that they should stay and go over the grounds carefully. Hoss had to make a trip to the casino. He wanted to talk with Mary McNab before Harry had a chance to speak to her, though it wouldn't really change things. If Harry's story was true, he still could have had the Wilson's van in his garage and moved it before going to be with Mary.

Mary McNab worked in the administrative office of the Leelanau Sands Casino. Hoss had only seen her once before, as a teenager. He scanned the four women in the room and was able to pick her out easily. She looked more like her father now—not a good look on a woman according to Hoss's taste.

She was in her mid-twenties, with eyes that took over, once they fixed on you, so you couldn't notice anything else. Her eyes gave away the fact that she was expecting him. Most likely that meant he was about to hear the story she and Harry had agreed upon. Was it likely he'd have given her name if he didn't think she'd corroborate his story? But here Hoss was puzzled, because he wouldn't have believed a daughter of Charlie McNab would lie for Harry Swifthawk, even if deeply emotionally involved with him.

Hoss went to her desk and said he had to talk to her.

Mary glanced first toward her co-workers and then up at a surveillance camera on the wall.

"We'd best go outside."

Hoss saw the camera and agreed.

A short distance from the casino's entrance Mary stopped and faced him. "Yes?"

"Was he with you last night?"

"Who is he?"

"You know darned well who I mean."

"Is this between us?"

"I can't promise that. It might have to come out."

She sighed in resignation. "Yes, until a little after four this morning."

"When did Harry come to your place?"

"One-thirty."

"You sent him home before your aunt got up?"

Mary nodded.

"When did the two of you make this date?"

Defiance appeared on Mary's face. There were too many questions.

Hoss tried again. "Let me put it this way. Did Harry call at one-thirty and ask to come over?"

Mary quelled her emotions. "No, he was supposed to come over at ten. We'd made the date the day before. I called him at one o'clock since he hadn't come yet, and there was no answer, but he showed up a few minutes later. He said he walked because his car wouldn't start. I don't know why he made the effort to come through the storm, because he just fell asleep immediately. I didn't think I'd ever get him to wake up without waking my aunt."

"We've been looking for a woman doctor who disappeared yesterday in Traverse City. You may have heard."

Mary nodded.

"You don't have to answer, but if you do, make sure you tell me the truth. Make sure you don't give me misleading information. Understand?"

She understood, but what she understood was based on centuries of her people dealing with whites. She was unable to understand that Hoss was only warning her that she might be charged with obstructing justice if she lied. Instead she heard a threat.

"I understand." Her voice had a hard edge.

"Did Harry say or do anything that would indicate he knew anything about this missing woman?"

"No. Nothing was said about her. He was troubled about something. But he wouldn't say what it was."

"How do you know it wasn't about Dr. Wilson?"

"I would have known if it were something as bad as kidnapping a woman."

"But no details?"

"None."

Hoss nodded. His expression said he was sympathetic with her wish for this conversation to remain confidential. "Thanks for cooperating. I won't say anything unless it becomes absolutely necessary."

Almost inaudibly she said, "Thank you."

Mary's story didn't strengthen a case against Harry, but it didn't disprove it either. Hoss had to use the john, so he followed her back into the building, reflecting on what he'd just learned.

❍

Harry Swifthawk had driven to the casino for two reasons: he suspected Hoss was going there to question Mary and he wanted to talk to her afterward to find out what had been said. He was also anxious to know if the truck was still parked there.

Yes, there it was, its tail end facing the highway still inviting the police to find it. No one had found it yet. Harry was puzzled. Hoss had questioned him about last night. What was that all about? He had expected questions about yesterday morning, but last night? He'd heard the cops had been looking all night for the missing doctor's van. Could Hoss think he had something to do with that?

He drove into the casino lot and parked. In the row of cars facing him was a green Chrysler van. That was the make and color the cops were looking for. He had an idea. This probably wasn't the van in question, but he could tell Hoss about it. He didn't want to be liked by the "Big Pig," but it just might get Hoss off his back.

❍

Inside the building, Hoss looked around at the humming activity of the gambling rooms. He was very happy the casino was not in the jurisdiction of the Leelanau County Sheriff. He didn't want to deal on a daily basis with all the problems it could generate.

He walked outside and stood for a moment struck by how fresh the air was after last night's storm. Men and women streamed past him into the building, headed for the gaming tables. Hoss enjoyed an evening at the casino now and then with K.D. and their friends, but he had no appetite for it on a morning like this. He walked out onto the entrance drive still looking up at the reassuring blue sky, then down to the parking lot where he saw Harry running toward him. Now what?

Harry feigned excitement. "I heard you've been looking for a green van, a Chrysler. I just parked over there," he said, pointing, "and as I'm getting out of my car I see this green van. Maybe it's the one you want."

"Show me."

Hoss walked beside Harry, wondering what all this meant. Why would Harry help him find the van?

Harry pointed. There was a green—. Yes! Those were the plate numbers! Hoss looked through the driver's window, careful to avoid touching the outside of the vehicle: manila folder on the passenger's seat, cup holder held a Starbuck's cup, the keys dangled from the ignition, two Barbie dolls on the rear floor, that was all. Hoss noticed it had been driven on a muddy road. The wheels and lower part of the body were uniformly covered by dark, sandy mud. Perhaps the dirt was unique enough to pinpoint the exact road.

Hoss faced Harry angrily. "You're telling me you didn't know this car was here until just now?"

"That's right." It wasn't going the way Harry had hoped.

"Wait inside the casino for me. I want to talk to you some more."

Hoss returned to his car and called the tribal police and his own office and set in motion the procedures which would find the van, an hour later, in the center of a taped off area fifty feet on a side, surrounded by dozens of curious gambling patrons and residents of Peshawbestown. Because his hobby was photography, Russell Preva had become the Department's designated photographer. He was busily at work within the cleared area, as was Don Silver, one of the deputies who'd received special training in the collection of evidence. Silver was drawing-up a flow chart for the systematic examination of the vehicle, while waiting for the full crime scene crew to arrive from the State Police Post at Acme.

Hoss went back inside the casino and began his interrogation of Harry by charging that the tire tread on the van was identical to the tracks he'd seen the night before outside Harry's garage. He was bluffing; he couldn't be sure of that.

Harry was dumbfounded. Then it was true; Hoss thought he was involved in the woman doctor's disappearance.

"That van wasn't at my house. It left no tracks on my property. Like I already told you, I don't know about those tracks, but anyone of our friends parking their trucks could have made them. Those treads all look alike unless you've got'em right there to compare."

He's right, thought Hoss, and that's why his testimony about the appearance of the tracks was worthless. Hoss then proceeded to question Harry from every angle he could, but the man stayed with his story about finding the van in the casino lot, swearing it was the truth.

"OK, so that's the truth. Now, tell me some more truth. Where did you go yesterday when you cut out of work? By the way, Crow's not backing you up on the lie you told Shorty McQuade. So, what do you say?"

Harry became very sober, his usual smart-ass attitude absent.

"Didn't feel like working. Just cut out for a while, that's all. But, I swear my leaving work had nothing at all to do with this missing doctor."

Dealing with Swifthawk was like trying to pick up mercury with a fork. Hoss didn't know what to believe. He dismissed Harry for the second time that morning.

❍

At two o'clock sharp, Kip Springer emerged from his campaign office, a store vacated when a Suttons Bay T-shirt shop went belly-up. Out of the corner of his eye, he identified the TV crew, but hastened on toward his own waiting car.

"Mr. Springer, Mr. Springer! Could you give us a couple of minutes?"

Kip looked up in apparent surprise and stopped.

"Mr. Springer, I'm Vince Lawton of Channel 8 News. We are covering the disappearance of Dr. Barbara Wilson. I'm sure you've heard about a member of the Chippewa Band finding Dr.

Wilson's van." He had adroitly avoided saying that the Sheriff had anything to do with the discovery. "You are running for sheriff in the upcoming election. How do you think the investigation is being handled, so far, by Sheriff Davis?"

The camera stared into Kip's face like a near-sighted Cyclops. Behind the camera a man was holding up a gold, reflective screen. It passed through Kip's mind that his tan would look good in this light.

Kip turned back to the reporter. "It's encouraging that the van has been found, but I have to be frank—I think the person who did this should have been caught by now." He grew stern. "I want that person to know that if he harms Dr. Wilson he will be making a mistake he'll regret dearly, because when I'm elected I will never give up until he is apprehended and punished. That's a promise!" He turned and resumed his dash to his car where one of his young campaign workers waited behind the wheel. "Where to, Mr. Springer?"

Kip thought for a moment. "How about the Leland Country Club."

❍

Donna had slept three hours. Hoss had heard an outline of her encounter with Wilson right after she'd left the Wilson home. Following this brief conversation, Hoss had told her to go home to catch some sleep and report to Headquarters at ten. She'd been waiting two hours. When she'd arrived, David Wick, the dispatcher, told her the van had been found and that Hoss was still at the site, so she knew she'd be waiting a while. She got some coffee and settled down to some unfinished reports that were in her file drawer. She filled in a few blanks, but soon found her thoughts drawn to the van having been found at the casino. That was a problem. It was fifteen miles from the Wilson house to the casino. How could

Wilson have driven the van that far last night without being seen by the lookouts?

"Wait a minute," she muttered to herself. If Wilson had killed his wife immediately after her appointment with Dr. Marsh, he could have driven the van to the casino that same morning, after disposing of her body. Was there time for that? He had to get back home in time to receive the call from the school at noon. She left Marsh's office at 9:30. Two and a half hours.

Donna sat down with a notepad and began to calculate the distances and the time needed to cover them. Her conclusion; Wilson had the time, but it was close. Then, she realized there was another problem; how could he get back from the casino after leaving the van? The shuttle bus. That was the answer. One runs constantly between the casino and Traverse City. He could have taken a cab from there.

Hoss came into the room. He hadn't had any sleep and he looked wasted. He noticed her sitting there and wearily gestured a greeting.

"We brought the van back and put it in the police garage. The crime guys will finish working over the inside, here."

"Find anything?"

"Not a damn thing so far except latent prints. There are lots of those—except on the steering wheel. That was wiped clean. Which means the prints that are in the van probably belong to everyone but the perp. Come on into my office," he said as he lumbered unsteadily in that direction.

Hoss hung his cap on the hook behind the door and sat heavily in his chair. Donna tensed, expecting the chair to splinter like a dry log under an ax blow. It held. Hoss closed his eyes. "OK, tell me about romancing Benjamin Wilson in the middle of the night."

"You don't know how close that is to the truth. That guy is very lecherous for a man supposedly distraught about his wife. I thought he was hitting on me the first time I interviewed him and that was confirmed last night. His wish to hustle me off to the bedroom was greater than his concern about my questions."

Hoss opened his eyes and looked at her. Even fatigued she was a very beautiful woman. He could understand Wilson finding her attractive, but as she said, where was the concern for his wife? "You never told me about him hitting on you."

"It was very subtle, only something a woman would notice and I didn't think too much.... No that's not true. I did think it was very strange, and I began to suspect him. I imagine I didn't say anything about it for the same reason a lot of women don't report harassment. They're afraid they may have provoked it—or people will think they did."

Hoss thought to himself, You're right there, lady. Just being you is a provocation. He closed his eyes again. "Onward."

"I've told you about his initial lie and my seeing his wet shoes. He'd been somewhere he didn't want us to know about. I'd caught him off guard so suddenly, he couldn't think of a plausible story and he knew he'd delayed too long, so he claimed he'd been out walking. That's all he'd say. You've got to understand I've got such bad vibes about this guy that I wasn't putting it past him to try to silence me. So I called Kate Schott right in front of him, so he would know my dispatcher knew where I was. When we were inside the house, he said, 'I'm surprised, Deputy Roper, that you'd think I'm dangerous. My feelings are hurt. I'm really a very gentle, affectionate man.'"

Donna laughed and shook her head, as if to say she couldn't believe how she'd overreacted. "It gets worse, but the details of how I finally lost my cool add nothing. The bottom line is, the way that man was coming on was not natural."

Hoss assessed her discomfort. It was apparent that Wilson had really unnerved her. "I believe you," he offered and appeared to change the subject. "I talked to a curator from the Metropolitan Museum once. He came here to give a talk at the Dennos Museum.

There was one of those wine and cheese things after his presentation, and K.D. asked him if he ever did any authenticating of art works, and if so, how he knew something was a fake. He said, 'After you've lived with a period of art for a number of years, you just feel what is true and what is not.' It was that kind of thing with Wilson, wasn't it?"

Grateful for Hoss's understanding, Donna felt her composure returning. "That's it."

Hoss remembered that he had intended to talk to Donna about leaving her assigned post but decided to let it go for the moment. "How are you going to proceed with Benjamin Wilson?" he asked instead.

Donna discerned that he hadn't said, "What suggestions have you got?" or "How do you think we should proceed?" She recognized, by the wording of his question, that she had achieved a new standing in the Department. OK, she'd run with it.

"I want to talk to the neighbors, get their stories. At the same time, I want to start a check on credit card and bank activity. Barbara Wilson's colleagues may be able to help me know who she is, or was."

Hoss was listening carefully. "Good, keep in touch."

"What's next on *your* agenda?" Donna asked, trying out a colleague's phrasing.

Hoss made room for her. "The TV guys and I worked out a program to show the doc's picture and ask for info about anyone seeing her or the van in the vicinity of the casino. Channel 4 also agreed to get your man on the tube to appeal for his wife's life. I've never known a case where that's made any difference, but it won't hurt to give it a chance.

That's about it until we learn what the lab boys find in the van." Hoss brought himself upright in his chair, preparing to rise. "I gotta get some food, how about you?"

"I ate something before I came in, and I want to get started on Wilson. Oh, there is one other angle I think might be productive. The psychiatrist, Marsh, could tell us a lot if he'd loosen up a bit. Thought I'd like to have another interview." She knew Dr. Marsh had irked Hoss and that the sheriff would rather leave Marsh to his vows of silence and act like he wasn't that important, anyway. One of those guy things.

Hoss smiled at her, knowing just what she was thinking. He laughed. "OK, only don't say that I sent you."

Donna laughed, too. "That's the last thing I plan to say!"

CHAPTER 7

SWIFTHAWK DROVE BY THE CASINO lot again in the early afternoon. The excitement caused by the discovery of the Wilson van had died down, the crowd gone. Again, it was only a parking lot in the same way a stadium is just a hill of seats an hour after a thrilling game. Two of his friends, both black-jack dealers, stood outside taking in a few lungs full of fresh air before their shift began. Harry paid no attention to them. He sought something else. And, there it was—still there—its ass end and plate practically hanging over the highway! How could that be? Over twenty-four hours! Had no one reported it missing?

❍

The Assistant Manager of the Peninsular Bank and Trust Company would be more than happy to cooperate with so comely a member of the law establishment, even if she hadn't just presented him with a court order for the Wilsons' bank records. He came damn near declaring that he would do anything she wanted. He had, in fact, provided Donna with two very interesting facts: Barbara Wilson had withdrawn six thousand dollars in cash from the bank the day before her disappearance and another two sixty from the ATM the following morning, fifteen minutes before her appointed meeting with Derek Marsh. Benjamin Wilson had said that she never carried any cash. Did he know about the six thousand? Why did Barbara Wilson need additional money in the morning?

Donna examined the couple's pattern of deposits and withdrawals for the past several years. Monthly transactions were boringly uniform. Half a dozen checks were written each month for the same amounts. The manager, who said his name was Cliff Bledsoe in a manner that suggested he wanted it to become very familiar to her, identified two of the debit entries as mortgage and auto loan payments, both held by the bank. Scattered were various amounts under two hundred dollars, most including cents.

"You say she has no personal account, only this joint account with her husband?"

"That's right."

"No business account? What about her medical practice?"

"Yes, of course, her corporate account, Barbara Wilson, M.D., P.C., but that's not really her account, it belongs to a corporation." He added in an instructive manner, "The court order doesn't apply."

Donna looked at the subpoena and read: "Deliver to the Leelanau County Sheriff's Department any and all information pertaining to the accounts and/or transactions of Barbara Shelby Wilson, M.D." Donna looked up at a man who was smiling patronizingly.

"I'm sure you know that corporations are separate legal entities. Barbara Wilson, M.D., P.C. has nothing, legally speaking, to do with the woman herself. If I were to…"

Donna, smiling familiarly, raised her hand and stopped him. She knew he was about to say that it would be illegal for him to show her Dr. Wilson's P.C. account. Once he did that, it would be difficult for him to commit the illegal act she knew he was about to do—just for her.

"Cliff," she purred, as if asking him for a special favor. "I could easily get another subpoena for the P.C. account, but that would waste valuable time, time that could make the difference between

Dr. Wilson being found alive or dead. Are you sure you can't help me out?"

When he went out to get the books, she chastised herself for making use of his sexual interest for her purpose. Many men are quick to claim that women get treated as mere sexual objects because they themselves want to hold on to that special power. OK, she conceded, one point for their side.

There was only one interesting item in Dr. Wilson's professional account, a monthly check to Dr. Derek Marsh. It was usually around five hundred dollars.

Only two checks had been charged against her account thus far this month. One was made out to Traverse Realty, which Bledsoe was sure was a rent payment and the other was for five hundred and twenty made out on June first to Dr. Derek Marsh. Donna flipped the pages of her notebook back to a calendar page. The first of June was on Tuesday, the regular appointment day. The bank posted the check on the fourth.

So, Marsh must have handed her the bill on the first and she must have mailed it the next day. Conscientious lady—and to think Russell Preva suggested Dr. Wilson became so caught up in shopping, she forgot to pick up her daughter.

Out of a pocket in the back of her notebook, Donna withdrew a card identifying her as a Leelanau County Deputy Sheriff. She wrote a number on the back and handed it to Cliff Bledsoe. "If any new information comes to your attention, I'd appreciate a call at our office. If it's after regular hours, you can reach me at the number on the back."

Bledsoe was a cute guy, maybe he'd think of the number at some other time.

❍

"Thank you for finding time to see me."

Donna sat opposite Dr. Derek Marsh in his office.

"I feel horrible about Dr. Wilson," Marsh said. He looked pale and anxious.

"We all do. We're still hoping to find her alive."

"I don't know anything that would help you with that."

The look she returned implied he hadn't given the police the chance to decide that for themselves.

He'd been speaking in a more casual and intimate way than at their previous meeting. He was, as Donna had hoped, relating differently than he had with Hoss present. She was surprised to find she was having a problem with that. Coming close on the heels of bending another male ego, it had her wondering if she might, indeed, be a sexual manipulator. She didn't want that to be true with this man.

She felt the pull of a natural attraction to him. She felt sympathy with his pain. What would it be like to have a person you were working with very closely disappear? Had there been something in the victim's life that he blamed himself for not taking more seriously, or was there perhaps a warning he'd neglected to give. He was suffering from something; she was sure of that. It was something he wasn't likely to talk about. In a normal social situation, one backs off when one senses that this is the case, but she had to save a woman's life, and politeness wasn't a luxury she could afford. What could she say which would cause him to expose his thoughts?

"It must be hard to have this happen to a patient," she ventured.

"Yes. I've had patients who have died of natural causes, and that is hard, but somehow this is worse, much worse."

"I'll be frank with you Dr. Marsh. I have reason to suspect that her husband isn't as affected by her disappearance as you are. I'm running with this myself, it's not the main thrust of the official investigation, you understand. If I'm way off base, I'll look foolish and my effort will be wasted, to boot. I need some guidance. That's why I'm here today."

"I see." He grew thoughtful. "Why, may I ask, have you come to that conclusion about her husband?"

"His behavior—toward me. The way he responded to my questions."

"Reading between the lines," he said smiling, "That's my line of work."

"You could say that."

"I'd say you're good at it."

Had he just confirmed her suspicion about the Wilson marriage? Yes, indeed, that's what it meant. Was he going to enlarge upon it?

Marsh watched her work with it. This was as far as he should go. It would cause her to go after Wilson with all her energy. Too bad in a way. He was very attracted to this woman and would like to have more of these intimate talks, but he could see that it wasn't wise. She was too sharp, asked too many questions. Maybe, when all of this was safely over, maybe then.

"As I've said before, I have no specific information which could help you. Honestly."

"It could be that there is some detail she has told you that—." He was shaking his head.

"Miss—. I don't know how to address you. 'Officer' seems too official. 'Miss' makes you a girl much younger than myself."

"Donna," she smiled, "but then I'll have to call you Derek."

"Please do. Donna, what you say may be true. Perhaps there is something that could help you, but I don't consciously know of anything, and I can't very well 'free associate' here with you about my patient. If I do have a revelation I believe won't breach confidence, I'll call you."

Donna took out a card and again wrote her home number on the back. In this case she was sure any call would be strictly for a professional purpose.

❍

The insinuation in Eugene's voice signaled one more bit of sub rosa political dirty work that he, Boyd Steward, would have to endure. As Attorney General, he had been a willing participant for years, but no longer. Thank God! He was done with it, but he was ashamed of how long it had taken him. Because of his change of heart, it was now almost unbearable for him to associate with his former conspirators.

Ever since he'd told them of his decision to leave Lansing, knowing he was no longer a player to be reckoned with, they'd silently bypassed him, leaving him out of the closed room discussions and decisions. That was OK. That was what he wanted. Still, it required all of Steward's self-discipline to stay and complete his term of office. He could, of course, plead the old stand-by "reasons of health" and depart quickly from the political latrine. He stayed on for only one reason—because his son was the Deputy Director of Health. It was a political appointment, and Steward didn't want to cause him trouble by rocking the boat.

Steward opened his desk drawer and extracted a Tums tablet from a roll and chewed it. He heard Lessum in the outer office lathering up his secretary. What a toad!

Eugene Lessum came through the door and closed it behind him. "Boyd buddy, how's it going?"

"Hi, Eugene, have a seat. What's on your mind?"

The rhythm was faster than Lessum had expected. Missing was the ritual exchange of jocularity that established membership in the club. Also, Steward's greeting, only perfunctory, lacked the requisite heartiness.

"You've no doubt heard of the lady doctor from Leelanau County who has disappeared?" He looked to Steward for a sign.

Steward nodded. "Saw something on the news."

“They found her car this morning in the parking lot at the casino—but no sign of her. Anyway, the local sheriff who’s covering it doesn’t know his ass from a hole in the ground. People are asking that the State Police step in and take jurisdiction. As you know, we can’t do that, but we can launch our own investigation.”

What’s this we business? The Attorney General can step in, not the fucking Administrative Assistant.

Eugene Lessum paused, waiting for Steward to comment. Steward continued to stare silently at his unwelcome visitor.

Lessum added, trying for a note of conviction, “I think it’s a good move.”

“What makes you say he’s mishandling the case?”

“He came up with some cockamamie plan last night to catch the kidnapper. He set up the largest-scale surveillance operation ever attempted in that area. It cost both counties a pretty penny in overtime pay and the abductor managed to dispose of the woman’s van, anyway.”

Boyd Steward filled his pipe and lit it before replying. “That doesn’t sound like such a big fuck-up to me. Tell me, Eugene, what’s the real reason you want this sheriff set aside.”

“I really do think he isn’t up to the job,” Lessum insisted in a weak attempt to seem honest, “But you’re right, there is another issue. The Leelanau County Administrator, the Prosecutor, Sheriff, Zoning Board and pretty near every other elected person in Leelanau County, while members of the party, tend to sound like the Sierra Club on environmental issues. They imagine they’ve got the most beautiful part of the state and they believe it’s their mission to keep it that way.” He laughed hoping to have Steward join him. Silence and a strained look of impatient disgust were all he got back.

“I mean beauty is just great, but it can’t stand in the way of progress.” He was sorry he had said this, even as the words left his mouth. “What I mean to say is—.”

"Looks to me like the people who live right there think otherwise." Steward said.

That stung. Lessum was not used to hearing such talk from guys on the team. Maybe Steward was no longer on their side. Lessum decided not to pursue it; he would apprise the Governor.

"As I said, I think it's a good move, but give it some thought, Boyd." Getting up, he said, "Gotta run, so damn much work. You're lucky you're retiring."

On his way out, Steward noted that Lessum hadn't any parting sweetness for his secretary. Boyd Steward smoked his pipe, attended to some paperwork on his desk and waited for the call he knew would come. It came fifty minutes after Lessum left.

"Boyd, glad I caught you." The deep velvet tones were wasted off the Shakespearean stage. "I was just talking to Eugene Lessum. Oh my, one has to endure such people in this job—such low wattage. He told me you were, and I quote, 'short with him.' My congratulations on your restraint. You're lucky to be retiring."

That was the second time in an hour Steward had heard that sentiment and he was aware it really meant: I'll be glad when you're gone!

"Boyd, you know the real reason we have to do what we can to support Ackerman's candidates. It's what Jason Ackerman wants, and we can't afford for him to become angry and take his business interests out of the state. You know we need him to stay right here and continue to contribute to our—all together, now—Campaign Fund. It's what we elected office-holders spend half our time and energy doing. Without Jason Ackerman, it means I'll have to spend two-thirds of my time collecting money for television ads. I can't afford that. Of course I know the State Police can't take over the investigation—that's not permitted. They can, however, launch a parallel investigation. I need you to put that in motion—with fanfare. And, if it's any consolation, you know they have the resources to do a better job. Speaking of doing a good job, your son, Bob, is really doing a helluva job for us over in the Health Department."

That was what Steward had been waiting to hear. He knew it was coming from the moment Lessum left his office—the threat.

"I can depend on you, Boyd, right? Just like old times."

Boyd Steward knew what he'd like to say. Instead, he said, "Like old times, Governor."

❍

The lake was flattening out after the storm. It took hours after the wind died before the water lost its energy. Jason Ackerman stood on the beach in front of his imposing house, surveying the changes the storm had made, the reshaping of the dunes, the texture of the sand and stones thrown up by the waves. It was here on the shore of this cold northern lake that he felt some equanimity. Not peace, he was never at peace. But here, he felt as expansive as these elements: wind, surf and overarching sky.

The heavy surf had beached several new pieces of driftwood. He picked one up and held it out at arm's length. It looked like a fish, he thought, a barracuda. He looked at his watch. Quarter to six. He intended to watch the six o'clock news, see if the Springer guy had been able to follow instructions. He climbed the steps to his house and threw the piece of driftwood on the pile of others he'd collected.

Claudia, the Mexican maid, met him as he came in, his six o'clock glass of Highland Park in her hand. Ackerman was comfortable with foreign servants from less wealthy nations—no inappropriate chatter, no back talk, and they were happy to have the work. He walked to his study where he picked up the remote control to his projection TV, sat in his large leather chair and pressed a button. On the enormous screen a bigger-than-life-size St. Bernard ran at him and slid across a freshly waxed floor to stop at a bowl of dog food.

The news came on and the anchor looked seriously into the camera and reported, "There has been progress in the case of the missing Traverse City doctor."

The report went on to say that the empty van had been found but there was still no trace of Dr. Wilson. Having no more real information, he passed the burden of filling airtime to the roving, on-the-scene reporter, who informed the viewers of the obvious fact that he was standing in the parking lot of the casino with a crowd of people, then spent the next five minutes interviewing willing spectators, none of whom knew more than he.

Ackerman didn't like the phrase "progress in the case. " Voters would hear this to mean that Davis was doing his job. But as he continued to watch, he began to reconsider. The van was empty. Where is the victim? The tension in the citizenry would mount. They would demand action. Still, the word "progress" should never have been used. Did the News Director think he was dealing with a fool?

A female announcer began to introduce the interview with Kip Springer. This also irked him. He had specified that it should be the male anchor. To his mind, a viewer reflexively regarded news delivered by a woman as filler and fluff.

He listened and watched carefully, his memory recording every word of the brief interview between Kip Springer and the reporter. It opened nicely, just as he had written the script, with Springer rushing officiously to his car, looking around surprised to see the reporter and interrupting his urgent business to respond graciously to a messenger from the people.

Ackerman's approval quickly faded. Springer was not saying what he'd been told. He was going very easy on Hoss Davis, voicing none of the criticism Ackerman had coached him to say. "I think the person who did this should have been caught by now." That was all, no detail about Davis botching the investigation. Ackerman acknowledged, however, that Kip's promise to the perpetrator that he would be caught and punished had clout. The overall effect, he concluded, was good enough—barely. Nevertheless, Springer hadn't performed as he'd been directed. He would have to learn that he got extra points for good, original ideas only after he had completed his assignment.

Switching off the set, he sat quietly. He felt good, the way he always felt when he was in a struggle with an adversary. Outwitting the opponent and the moment of triumph, that's what it was all about. It had nothing to do with real gains, because he had no real needs. No needs, only old gnawing, unfinished personal issues, ones he never addressed head-on. Vaguely he knew this to be true, but only vaguely, because like most people, he'd worked out a program that sustained him. He wasn't about to question it—just keep on winning.

Just then one of his prizes entered the study, came over to him and kissed him. Lauren had been twenty years younger than he was when they married eleven years ago. Now she was only about twelve years younger by his perception. It would have been nice if it meant he'd grown eight years younger, but unfortunately that wasn't the case.

Claudia appeared at the door of the study just as a possessive hand was sliding up Lauren's leg. Claudia, familiar with this scene, delivered her message and withdrew. The message was that Ted Ross, one of the co-investors in Ackerman's land development syndicate, was on the phone and said it was important.

Filled with sudden irritation, Ackerman considered making Ross wait until he was finished with Lauren, but instead he left the hand where it was and answered the phone with the other.

"Yeah, Ted."

"Jason, we have a problem, possibly a serious one. I just learned of it a few minutes ago, when I came over to the Greenleaf Properties Office. Carl, our manager, thought at first he could handle it himself, but realizing its potential for trouble, decided he had to tell one of the partners."

Ackerman was getting impatient with this beating around the bush and was about to say so when Ross continued, "We had a break-in—well, actually, a walk-in theft. Yesterday our secretary sees this guy drive up to the office building in one of our trucks and get out. He's wearing coveralls like the guy wears in our garage. She doesn't recognize him, but she figures he must be newly hired. Guy comes in and tells her he's supposed to take your computer into Traverse City for repair. She shows him your office and goes back to work. Couple of minutes later he comes out of your office carrying the computer, puts it in the truck and drives away."

Ackerman was listening with full attention. His left hand, still between his wife's legs, felt nothing.

"When Carl came in to work, the secretary mentioned that your computer had been taken away for repair. He checked and sure enough it was gone. He asked the garage man, who knew nothing. Then the two of them did some checking. It looks like a coverall with the company logo on it is missing.

Ackerman's thoughts raced ahead. "Tell Carl not to report it to the Sheriff's office."

"He didn't. He's smarter than that."

Some years before, Ackerman had concluded that the whole Leelanau Peninsula offered almost infinite opportunities for profitable development. It could be made into a major American resort, a mid-western Aspen. The profit potential was mind boggling, especially for those in at the beginning. With this aim, he'd formed an investment group called Leelanau Development Corporation. Since then, he and his partners had been blocked in every attempt to get their project underway by the zoning committees of the county and its three largest towns. The residents of the county presented as large a problem. A large majority supported the zoning restrictions.

Ackerman decided the county officials would have to be replaced. The attitude of the residents toward his group must also be sweetened. To accomplish this, Ackerman adopted a new stratagem. First, the name of the partnership was changed to Greenleaf Properties. Then an undesirable parcel of land removed from any beach or village was purchased. Here they were granted approval for a condominium project. What they created was an ideal community complete with parks and a recreation complex that included a health club with a full time staff. The quality of the units and services and the beautiful landscaping far exceeded the price they asked. The County Administrator, Howard Stites, curious about what Ackerman was up to, had the Building Department run a cost estimate on Ackerman's project. The calculation showed the syndicate was losing up to twenty-five thousand on each of the twenty units – half a million worth of public relations for their future projects.

In addition, Greenleaf Properties became a heavy contributor to community fund-raising efforts. They topped it all off by providing a bus, the company's logo on the side of it, of course, for transporting seniors to medical appointments and community activities. The strategy paid off. Last spring a Chicago based polling service was hired to conduct a surreptitious survey of the county's residents. They found that sentiment, once vehemently opposed to Leelanau Development Corp., had become quite positive towards Greenleaf Properties. All the syndicate needed now was to get the incumbents out of office and Greenleaf Properties would roll up its sleeves. The current residents would wake up one morning to discover that their precious peninsula had changed for good and there wouldn't be a damn thing they could do about it.

Ackerman knew the locals were fond of telling tales of jokes on other people, a folk thing, he figured. The story of someone pulling a boner spread through the county faster than deer hunters on opening day. The syndicate was spending a lot of money to establish the image of competency. The story that some bozo could walk right into their office and walk off with a computer and a truck was a tale he didn't want circulated.

"Make sure Carl says nothing to anyone about this," Ackerman reasserted, "and let that dingbat secretary know her job depends on her silence. What we do publicly is ignore the whole thing. If the truck turns up, we say it was loaned to one of our men and then stolen from him. The serious problem is the computer. If someone got into the files it would be very bad for our plans. The thief probably just wants to sell it. The average buyer, not having the password, would have to replace the drive and throw the old one away, along with our files. Some hacker, however, might be able to find a backdoor and get into information that would hurt us badly. We need to get the computer back."

Ross listened and admired Ackerman's quick evaluation of the situation. He doubted if he would have thought of sacrificing the truck as part of the price of good public relations. It was reassuring to have one's money riding in the same wagon as Jason Ackerman's.

Ross said, "I'll take care of it," as if he'd had some part in the decision.

Ackerman hung up and was soon back up to speed in his domestic project.

❍

Eagerly, Marti mixed her colors on the palette. It was another beautiful sunset and the unfinished canvas of the hill behind her house waited. Satisfied, she turned to study the hill once more before touching brush to canvas. Something was interrupting the mood she was trying to evoke. Some color ... yes, over along the right border of the field, about fifty yards away, her eye caught something black. What was it? She strained to see in the diminishing light, but was unable to distinguish any detail. It hadn't been there yesterday, of that she was sure. Could it be a piece of paper that had been blown there by the winds of the storm? No, it was more substantial. Since her mood for painting had been broken, she might as well get her bird-watching binoculars and have a look.

The binoculars weren't where she usually kept them, so it took a while to find them. By the time she was able to get back outside and train the binoculars on the black object, it was dusk. The glasses were of a high magnification and as a consequence admitted little light. The object looked closer, but it was too dark to make out detail. What was it? An answer suggested itself that frightened her. Suddenly, the fields around her seemed too quiet. She laid the binoculars on the chair in order to have both hands for the crutches and got back inside the house as quickly as she could.

❍

Hoss sat in the Sheriff's Department garage with Shorty McQuade. The lab people had gone for the day, but they had found something very significant—four short, wiry, curly, black hairs. They had been pressed into a fold of the black upholstery of the driver's seat. Dr. Wilson, her husband and their daughter were blond. This evidence had been flown to the main lab in Lansing.

Hoss and Shorty continued to sit after everyone had gone because they were too tired to move. Neither had slept for thirty-six hours. They were tired, but a little high. The evidence specialist had assured them that the hairs were completely adequate to identify the DNA pattern of the person they came from.

"In other words," Shorty exclaimed in a raspy voice, "out of all the people in the world, we'll know who the hair belongs to. We just won't know his name."

"I know his name!" Hoss returned with emphasis. "I'll never cease to be amazed by the mistakes people make. Harry was so careful to avoid leaving a clue. There was literally nothing else, no prints, no fibers. Well, almost nothing else. He forgot to sweep his driveway all the way out to the road. Like I told you after I saw the tread pattern on the van, I'm sure they're the same as those on his driveway. Useless in court, however, but it should be enough to get a court order to take a pubic hair specimen from Harry."

Shorty began laughing and couldn't stop, partly from fatigue and partly because of the mental picture he'd formed. Watching him, Hoss first smiled and then began to laugh, also. "What's so damn funny?" he yelled.

Shorty got control of himself long enough to ask, "Which one of us is gonna pluck that specimen?" They broke up laughing again like happy drunks.

"I think they've got special technicians for that," Hoss said.

They would have started laughing, again, but the telephone rang on the garage's extension.

Kate Schott, the evening dispatcher said, "A woman named Marti Jensen says she needs to talk to you. Important, she claims."

Hoss didn't want to have to deal with Marti tonight, but couldn't ignore her either. "OK, Kate, put her on."

"It's me, again, Hoss and I need you to come up to my place again … right now."

If it had been someone else pulling the same prank a second time, Hoss might have dismissed her coolly, but he tempered his response. "What's the problem?"

"Hoss, I was outside just now and I noticed something near the top of the hill by my house. It's black. I know it wasn't there yesterday."

What was going on here? His mind was so soggy from lack of sleep and overdosing on coffee that he was having difficulty thinking. Was she making another attempt to seduce him, or was she spooked, thinking there might be a kidnapper roaming the county?

"What do you think it is, Marti?"

"I can't see it clearly enough to say for sure." She paused then said sheepishly, "I was wondering if it could be … that doctor."

She was almost apologetic. Was it because of the transparent ploy she'd used to get him alone the other night, or was she embarrassed that she was nervous being alone? Hoss reviewed in his mind the description of the clothes Dr. Wilson had been wearing when she left home Tuesday morning. Gray—gray dress, nothing black.

"I really doubt that, Marti, but I tell you what I'll do, I'll come up there first thing in the morning and take a look. Just lock up tight, so you feel comfortable and I'll see you in the morning."

"But, if it is her body, wouldn't you want to know tonight?"

Was there something teasing in her voice—the old Marti setting him up?

"She wasn't wearing black, Marti. I'll be there first thing. We can have a cup of coffee."

Again the mixed feelings. One part of him wanted her to leave him alone. That part guarded against unneeded complications in his life. As for the other part … well…. Which was greater? He was too tired to decide.

And what did you expect, she thought, when she hung up. How would you have reacted if you were the sheriff and this broad calls saying, "There's something black and I don't know what it is, but it may be a body?" Especially after you'd already pulled one stunt to lure him up here!

She'd left the binoculars on the chair outside. If she didn't have the damned cast on her leg, she could dash out and get them. But there was no way she was going back out there. They would just have to stay where they were. A little dew would do them no harm. She checked the two doors. She did own a gun—a shotgun left behind by a one-time roommate.

She didn't like guns and had intended to get rid of it but hadn't yet. She went into the pantry off the kitchen, found the gun and a box of shells and brought them into the kitchen. She had loaded it only once before and it took several minutes until the procedure came back to her. She decided not to pump a shell into the chamber but placed the loaded gun behind a kitchen door and put the box of shells into a drawer. A dog—maybe she should get a big dog. She'd never had one, because she wanted to be able to leave at any time without having to provide for a pet. She wished she had one now.

A pot of bean soup simmered on the stove in the sparsely furnished kitchen. She mixed a salad and put two slices of Jack Taylor's cherry-walnut bread on a plate. A third of a bottle of cabernet rounded out supper. She usually put on some music while she ate, but didn't tonight, because she wanted to be alert to sounds around the house.

Pouring the wine, she thought of the fear the stupid object on the hillside had aroused. The odds were that it was nothing, as Hoss had said, just trash. What was causing the jitters wasn't the black object, she realized, but the image she'd had when first she'd heard of Barbara Wilson's disappearance. It was that of a lone woman being overpowered and abducted. She recognized that such a fear had been in the back of her mind since she'd first returned here and rented this isolated farm. She'd kept telling herself there was nothing to worry about here in this sleepy county.

Marti had been on her own a long time, but never really alone. There had been roommates or lovers or dormitories or close apartment neighbors, always people about. She'd enjoyed that, but she'd also yearned for time and space to be alone and work. The older she got, her painting satisfied her the most. She'd had enough entertainment for a lifetime - more than enough. Still she needed to have a man in her life. When there was no one, she began to feel dried up. That had prompted the clumsy scene with Hoss. In some ways, he was still a little boy. She knew he had an itch for her, but he was afraid of what would happen in his marriage if he yielded to it. OK, she was cool with that, but she wasn't going to help him with his decision. If he wandered her way she'd enclose him in her need. In the meantime, she thought she'd just make a trip into Traverse City tomorrow night and see if anyone at Larry's Oyster Bar might be lonely.

Cheered by this plan, she cleaned up the supper dishes, got the book she'd started reading, and settled down in the living room. Her meal, her plan for tomorrow and the book were forces for contentment, but she still had an ear cocked for strange sounds. So poised, she fell asleep in the easy chair.

Marti awakened suddenly. What had awakened her? A sound! Was it a car door closing or was it only a dream? It was dark outside now. She reached up and turned off the lamp beside her chair. Only a faint light coming along the hall from the kitchen entered the dark living room. What was that? A footstep on the porch! Who was it? Her breathing stopped. He was here to kill her, because....

Two raps on the door, then Hoss's voice. "Marti, it's Hoss."

She grabbed her crutches and quickly went to the window that opened onto one end of the porch. She could see Hoss standing there by the dim light coming through the glass of the front door She began breathing again and went to the door and opened it.

"For Christ sake, Hoss, couldn't you have called first? You scared the living shit out of me."

He saw that he had. "I'm sorry, I guess I didn't think."

Her acute fright subsiding, she invited him in.

"You changed your mind?"

"After I got home and had something to eat, I felt less tired and began thinking that you were really scared, and..."

"And," Marti said, "I wasn't just making something up to get you up here and into my bed. Is that what you were about to say?"

Hoss smiled and shook his head. "No, but it crossed my mind. What I was about to say was that you wouldn't get worked-up for nothing."

Marti moved aside. "Come on in."

Hoss stayed where he was, just inside the door. "I'm going to have a look at your body." He stopped and blushed at the slip. "*The* body—and then get on home and get some sleep."

Her teasing smile said, "Now, we both know what you really want to look at." She continued aloud, "OK, but I'm coming with you."

Hoss pointed to the crutches. "Can you manage climbing the hill with those?"

"I wasn't thinking of climbing. If a girl gets turned down on her wish to be carried to bed, the least she should be offered is a lift up a little hill."

"You take the flashlight," he said, and gathered her up in his strong arms, cast and all, as if she were a child.

The sky was astonishingly clear, one of those nights when there seem to be many more stars and the moonlight is so bright one can go about as well as by day. A silver world, not day or night, but slipped in between, creating the notion that whatever happened in it was not to be judged by standards of the day. For lovers a magic light, but eerie to those thinking they might discover a dead body in the silver grass.

As they approached they could see the dark form against the light background of the field. It had the shape and sheen of a wet seal. Marti turned on the flashlight.

"Plastic. It's a plastic…." Her voice broke off as they both saw the pair of feet protruding from one end of the rolled sheeting.

"Oh, Hoss, it's her!"

Hoss put Marti down and held her until she was balanced on her feet. He took the light from her and played it over the body and the earth around it. He carefully pulled the plastic back from the head.

"It's Dr. Wilson, all right. There's a wide wound on her head."

Hoss left Barbara Wilson's face uncovered and began to make a wide circuit around the corpse, focusing the flashlight on the ground.

In the bright moonlight, Marti looked into the dead woman's face. The head was turned in her direction. This stranger seemed to stare back at her imploringly. The laceration Hoss had noted looked like a small black skullcap. Her clear, pale skin radiated a cool glow brighter than one would expect from reflected light. The eyes were open and Marti imagined them appealing to her. Appealing to her to understand what had happened to her, to know her final terror, one woman to another.

Hoss picked Marti up and hurriedly made his way back down the hill. He was eager to get to his phone, eager to report the discovery and alert the crime scene unit that their rest was at an end.

Hoss's voice was in the background, talking on the phone, but Marti was looking back up the hill toward Barbara Wilson. Soon there would be a swarm of men here impersonally going about their business of examining everything about this woman, but they wouldn't experience the communication Marti sensed she'd had with her. She felt guilty leaving her there alone in the moonlight on the cold ground.

CHAPTER 8

"THE SON-OF-A-BITCH SCALPED HER! Can you believe it?"

These were his first words when he saw K.D. was still awake. It was three a.m. The County Medical Examiner had done a preliminary examination, photographs had been taken and the body removed to Munson Hospital for the post-mortem in the morning. Hoss decided to post a deputy at the farm and await daylight to complete the examination of the site. This done, he went home. His body was beyond collapse, but his mind raced.

K.D. was overwhelmed. "What happened?"

"He probably suffocated her, scalped her and then dumped her body on the old Johansen farm on Swede Road."

"What do you mean, scalped?"

"Like he cut away a piece of her scalp." He held his hands up and made an oval three by four inches.

"You mean scalped like in the old west? Harry Swifthawk?"

"You're damn right!"

"You think it's him because of that? Because he's a Chippewa? I mean I'm not sure they ever did that."

"I don't mean he did it because he's a Chippewa, I mean he did it to give me the finger."

"Wait a minute, I know he is always baiting you, but it's hard to believe he'd go that far."

"Yeah, of course, but you see, I don't think for a minute Swifthawk intended to kill the woman. Robbery was no doubt the intent, but something went wrong and he suffocated her by accident."

K.D. was frowning. "I don't get it, then why draw attention to himself with this 'scalping' as you're calling it?"

This last challenge visibly stymied Hoss. His reply lacked the earlier certainty.

"How do I know his reasons? There is the evidence of the tire tracks at his house. He pointed out the van in the casino lot, and why did the killer cut out some of the woman's scalp if it wasn't meant to mean scalping? He thought he could wave it in my face, because he thought he had an alibi; he was at work. When I faced him with the news that this alibi was not going to hold up, he couldn't say anything. I know he's trying right now to get some girl to lie and say he was at her house. He'll have trouble with that, because the word will be out around the reservation that Harry is in deep, serious shit. No gal wants to get herself involved in a murder. But, at the time he killed Barbara Wilson and cut out a piece of her scalp, he thought he had a solid alibi."

Hoss let his bulk fall onto the bed beside his wife.

"My mind's not closed," he added in a calmer voice, "But the evidence is strong enough to arrest him and get a sample of his pubic hair to see if there's a match with the hair we found in the van."

K.D., on one elbow, studied her husband. His voice had been loud—strident. This was rare in him. Was it his fatigue? Did he really hate this troublesome Swifthawk fellow, or was there something else?

"Marti Jensen owns the Johansen farm," she ventured.

"She's the one who spotted the body. She didn't know what it was, just a strange object on the hill behind the house, so she called and reported it."

"That's where you went after you came home?"

"It kept bothering me. I had to see what it was."

"But you were so tired when you got home. Why didn't you ask her to go take a look herself?"

"I knew she couldn't climb the hill, because of her crutches."

"Crutches?"

Hoss saw the hole he'd stepped into, and he sensed K.D. saw it too.

She understood a little more now about his unsettled mood. Certainly he felt the stress of the responsibility for the Wilson case and the failure of his attempt to find Barbara Wilson while she was alive. Now, however, she realized that Marti Jensen must be added to the equation. K.D. had long known that the attractive eccentric fascinated Hoss. It was the kind of fascination that a mind-altering drug might hold: you may be wary of it, but you wonder, nevertheless, what it would be like. When the news came around that Marti had moved back into the area, K.D. noticed Hoss's reaction. While he tried to hide it, she could tell his interest was instantly aroused. K.D. wondered just how much involvement there had been between her husband and this woman who had always scoffed at what their community called "common decency." Was Hoss bothered by guilt? Was that the reason he hadn't mentioned having seen Marti? Was that the reason he hadn't said, after dinner, that he was going to her farm? Was it guilt, or was it only a wish to keep the contact a secret, so he could continue it without discovery?

"When we pick him up, we can get his DNA profile. That should wrap it up." The conviction he tried for had a false ring.

K.D. didn't reply. She got up and went into the bathroom and closed the door. She paused in front of the mirror and quietly studied her face. There was a mixture of sadness and fear there. She knew the fragility of anyone's contentment. As a volunteer at the rehab unit of the hospital, she'd heard many stories of peoples' lives altered suddenly and drastically by an accident or illness. It didn't matter that you had been a hard-working, responsible person. It didn't matter that you had been fair and gentle in your dealings with others. None of this protected you.

At forty-two, she still had her looks, thanks to inherited bone structure. She was very fit, but there was no denying the lines and lack of life in her skin. Gone was the elastic vitality of youth. Marti's could be no better, she reassured herself. Marti, however, was unknown and exotic fruit, while she was familiar fare.

How stupid! While she was deeply affected by this situation, at the same time she experienced it as banal, common to the point of ugliness. It came to her suddenly why Hoss focused on Harry Swifthawk. She had found his vehemence strange, bordering on racism, and she had never heard anything like this from him before. But it was the simple old human formula, wasn't it? When you can't deal with your own conflicts, look for the stranger toward whom you can direct your frustration. Harry Swifthawk, as a member of a group already historically suspect and currently arousing envy because of its gambling bonanza, made the perfect scapegoat. Add the fact that Harry was personally disreputable and had thrown down the gauntlet to the non-Indian community—and Hoss in particular—time and again.

She had to help Hoss get control of his distorted feelings before he did something foolish that would hurt him.

❍

"He's hiding. We've asked around the reservation, but no one knows anything," Shorty reported. "It's hard to know if that's completely true, or no one wants to be the one to turn in one of their own. I think the guys on the Council want us to find him, but we gotta do it ourselves. So I've put out an APB,"

Standing on Marti Jensen's porch, Hoss listened to the news that Harry had slipped through their fingers. Shorty waited for instructions, but Hoss was lost in thought. He was thinking about the six thousand in cash Barbara Wilson had withdrawn from the bank the day before she was abducted, and the two hundred and sixty out of an ATM the following morning. He'd only learned of it this morning at breakfast when Donna called him. The point was Harry must have the money since nothing was found on the body.

Hoss returned his attention to Shorty. "I'm not surprised he decided to run. When you find him, be sure the location is searched for cash. Dr. Wilson had over six thousand on her when Harry snatched her."

Shorty left with an uneasy feeling that his assignment to find Harry was a land mine on his final stretch of road to retirement. But, Shorty knew Hoss wanted Harry very badly and that was enough for him.

Hoss walked up the hill where the crime scene investigators were still at work. Doc Bahle, the Medical Examiner, had told Hoss the night before that as far as he could discern on a preliminary exam the cause of death was anoxia. Doc didn't like her color. There were no marks on her throat, so it would imply suffocation. The post-mortem would tell them. Also, there were no signs that she had struggled—no skin or fabric under her nails. Hoss had asked Bahle about the possibility of sexual penetration but was told that, too, would have to await the autopsy.

Hoss made his way through the thicket of weeds separating the field from the dirt road that Swifthawk must have driven up. OK, he was thinking to himself, take it from the beginning. Suppose Harry was pissed off by my remarks about his behavior being childish and that made him try something to top the theft of the gasoline. He drives into Traverse City and sees a lone woman getting money from an ATM. He follows her to the Peninsular Power Building and figures she'll be back out soon. When she returns, he jumps into her car, probably armed and wearing a ski mask. He makes her drive to his place—no, that wouldn't work, because she'd be able to identify it later. Certainly he never intended to kill her. Possibly he intended to take her someplace like a woods, where he'd leave her tied up to delay her raising an alarm until he could get rid of the van.

Hoss sensed discordance. How would abducting a woman in Traverse City, outside of his jurisdiction, constitute revenge for his remarks made to Harry? K.D's reminder that a person is innocent until proven guilty and how he might just be ladling a little of his earlier aggravation with Swifthawk into the present case nagged at Hoss, but he brushed aside the interfering thoughts. He was convinced Harry was guilty. They had the pubic hair, and there would be a match! Still, he'd lost his buoyant feeling.

❍

It was at breakfast that Lauren Ackerman told her husband that she'd heard the woman doctor's body had been discovered.

"Where did you hear that?"

"Claudia heard it on the radio this morning."

"Who found it and where?"

"I think she said the Sheriff found it on a farm last night."

Ackerman got up and rushed to his study. He dialed Eugene Lessum's cell phone number. The Governor's Administrative Assistant answered in his car on the way to the Executive Office Building in Lansing.

"Eugene, this is Ackerman. The body of this Wilson woman was found last night. I don't know the details, but it's imperative that we act now to get the State Police on the case. In the meantime, call Jerry Beasley in Traverse City and have him leak the news about the State Police. We've got to get it on the next news break."

Lessum was angered by the guy's arrogance, but...

"Consider it done, Jason."

❍

Shelving any illusion of being a free man, Boyd Steward waited on the line to be connected to Col. Mel Pollock, the Director of the of the Michigan State Police. He had built a warm relationship with this colleague over the years. During his many years of public life, Boyd had asked others for many favors of a stinking, political kind, but never of this man, and he hated to do it now. It would have been nice to retire with at least one person knowing you for the kind of person you wanted to be. Mel would know in an instant that what he was being told to do was a political knife in the back of Hoss Davis. And, if Mel refused to go along with the program, Boyd would have to outline the demise of Mel's own career for him.

"Boyd," a cheerful voice anticipating warm friendship came through the ear piece, "Just this morning, Ralph Biggs suggested I call you to get up a poker game for this coming weekend. How about it?"

"Great idea. You name the place and time and I'll be there. I'm batching next weekend. Sarah's visiting our daughter in St.Louis. She's in medical school down there, you know."

"That's right, how's she doing?"

"She's getting straight A's in moaning and groaning."

"Aren't they wonderful! Hey, what can I do for you, today?"

Steward took a deep breath, as if he were about to step out the door of a C-54 with a well-armed enemy waiting below. There was nothing to do now but jump and hope for the best. "There's a situation up in Leelanau County, as I'm sure you're aware. I understand your crime lab is already involved."

Pollock listened without comment while Steward read the orders. He was silent for a few painful seconds after Steward finished.

"Was this your idea, Boyd?"

Boyd Steward heard the coolness in this question. He would have liked to be able to tell this old friend that it wasn't at all his idea, but he knew that if he wanted to protect his son, he must avoid any hint that the plan originated higher up.

"Yes, it is. I'm concerned, you see, that this killer be caught as soon as possible. An object lesson—swift justice—reassure the people. There hasn't been much crime in that rural area, and I want it to stay that way."

Again Pollock was slow to respond. "I was talking just yesterday with the Commander of the Traverse City Post, Lyle Steele, about this. He tells me Davis is well liked up there. I didn't get the impression he has a reputation for incompetence, either. Where did you hear that, Boyd?"

"I didn't say he was incompetent, I'm just saying I want us to have our best team on the field." Why did Mel have to make this so hard?

"I've met Davis, as a matter of fact, I think you'd like him. Kinda guy you'd want at a poker night," Mel continued.

"Because he's a nice guy, doesn't mean he can do the best job," Steward argued, becoming angry with Pollock's resistance.

"What I'm saying, Boyd, is, for no fault of his own, this won't look good for Davis, and he's running for re-election."

Boyd Steward counseled himself to be calm. Mel Pollock was only speaking as he wished he could himself. "I appreciate your input, Mel. Really I do, but I've decided it's time the state entered the investigation, and I want your department to step up to the line as of this minute. Do the kind of job we all know we can expect from you." The tone was final, no room for a rebuttal. Steward attempted to end the call on a lighter note, "Let me know about the poker game."

Boyd Steward hung up. He was certain it would be a very long while, indeed, before he heard from Mel about a poker game.

❍

Hoss's mood lifted a bit as he drove from Marti's farm to his office in Leland. It came from recalling his contact with Marti last night—her appeal for his help, carrying her up that hill and the smell of her hair tucked in beneath his chin—and knowing that she watched him as he went about directing the investigation. The experience they shared last night brought them closer together. He no longer thought of her as an exciting tease. He could see her as a companion. He had no doubt that she was well aware of the change in his feelings.

He parked in his space at headquarters and went into the building.

CHAPTER 9

HOSS WAS COMING DOWN THE hall to the dispatcher's office when he heard David Wick say, "Hold on, he just walked in." David held out the phone toward him.

"It's Don Silver. He's calling from the State Police lab."

"Hi, Don."

"Hi, Hoss, I'm at the lab. Wanted to catch you before you go pulling down our pal Swifthawk's pants. The hairs we found in the van aren't his—or anyone else's. They're dog hairs."

"Dog hairs! Are you sure?"

"I'm sure. The only question is what breed, and we'll have to get the FBI lab's profile on canine DNA sub-classes to determine that."

Hoss was deflated. "That's not good news, Don." He tried not to reveal the full degree of his disappointment. "What it comes down to is that we didn't find anything of value."

"Well, I wouldn't put it that way," Don argued, "It is evidence."

Don's reply surprised Hoss. He had only been thinking of evidence against Harry. "Right, Don," he managed. He fell to wondering if the Wilsons had a dog. "I wonder if Donna knows?" he muttered.

"How's that?" Don asked.

"Sorry, Don. Thinking aloud. Thanks for calling with the information. Please go ahead and have them nail down the breed. I'll call you later."

One thing was sure: it hadn't been old Yellow in the van.

The phone rang again. K.D.'s voice had that edge which Hoss associated with bad news. "They just said the State Police are beginning their own investigation of the Wilson case. It was on Channel 8."

Hoss was stunned. "Starting their own investigation? You're sure they didn't say they were cooperating with the Sheriff's Department? What exactly did they say?"

"This newsman said they learned that the Attorney General had directed the State Police to begin an investigation of its own so that their greater resources could be utilized, because such a vicious killer must be apprehended immediately … or something to that effect."

Hoss said, "I see" and fell silent.

"You haven't heard anything then?"

"No."

She could barely hear his answer. She knew what a blow this was to him. "Darling, I'm sorry. Maybe you could call the Attorney General yourself."

"Damn it. I've never heard of anything like this before."

K.D. began to blurt out what was on her mind, then hesitated. She modified her thoughts to a single sentence. "I know what it is, Hoss. Someone doesn't want you to get the credit for solving the case."

To herself she thought, The Attorney General wants Kip to win the election.

But even as much as she had said was too fast for Hoss. K.D. was always seeing shadows among the shadows. Shadows he couldn't see at all.

He said, "Honey, I'll try to find out more about it. I'll talk to you later."

K.D.'s mind was already racing ahead to motives and images deep and dark. She said nothing since she knew from experience that Hoss would hear her speculations with discomfort. She always came away from these exchanges feeling unhealthily paranoid. Nevertheless, in her own mind suspicion was rapidly gelling into certainty.

❍

When Jason Ackerman was seriously worried, he went for a long drive, alone. He had long ago forgotten the origin of this inclination. It had, in fact, begun a couple of months after he had been awakened by his mother's crying out when she discovered his father dead next to her in bed.

Jason's life before the morning of his father's fatal heart attack had been perfect. He hadn't appreciated that fact, of course, since all he knew were doting parents spending lots of money, much of it on him. The abundant money came from his father's successful Chicago law practice. The manner in which all of it was readily spent on anything and everything for the good life was dictated by his father's compulsion to live out a fantasy of limitless wealth.

Jason hadn't understood this. He believed—and why not?—that servants and private school, his golf, tennis and ski lessons, and the constant flow of the latest, expensive sports equipment were the natural rhythm of life. As a child, such things as savings and insurance were beyond his knowledge. They were not real to his father, either, not something to be taken seriously when there were more entertaining ways to spend cash.

That's why Jason's life changed so precipitously that morning. The sudden loss of the father's income left Jason and his mother penniless. No longer would he be able to attend private school with all his friends. No longer would he be welcome on the tennis courts or links of the country club where he'd been praised for his rapidly developing skills.

The advent of this sudden change in his life, coupled with the deep mourning for his father, had produced a depression of suicidal degree. Nothing interested him or could even motivate him to move. Nothing, until he saw his father's car keys lying on the hall table. He had rudimentary driving skills, but had never driven a car alone. His mother, preoccupied with her own concerns, was unaware of his backing the car out of the garage and onto the street.

Jason headed toward the open country north of their Lake Forest home. Superimposed on his depressed feelings was this new sensation of independence. The powerful car would go anywhere he commanded; he had but to turn the wheel.

That day, driving alone, he experienced the epiphany of his life. He suddenly saw that life was all about money. One had it in quantities that made a difference, or one didn't. He did not then, or thereafter, question his father's behavior. He didn't question his father's denial of his cardiac condition or his failure to provide for the family. He concluded it was his mother's fault for not taking better care of his father. Women were not to be trusted with anything serious.

In that moment, his character fused around the idea that his father's only mistakes had been too little money and too much trust in a woman, and he resolved with religious intensity never to be in either position himself. With that resolution, his depression began to lift and his energies became boundless in the pursuit of his own wealth and success. This mind-set had served him well. Still, occasional thorny problems arose. At those times, without being consciously aware of the connection to his past epiphany, Jason Ackerman found he had an urge to go for a drive, alone.

His present concern was the computer.

The computer records of memos and correspondence that would reveal very clearly what Greenleaf Properties had in mind for Leelanau County. The devious steps the plan outlined to achieve their goals would be certain to anger the citizenry. If the content of the computer's files were to become public knowledge, he and his co-investors may very well have to say goodbye to those plans and the money already spent. The potential loss represented a small part of his net worth, but Jason Ackerman didn't like to lose. It was more than that: he was terrified of losing.

As if Providence had heard the terror in his heart, the car phone rang.

"Mr. Ackerman, this is Carl. We found the truck. One of our guys spotted it in the parking lot of the casino. I sent him back there to keep an eye on it until I could talk to you."

Ackerman's energy surged. "Good man, Carl! Now I want you to go over there and take over from him. I don't want any screw-up on this. We don't give a damn about the fucking truck, but we need the computer. If it's in the truck, great, but if it isn't we have to find the guy who stole it. Understand?"

"Right, I understand."

"If the computer isn't there, stay near the truck and watch to see if someone tries to move it. If they do, follow them."

"Right."

Ackerman smiled to himself as he hung up. It was just as if things happened when he wished them to.

❍

Barclay Scott, who owned the Riverside Inn, had bought the old Kalcheck farm six years earlier. He had bought it with the plan of someday building a home on its highest hill. Deep inside the woods that crowned the second highest hill was an unused sugar shack built by Amos Kalcheck with inch-and-a-half planks of native cedar nearly seventy years earlier. It remained as snug and dry as on the day Amos put it up, a fact appreciated by the man who had just taken up residence there.

Harry had moved in that morning. Buddy had awakened him with the news that the woman doctor's body had been found and an arrest warrant issued for him. Harry had but one thought—get away. He felt sure that once Hoss had him, he'd never be free again. He also needed time to think. He was badly confused.

He had been assuming all along that Hoss was interested in him and his garage because he had linked him to the theft of the computer and the truck. Had he been totally wrong about that? Had Hoss only been thinking of the woman doctor? One thing was sure, he had to hide out until he knew more, and he couldn't delay long enough to brush his teeth.

He instinctively knew—knowledge instilled by hundreds of stories spanning generations of the Chippewa's experience with white justice—that once you were in a white man's jail you didn't stand a chance. He had to remain free, or he wouldn't be able to help himself. Hoss had a reputation of being fair with the people of the Band, but Harry knew he had jerked Hoss around too many times over the years to expect fairness. Maybe that was his own fault, but there it was.

Harry had brought bread, cheese, smoked whitefish and two six packs with him to the sugar shack. He now sat on the bench outside the door and popped the cap on the second beer of his lunch. Sitting there in the shade of the giant maples and listening to the wind ruffling the leaves overhead, it was incongruous to think that out there in the world below this hill men were hunting for him. Although he couldn't be seen from the valley, he was able to catch glimpses, through the foliage, of the occasional car as it passed along Jacobson Road, coming and going between the reservation and Leland. He was reminded of the times when, as a child, he would climb a tall tree and look down on the adults looking for him and calling his name, unaware of his presence above them.

More disturbing to Harry than Hoss's pursuit of him was his growing fear that someone else might also be searching for him. The truck had sat in the casino lot for two days, and it was still there this morning when he'd left home to come up to the old sugar shack. It must not have been reported stolen to the Sheriff, after all, or it would have been found by now. Why hadn't Greenleaf Properties notified the police? That had been what Harry expected and wanted. Harry was puzzled. Did it mean they didn't want the police to know about the theft? Otherwise, wouldn't they want their stuff back? Sure they would. He'd known of people not reporting a stolen car because there was a hidden stash of dope inside. Could there be something like that inside the truck? The glove box? Under the seat? Well, he wasn't about to go near the damn thing to find out.

There was the computer. He'd transferred it to the trunk of his own car before he ditched the truck at the casino so that when Hoss returned the truck to those Greenleaf guys, they'd still be angry at him because he'd failed to retrieve the computer. Harry had no experience with computers. This one looked to him like the standard type he'd seen in offices. He'd never heard of anyone stashing dope in a computer, but he supposed there'd be room. Maybe he'd take a look, later.

Mary McNab's cell phone was in his car. When he'd told her this morning that he was going to hide out, she made him drive by her house and get it so she could keep in touch. His train of thought and his mounting anxiety about the stolen truck brought him to the point where he had to know if it was still parked in the casino lot. He got the phone and returned to the bench and entered Mary's private number at the casino office. Her voice was friendly when she answered, but as soon as he spoke her name it became officious.

"You can't talk, Mary, is that right?"

"Yes, Sir. What can I do for you?"

"Mary, I need to know if a certain truck is parked in the casino lot." He described the truck and its exact location.

"I'll have to check on that when I have time, Sir," she said. "I'll call you back. What's your number?"

Harry started to look for a number on the instrument in his hand but realized before embarrassing himself that it was part of her act. Instead he said, "Just dial someone who can't get you off his mind."

Mary liked that. She came near to spoiling her performance with a delighted laugh.

Ten minutes later, she left the office as if on a routine errand but instead went outside to check the parking lot. A large RV blocked her view of the place Harry had said the truck would be, making it necessary for her to walk all the way out into the lot. Walking past the RV, she came directly upon the truck, its grill toward the casino, its rear end toward the highway.

That she had deliberately come to look at the truck, was obvious to anyone who saw her, including the man parked three cars away, eyes fixed on her like those of a hunting hawk.

Satisfied that she'd located the truck Harry described, she began to walk away.

Carl didn't really expect whoever had stolen the truck to return, but if he did, Carl imagined him cruising by slowly in a car and he was ready to follow. Now here was this Indian woman who obviously was checking out the truck. If he let her walk away, he'd lose her. He quickly slipped out of his car and began to follow her. Mary sensed his presence and turned to look at him, then began walking faster. Carl ran quickly and was beside her before she could take half a dozen more steps.

"Get in my car," he commanded evenly. He moved the hand inside his windbreaker forward showing Mary, by its outline against the thin fabric, the object that backed his words.

He was a good twenty years older, slightly built and only Mary's height, but the certainty of his will and the gun told her she was no match for him. She was imbued with the same conviction Harry held: never become a white man's captive! On the other hand, she was afraid that if she started running, he would shoot her. No one was nearby, and the sound of a shot would be lost in the traffic noise from the highway.

The man motioned with his head toward his car. He displayed a desperate quality that frightened her, as if his life depended on her capture.

Just then a car turned slowly into the lane, looking for a vacant space to park. There were four men in the car. Mary waved to the driver and motioned for him to approach. The man with the gun could do nothing but stand and watch her as she walked over to the driver's open window and said, "There are empty spaces at the side of the casino, just follow me."

The man continued to stand and watch as Mary led and the car followed. On one of several over-the-shoulder glances, she saw his car drive out of the lot and turn north on Highway 22. An involuntary shudder passed through her. She was sure she had just had a brush with death.

Immediately she called Harry from a lobby phone in the casino. He listened to her story, his anxiety and anger mounting as she described the attempted abduction.

"Mary, I'm sorry I put you in that spot, but I never anticipated anything like this."

"Sorry isn't good enough. Your problem is that you never anticipate the consequences of what you do." Her pent-up frustration flared. "Are you going to tell me what this is all about?"

"Are you where you can talk freely?"

"Yes."

"I feel like a stupid kid, but what happened is I got carried away. The Sheriff said some things to me that made me want to get even with him. I knew that this Greenleaf outfit was a high-powered business that would climb all over Davis demanding he get their truck and computer back."

"Truck and computer? Let me get this straight. You actually stole them?"

"Well, not really. I mean, I didn't want the damn truck or the computer. I only wanted to cause trouble for Davis."

Mary was speechless. How could she be involved with such an impulsive, childish man?

"That is so fucking stupid! You could spend years in prison because of this 'prank.'"

"No argument, but I naturally thought they would go screaming to the Sheriff, but apparently they haven't. I don't know what this means, but the way that guy came after you, it's pretty damn serious."

"Now you think of serious."

"When I went into that office, I was wearing that droopy mustache I wore at that costume party we went to and I wore sunglasses and a stocking cap with my hair all tucked up inside. There is no way that secretary can identify me, but now they'll know who I am, because they're going to find out who you are."

Harry was staring into the distance at nothing, his mind racing through the likely progression of events to follow. He repeated again, "I'm sorry as hell to mix you up in this, sweetheart."

She said nothing.

"Like I said, I don't like it that they didn't report the theft. Also, I don't understand this hardcore gun thing in the parking lot. We've got to assume they'll make another attempt to get you, because they'll want you to tell them where I am. The point is you've got to get away from there. You've got to get out of town."

"What? I can't do that. Who will take care of Aunt Clara and what about my job?"

"You can get one of your friends to look after Clara and you can take a leave of absence," Harry reasoned.

"You pull an adolescent stunt and then you want me to change my life all around because of it. No way, Harry! I'll take care of myself."

"Honey, I said I was sorry, I did a stupid thing. This mess has made me look at things differently, honest. It's just that right now, I'm afraid for you."

Mary calmed a bit but remained very skeptical about Harry's claim to have changed. Most likely he was worried that these people would make her reveal his hiding place.

"I'll tell you what," Harry offered, "I'll get Buddy to stick close to you. Have him call me on your cell phone number. Just don't get mad and put yourself in danger because of it. Promise me."

He sounded sincere, she argued with her better judgment. "All right ... for a couple of days."

"Good. Maybe by that time I can figure out what's going on. They could've had the truck if they wanted it, but apparently that's not important to them. It must be the computer they want back so fucking much."

❍

A day had passed since the warrant had been put out for Harry and they were no closer to finding him. Hoss had hoped that he'd be able to close the case before the State Police could even get up to speed. He believed both Mary McNab and Buddy were certain to know where Harry was hiding. One of them probably took him food each day. There was one more thing Hoss could try; he asked David Wick to connect him with Shorty.

"We're going to do something that's not quite according to the rules. I want you to go to the casino and follow Mary when she gets off from work. Tell Russ I want him to keep a watch on the road leading to their trailer and tail Buddy if he leaves. We may get lucky."

"OK, Boss. Incidentally, I think I know how Harry got the van into the casino lot without being seen by any of our guys. Fella works on the casino grounds noticed that there were fresh tire ruts on what used to be an old road that leads from the back of the parking lot up into the woods behind. I went and had a look. I could follow the track all the way through the woods and out to where the old road joins Peshawbestown Road as it runs along the top of the ridge. There are new ruts and the soil looks like the black dirt we found on the van's wheels."

"Good work. Sounds like it's something only a person familiar with the reservation would know about, wouldn't you say?"

"I'll agree with that."

Only minutes after he hung up, the expected call came from Lyle Steele at the State Police Post in Traverse City. Lyle was as tactful as he could be. His voice conveyed an apology, which he officially couldn't give. He said he had been ordered to begin a parallel investigation and requested access to any information Hoss's department already had. After having delivered that message, it was apparent in his tone of voice that he was happy to be able to move on to small talk about a mutual acquaintance.

So there it was. Clearly it had not been Lyle's idea, nor, Hoss thought, that of anyone in the State Police organization. They had enough work of their own without looking for more. The Traverse County Sheriff hadn't made any mutterings of disapproval either. Hell, he had been cooperating with him! It had to be coming from higher up the political ladder. Now Kip Springer's appearance on television made sense. Initially, Hoss had not questioned why Channel 8 chose to ask Kip his opinion about how the case was being handled. They're always chasing after candidates with their mobile camera. It never occurred to him that "breaking news" just might be choreographed. Maybe K.D.'s suspicion was right after all.

Any remaining doubt vanished when he walked into the Riverside Inn for lunch. Barclay Scott was standing at the bar looking up at a TV screen. He saw Hoss enter and said, quickly, "Hoss, come look at this!"

Kip Springer was coming down the front steps of the State Police Post in Traverse City. A smiling Kip walked over to the reporter who asked, "Mr. Springer, we understand that you have been conferring with the Post Commander about the ongoing investigation into the murder of Dr. Barbara Wilson. Can you tell the Channel 8 viewers if there has been any breakthrough in the case?"

Kip, looking very much the insider, answered, "The State Police, as I'm sure you know, only very recently began their investigation. I'm not at liberty to say anything about the stage of the investigation, but I'm sure things will begin to move rapidly now. I was sharing some of my ideas about the particulars of the case with Commander Steele."

"Commander Steele asked for your input, then?"

"Commander Steele welcomes good ideas, especially from those in law enforcement. I would like to take this opportunity to appeal to anyone who thinks he or she may have any information at all about this dreadful murder to call the State Police here in Traverse City. If we act together as a community we can make it very difficult for the criminal element to get a foothold here in this beautiful corner of the state." Kip turned and hurried to his waiting car, while the reporter repeated the usual closing statement, identifying himself and his whereabouts.

"Others in law enforcement?" Hoss repeated. "I wonder if the boys over at Springer Lumber know they're in law enforcement?"

Barclay drew off a glass of Sam Adams and put it on the bar for Hoss. "D'ya ever get the impression that the whole fuckin' world is done with mirrors? Hell, I know that half the time I'm not sure I'm real myself."

CHAPTER 10

DONNA STOPPED TO FILL UP at Snelling's Marathon station on Highway 22 at nine A.M. It was there Chris Snelling told her he'd heard on the radio about the State Police starting their own investigation.

"Guess we're too slow for 'em here on the peninsula," Snelling had concluded.

Donna hadn't seen or talked to anyone in the Department since she'd spoken to Hoss at noon, the previous day. Donna knew he must be pissed-off. Her first thought was to call in to headquarters, but after she'd signed for the gas and returned to her patrol car she had an idea. Did the presence of the State Police mean that Hoss would back off and let them run with the case? She didn't know. She knew, however, that she didn't want to back off of her investigation of Benjamin Wilson; she felt sure he was guilty. If she could get the proof she needed, the Sheriff's Department would get credit. Besides, no one had contacted her and told her to lay off. She decided to avoid that contact.

She parked her car in the driveway of the neighbor just to the south of the Wilson house, the Jacobs, Sarah and Richard. Donna had called the night before and made the early appointment. Before she could open the car door, David Wick's voice came on the radio asking for her response. She got out of the car, instead, and turned off her cell phone.

Sarah Jacobs answered the door, wearing an elegant robe. Sarah definitely went with the robe, dark brown eyes, gray-streaked, dark hair sleekly pulled back.

She led Donna to a breakfast room that had a view over Grand Traverse Bay. She brought a coffee carafe to the table and smiled at Donna.

"Where do you want to begin?"

"First of all, I want to thank you for seeing me this early and on such short notice. As part of our investigation into Dr. Wilson's murder, I'm trying to understand who she was—her personality, her activities, her friends … her marriage."

Sarah smiled, "You mentioned her marriage last, but my hunch is it ranks first in your curiosity. Am I right?"

With this, Donna understood that Sarah Jacobs was not one to let you stand back with note pad and pencil. She demanded conspiracy in the root meaning of the word.

"You're right."

Sarah nodded, not so much at Donna's admission as at the understanding she knew they now had.

"I don't suppose one should call it a marriage made in hell." She paused to sip her coffee and let the statement have an effect. "It was cobbled together in a laboratory, someplace where they graft different species together—a laboratory run by a scientist who knows nothing about people."

With comic understatement, Donna asked, "It's your opinion, then, that they were ill-suited?"

"I can't say there is anyone I could imagine as the perfect mate for either of them. Benjamin is not complicated, if you don't look too deeply. Your basic predator. Other people are to be used. He latched onto Barbara for her paycheck." Sarah studied Donna. "You're saying to yourself, 'This bitch has an axe to grind.' Am I right?"

Donna returned a faint smile in answer.

"I don't. The only reason I'm blabbing so freely is because I liked her and I want to help you if I can. You can believe that or not. Anyway, I've known them since they moved here five years ago, and I've been with them in a variety of situations. I think I know him pretty well. You've talked to him, I assume."

"Yes, twice."

"I'll bet he had trouble telling you that his wife was missing, because he was so busy trying to put the make on you. Am I right?"

Donna couldn't help herself and laughed aloud. "Right, again."

"And he's such a creep, you weren't even flattered." Sarah didn't demand confirmation this time, but continued, "So that's what I mean, there's no mate for him, because he doesn't need or want one, only someone to feed off. She on the other hand, wanted one, but was just as incapable of having one as he, but for other reasons. She never smiled...no that's not true, she tried to smile, but it was only like a tic or twitch. It was there for a moment and gone, like summer in Siberia. Would you care for a chocolate-chip cookie?"

"No, no thanks."

"It made me sad to be around her. It was like standing by and watching an injured animal trying to drag its broken body off the pavement. She wanted so desperately to feel at peace, to feel whole. She was always trying one gimmick after another—mystical garbage—so against my grain I had to force myself to sit and listen and nod. I'm talking stuff like numerology, pyramids, crystals, reincarnation—all that nonsense. At the same time, here she was a scientist. I suspect medicine was the ballast that prevented her from floating right over the moon."

Donna listened and tried to evaluate how much of this woman's information could be trusted.

"I don't claim to be a shrink," Sarah continued, "But I sensed something tragic had happened to her as a child. I thought it likely involved her parents, of course. I was right."

"Yes?"

"Her father committed suicide when she was ten."

"How do you know that?"

"I asked her."

"Asked her if her father committed suicide?"

Sarah's smile was part wink. "Well, I didn't approach it that directly, but I got her talking."

"And you don't claim to be a shrink?"

"Hey, you know what? She told her shrink that she told me about her father, and he advised her not to talk to me any more about personal matters. He said it was draining something from the treatment with him."

"What did you think about that?"

Sarah gave a knowing look. "You know what I really think? I think there was something going on in those sessions that he didn't want her to talk about."

Donna was surprised. "You mean going on between them? Something sexual?"

Sarah, seeming to decide she had said too much, joked, "Maybe he was only afraid I'd ask for my share of his fee. To be honest, I don't know anything about him. All I really know is that he's new in town and he's divorced."

Neither spoke for a moment, then, Donna took up an earlier topic.

"You say Mr. Wilson was on the make."

"Do I know of any affairs?"

"Right."

"Actually, no. I've only heard some rumors"

"About whom?"

"Didn't you know that repeating rumors causes one's double chin to grow?"

"Then you're not going to help me?"

It was an appeal Sarah couldn't ignore. "No names, but I understand there's a well worn path through the underbrush between the Wilson home and a certain natural cedar house on the next street."

Donna left Sarah Jacobs and drove into the street one block higher up the hill above the Wilson's with only a house description, no name. The houses were older here, the lots larger. At the end of the street, and about an eighth of a mile from the Wilson's back door stood a weathered, cedar building of a design that would have been radically contemporary thirty years ago. Donna knew that with the State Police taking over, she had no time for the formality of an appointment. She parked the patrol car, strode quickly to the front door and pressed the bell.

The woman who opened the door was dressed in an interesting caftan. Donna couldn't help considering the irrelevant question about its origin. The woman smiled.

"Ivory Coast. And, the import duty has been paid, officer."

Donna, taken by surprise and speechless, looked into the warm and easy smile of a woman in her early fifties. Instantly, Donna knew she had seen that face and smile before. Yes, it had to be her, the woman in the painting hanging in Larry's Oyster Bar. There, she was pictured seated sideways in an armchair, her legs over the arm, hair piled loosely on top of her head, skirt falling to mid-thigh, drink in hand, laughing freely at something—perhaps life. A good-time gal. The person she'd asked about the portrait didn't know the identity of the subject, but knew it had been painted by Lawson Giles, a local artist who'd moved on to New York success.

Donna collected herself and hurriedly explained who she was and what investigation she was part of. She was aware she'd left out a normal piece of an introduction—the other person's name—

and knew she couldn't very well ask for it and maintain any semblance of authority. A call to headquarters would have given her the name from the address, but calling headquarters was no longer an option.

"Please come in," the woman said and led her back to a sitting room with yet another terrific view of the bay.

"We can be more comfortable here."

She left Donna and went into the kitchen. On a coffee table, Donna spied a brochure from a local film society. The address label said, Mandy O'Brien. Donna was relieved.

Mandy O'Brien returned with a half bottle of white wine and two glasses. It was too early in the day for wine by Donna's schedule, but not apparently by Mandy's. Donna made the obligatory "on duty" refusal and was emphatically overruled.

"If you don't have a small drink with me it will subvert the establishment of rapport. The interviewer must, even at the cost of imbibing unspeakable liquids, establish rapport." She paused. "You said you were investigating Barbara Wilson's murder. The only reason you could want to question me is because of my relationship with Benjamin." She noted Donna's surprise. "That's right isn't it?"

"Ah, yes."

"Well, it's true. I met him three months ago and we became involved. I didn't know Barbara."

Donna was knocked off balance by this candor. It caused her to veer away from the woman's confession for the moment with a question she'd earlier planned to ask, but as she was asking it, realized it was decidedly inappropriate now.

"What were his feelings about his wife?"

"Well, I don't suppose they could have been very deep, do you, or why look my way?"

Donna couldn't answer before Mandy said, "Of course, how dense of me! He's a suspect isn't he? A spouse always is. You're wondering if he acted in any way to make me suspect he killed her." Her expression became serious and she stared at Donna. "Hell, you're wondering if we hatched up a plot together to kill her." She added lightly, "Should I have a lawyer present?"

"I'll answer my own questions," she went on, without waiting for an answer. "No, we didn't plot to kill Barbara, and no, he never said anything to lead me to think he did it or wanted to do it."

Donna realized she had no way of judging the truth of these frank statements. The woman's style of relating was foreign to her.

"This relationship you have with him—. Is it serious?"

"Is that really relevant to your investigation?" Mandy asked and then shrugged. "It doesn't matter. No, I had about made up my mind to end it. When this trouble descended on him, I thought I'd wait until he had things back together a bit."

Donna had more information than she dreamed possible, but there was still the major question concerning Benjamin Wilson she hadn't asked.

"Do you know where he was on Tuesday night, the night of the day Barbara was abducted?"

"Where did he tell you he was?"

Donna answered immediately. "He said he was out walking."

Mandy said nothing and Donna prompted, "Do you know where he was?"

"My memory's slipping."

"But, that was only two days ago."

Mandy shrugged. "They say short-term memory is the first to go."

Donna didn't understand. Why had this woman who had been uncommonly forthcoming suddenly clammed up?

"This part of the investigation has been assigned to me and the time allowed me is very short. I...."

Mandy sighed and said, "Just a moment," and went into the kitchen, closing the door behind her.

Donna pondered what she'd just learned. An affair with Mandy O'Brien. Did that give Wilson a motive for murder? Not in the days of "no-fault" divorce—unless he wanted the undivided assets. Why wouldn't Mandy answer her question about Tuesday night? Why had she gone out of the room?

Mandy came back in and sat down, saying, "I don't like to contradict friends until I know the reason for their story. I just called Benjamin. The reason he wouldn't tell you where he was that night was to protect my reputation. Yes, he was here that evening. He had just gone home when you knocked on his door."

Donna was taken aback. This wasn't what she wanted to hear in order to advance her case against Wilson.

"When did he come over here?"

"It was early. He had taken his daughter to stay with some friends of hers and he came from there. I cooked dinner for us. I'd say it was around six, six-thirty."

"But, how could he come over here for dinner? I mean, suppose we found her alive, wouldn't he want to know?"

"I see what's bothering you. May I call you Donna?"

Donna nodded.

"Donna, he knew something bad had happened to her. She'd been missing too many hours for the cause to be benign. He said as much to me on the phone when he asked if he could come over to be with me. He was feeling alone and scared. He checked his answering machine several times while he was here."

"I see," Donna muttered. Suddenly she, too, was feeling alone. She'd been keeping company with her theory about Benjamin Wilson and it had just gotten up and walked out the door, leaving nothing to take its place. Like a falling person reaching out for something to break a fall, she asked, "Mandy, what do you think happened to Barbara Wilson?"

The other woman remained silent for a time. When she did speak it was without emphasis. She had nothing to sell.

"I didn't know her and I had little curiosity about her, but there were things Benjamin said that caused me to think about her more than I intended to. To my mind, she was a very unhappy woman looking for a cure and very vulnerable to anyone who offered one. My gut feeling was she had become involved with her psychiatrist. But, I don't know if that—even if it were true—could have anything to do with her murder." She noted Donna's troubled look. "Honey, you asked, and that's what I think."

Donna drove slowly down the hill. Mandy O'Brien's testimony cleared Wilson for the critical time the body was being placed on Marti Jensen's farm. That is, if Mandy was telling the truth. Donna thought she was. She would have to check the phone records for Wilson's call to Mandy that night and the calls Mandy claimed he made to his answering machine. Donna felt certain the calls had been made. That about wrapped it up for her ... and the Sheriff's Department. At the bottom of the hill she turned north on Highway 22, which ran along the shore to Suttons Bay. From there, she'd drive on to Leland and headquarters. As she drove, the conversations she'd just had replayed in her mind. An unexpected subject had come up in each of them, each woman's suspicion about the psychiatrist, about Derek Marsh. Donna thought back to the expression she'd seen on his face when she and Hoss were leaving his office. She hadn't understood it at the time, but now it came to her that it was a look of great relief.

She made a quick decision and pulled off the highway and onto the shoulder and began to rethink her next move.

CHAPTER 11

LATELY, ONLY WHEN WORKING UP a heart pounding sweat while leading the aerobics class did she find relief from her worry about Hoss. Class over, mopping her face with a towel, K.D. listened to Martha Kovaric, who had come up to her.

"K.D., next week will be my last class. Jerry and I are moving."

"What?"

"Yes, I know it's sudden. Everyone says that, when I tell them. We've sold the farm."

Martha and Jerry Kovaric were as much a part of Leelanau County as cherry trees. They owned a centennial farm K.D. would have died for—the beautiful property that is; she had no desire for the hard life of farming. The farm, over a hundred years in Jerry's family, spanned two hundred and forty acres of rolling land, much of it affording spectacular views of Lake Michigan.

"That's very sad news. Why did you decide to do this, now?" K.D. asked, trying to keep her true feelings of incredulity out of her tone.

"Jerry thought we couldn't afford to pass up the offer we got."

"I didn't even know your farm was for sale."

"It wasn't, but an apple grower from near Paw Paw called us and said he'd been told by a Leelanau County friend that our farm would be perfect for apples, and he made us an offer that was much higher than the going price of land." Martha paused and reconsidered her statement. "That is, much greater than prices a year ago. Several cherry orchards have sold recently for prices nearly as high as we got."

"I'll miss you a lot, Martha. We all will."

Why had the price of farm property shot up? It occurred to K.D. that another member of her class had sold farm property recently.

Martha gathered up her gear and was starting to leave. K.D. stopped her. "Who bought your farm, if you don't mind telling me?"

"Of course I don't mind. Alex Campbell, Campbell Orchards in Paw Paw, like I said."

"Thanks," K.D. replied. She began thinking about the best method to check out her new suspicion.

❍

Donna stood on Judge Burdick's porch waiting for someone to answer the door. She was anxious. The thinking she had done while parked at the roadside, remembering the suspicions both women held about Dr. Derek Marsh, led her to now consider him her prime suspect. She strongly wanted to follow this new lead and was afraid Hoss would tell her to drop it. With the State Police actively entering the investigation, it made little sense for the Sheriff's Department to continue straining its limited resources. She wasn't consciously aware that a good portion of her desire to investigate Marsh came from a feeling of betrayal. She had opened herself up to an attraction for him. She was well on the way to being smitten.

To pursue him, now, became a way to deny the emotional blunder she'd almost made.

That earlier, roadside contemplation of the path the investigation would have to take, told her she would need subpoenas. Records must be searched that would be carefully guarded from her view unless she was armed with the necessary papers. Hoss usually took care of that, Hoss and Peter Dreisbach. Afraid to contact Hoss, she'd made the call to Dreisbach on her own. She hoped he would assume the request came from Hoss. That's not the way it went. After she'd laid out her plan to the Prosecuting Attorney, she'd waited through a silence long enough for her to suspect he was trying to reach Hoss on another line.

Finally he said, "Have you been in touch with Hoss today?"

"No, I haven't, I was given the assignment to investigate Wilson and Marsh yesterday and I've been working on my own."

Pete Dreisbach also couldn't read Hoss's intentions, but strongly wanted to see the case solved by him. Those who wanted to discredit Hoss belonged to the same faction that was, also, out to replace him in the coming primary. He had talked to Judge Burdick on the phone earlier in the morning and knew that the Judge was irked with what he viewed as a politically motivated move to bring in the State Police. He was sure Burdick would sign the subpoenas.

"Where are you now?" he asked.

"Do you mean the telephone number?"

"No, I mean, are you here in Leland?"

"No, I'm in Suttons Bay."

"Good, I can save you some time. I can meet you in Suttons Bay and give you the papers. You have to take them to Judge Burdick's home and get his signature. He doesn't have court today, but I'll call him and tell him you're coming."

They agreed to meet in front of the Mobil station. Donna reviewed the conversation after she'd hung up. Did it make sense that Dreisbach really wanted to save her time by meeting her? Why hadn't he simply said, "Yes, I'll make out the papers. They'll be here in my office." But, he'd said, "Good, I can save you some time." Could it be he didn't want her to come to Leland - come to Leland and risk seeing Hoss? Donna was puzzled, but hey! Whatever. Her investigation was still alive.

❍

Alex Campbell. There it was in black and white. K.D. had walked from the Old Art Building, where the aerobics class was held, to the County Building and the County Clerk's office and now had the records in front of her. Alex Campbell was the new owner of both farms once owned by former members of the aerobics class.

"Helen," K.D. called out to the Clerk, who was busy at another desk, "do you know where this property is? It's the farm that was owned by Jill Jameson until recently—4033 Petersen Road—and bought by a guy from Paw Paw named Alex Campbell."

Helen Barber looked up; her eyes focused on infinity as she oriented herself to the question. "Sure, I remember picturing it when the new deed was registered. It's that hill you can see after you pass The Happy Hour Tavern as you're driving north. Beautiful view from up there."

"Is it an orchard?"

"Not at all; it's totally wooded."

"Really."

"He's been busy buying other property here in the County too," Helen Barber added.

"You don't say. What other properties?"

Helen and K.D. spent the next quarter hour finding the location of Alex Campbell's purchases. In the end, it was clear to K.D. they all shared one feature, they had great views of Lake Michigan.

That does it, she concluded, Jason Ackerman was buying up property under another person's name. She was as sure of it as she was that Ackerman wasn't her fairy godmother.

❍

The cooling, morning breeze off the big lake gave way to the mid-day sun causing his scalp to prickle. He wasn't wearing his hat. That was because he had only gone down his long driveway to put a letter in the mailbox when his wife called to him to go on to the store at Cob Corners to get her some sugar. He'd done that and was now walking back home. He passed his free hand over his head, feeling the heat in his scalp.

Joseph Stillwater had run into a cousin at the store who'd told him about his nephew's trouble. According to what the cousin had heard on television, a manhunt was in progress to find Harry. He was wanted as a suspect in the murder of a young woman doctor in Traverse City.

Joseph wondered, as he made his slow way home along the hot, dusty road, if he should tell his sister-in-law. Her kidneys were failing, and she'd been sinking for months; the last few weeks there'd been a rapid decline. This news about her boy would really hurt her, even though Harry had left home—left her—twelve years ago and had not been in touch with any one here in the Elk River Band since he'd sent that one letter. That must have been back eight years, Joseph figured.

Harry's letter said he was well and was getting married to an Anishnabek, "one of the people". It had been posted from Suttons Bay forty miles away on the peninsula. They'd all concluded he was living with the Band at Peshawbestown. Later this was confirmed when one of Harry's former friends saw him there at the casino. They also learned he had changed his name. Clearly, he wanted to break his ties with his home, so no effort had been made to contact him.

Joseph shifted the five-pound sack to his other hand and continued on. He had been surprised, back then, by the tone and content of Harry's letter to his mother. It seemed to say that Harry had settled down, that the wild, rebellious kid had mellowed. This news of a manhunt was more in keeping with what Joseph had feared for his nephew.

Harry had run away from home twelve years ago, because a young woman's two brothers had threatened to kill him. The young woman from Elk Rapids had been coaxed to take a ride on Harry's motorcycle, a drunken ride that ended in a skid on a gravel-strewn curve on Highway 31 south of town. The woman's leg was so badly broken that the best efforts of the doctors at the clinic in Petoskey still left her with a permanently shortened and deformed leg. Bad as that had been, Joseph had always feared that even worse lay ahead for Harry.

Harry grew up fatherless. Constant taunts from other children that his father had been a drunk had made him angry and wild. Joseph had no doubt this was the source of Harry's problem. He had done the best he could to fill his dead brother's role in the boy's life. When Harry was fourteen, the coming of age for a Chippewa boy, Joseph had told Harry the facts, as he knew them, about his father and his father's death, hoping that a better understanding would temper Harry's wildness.

When Harry was one, his father, Will Stillwater, had gone to work on a fishing boat out of Northport, because the lumberyard in Elk Rapids, where he'd worked for eight years, fired him.

At the end of that summer, Will got involved with a white woman in Leelanau County and got her pregnant. Her husband found out, and Will, afraid of what he might do, hightailed it back home. He'd told Joseph all about this the night he returned.

Will had only been back a month, much of the time spent at Clawson's Bar, despondent to be jobless and blowing the little money he'd saved from the fishing job, when he was killed.

On that night, as closing time neared Will suddenly became very quarrelsome and the bartender told him he'd better go home. Will left after making a slurred attempt to tell off everybody in the place. It was not an atypical occurrence. Will left the bar alone. Those leaving the bar at closing time found him dead in the parking lot. He's been hit over the head with a very heavy weapon that shattered his skull. The coroner said it must have been something like a crowbar.

If anyone had been angered by Will's closing performance in the bar, they couldn't be treated a suspects, since they'd all left the bar together. No one was ever charged.

Relating this story to Harry had caused a change all right, but not the one Joseph hoped for. Harry remained unpredictably wild and destructive. A new focus, however, emerged for his anger. What had been randomly expressed, earlier, became aimed at the whites—like the ones at the lumberyard, who'd fired his father. A fire there destroyed one of the buildings. Joseph felt sure Harry had set it.

The shade of a roadside maple provided a resting place. Exertion these days got him out of breath. He was sad about Harry being hunted and he was sad for the young woman doctor who'd died and for her family. But he concluded there was nothing he could do to help Harry now—nothing any of them could do. He decided to say nothing to his sister-in-law about what he'd just heard about Harry.

CHAPTER 12

IT WAS GOING TO BE a long day, at the end of which Donna thought she could be fired. If ever there was a time to inform one's boss of one's plans, it would be before making a two hundred and fifty mile unauthorized jaunt in a Sheriff's Department vehicle with a subpoena she'd acquired behind his back. It was 3:00 P.M. She had made the four-hour drive from Traverse City to Birmingham, a Detroit suburb, in time to keep her appointment with Charlotte Waring, the Executive Secretary of the Oakland County Medical Society. Carrying a subpoena and her notebook, she entered the building.

That morning she had carried the same subpoena into the office of the Grand Traverse County Medical Society in Traverse City, her immediate destination after thanking Judge Burdick for his signature. Sarah Jacobs had mentioned that Derek Marsh was new to the area. Donna wondered where he had moved from and why he would have left his previous practice. After all, it wasn't as if he were a young doctor who had come to town fresh from his years of training.

It was there, after handing the subpoena to the Society's secretary, that she met with open resistance to her request for information. The woman examined the subpoena and said imperiously that the request would have to be referred to the

Society's legal counsel. The woman added that she knew for a fact that he was out of town. This last bit was said defiantly.

Donna maintained her poise and pleaded the urgency of her inquiry. The woman was unmoved.

At this point, Dr. Fine, the Medical Society's President, came into the room and seeing a Sheriff's deputy asked the reason for her visit. He received one of Donna's most winning smiles as she turned her request toward him. He asked the secretary to get Dr. Marsh's file.

A few minutes later, Donna was standing next to the good doctor looking down at the four items in Derek's March's folder. One was the membership application Dr. Marsh made when he moved to Traverse City from Birmingham the previous year. The next was the letter they had received from the Oakland County Medical Society in answer to their routine inquiry about Marsh. This letter stated that while practicing there, Dr. Marsh had been charged with sexual misconduct by a patient. The District Attorney had, after investigating the woman's claim, dismissed the case. The Oakland County Medical Society's own Ethics Committee had then met to review the case, but adjourned without taking action. The report of this meeting had been sealed in accordance with the policy of the Society in cases where no action was warranted.

The third document was a summary of the decision of the Grand Traverse County Medical Society stating that since another county society had found no reason to censure Dr. Marsh, the Society would grant Marsh membership. The final document was the copy of a letter from the Society's Community Mental Health Committee welcoming his membership on that committee.

At that point, Donna's interest shifted to Birmingham. From her patrol car she'd called the Birmingham Police Department. She was transferred to the records division where a young guy with a tone of familiarity in his voice answered. She identified herself, matching his tone with warm intimacy in hers. She said she hoped he would do her a favor and then asked about the case of Dr. Derek Marsh.

"Let me see what I can find."

After several minutes he was back on the line. "All I have is a charge of sexual misconduct brought by a Harriet Carter against her psychiatrist, Derek Marsh. It was investigated and dropped for lack of evidence. The DA's office has the full investigative report.

"Are they an easy bunch to deal with?"

"They won't talk to you over the phone. You'll have to go there with your subpoena."

"And then?"

"I'm sure you must own a sleeping bag."

"Thanks, friend."

It was eleven o'clock when she hung up and pondered the best way to proceed. She needed a lot more detail. It sounded like the Oakland County DA's office was not for those with no time to waste. But, if she could read the minutes of the Medical Society's Ethics Committee, she'd get right to the heart of what she wanted to know. She called and made the appointment with the Society's Executive Secretary and began the long drive down the length of the state.

Charlotte Waring was one of those secretaries who are the true administrators of the organizations for which they work. She would place documents in front of the Society's current President and say, "Sign here." Of course it would be phrased with an awareness of the ego she was dealing with. Secretaries like her gave groups, such as a medical society, continuity. She would remember discussions from ten years back and be able to put her hands on the relevant materials in a moment ... if she wanted to. She dated back to the good old days of the medical fraternity, back when medicine was almost above the law.

Charlotte Waring wore a dark blue suit, its severity relieved only by a gold pin on the left lapel in the shape of a treble clef. Her pale, clear skin had taken on the fragile, tissue paper appearance of someone well past seventy, but there was nothing fragile about her presence.

She kept Donna standing before her while she answered a phone call. When she put the phone down, she looked up at Donna in sober, silent inquiry. Donna felt like a supplicant asking the papal secretary for an appointment with the pontiff. All was conveyed thus far without words.

Donna sized up her own position with Ms. Waring. On the one hand this woman would like to give the law the finger—for old times' sake. On the other, she might be sympathetic with another woman. Don't count on it, but it was, Donna decided, her best bet.

Donna gave Charlotte Waring the, "I'm a young woman trying to make it in a man's world, and you're a model of how it's done" look of sincere admiration. It was easy, because Donna did respect the character this woman projected; however, she did turn up the dial.

"Thank you for finding time for me today, Ms. Waring. I drove down from Leland this afternoon, because it's very important that I get this information today. You see, I've been given a part of a murder investigation. A doctor up in Traverse City was kidnapped and murdered, Dr. Barbara Wilson. Maybe it was carried in the papers down here?"

Charlotte Waring nodded.

"Dr. Wilson was a patient of Dr. Derek Marsh. He was the last known person to see her alive. She disappeared right after her appointment with him. He, as you might imagine, is a suspect and this part of the investigation has been assigned to me. I've been running into quite a bit of passive foot dragging on the part of everyone I've encountered. It's nothing new to me, being a woman deputy. Men seem to regard me as a bit of fluff to be flirted with and otherwise ignored, but recently I've encountered a different kind of resistance… uh, from the medical establishment. Consequently, I've been able to make less progress than my sheriff expects."

After this exaggerated version of the facts, Donna laid the subpoena on the secretary's desk.

"All records are covered by this, as you can see. Even so-called sealed files. What I need is the entire record on Dr. Marsh, and especially the record of the deliberation of your Ethics Committee."

Charlotte Waring read the subpoena and considered what she was going to do. Donna's reference to the scant respect she'd been given by men resonated in her own experience. On the other hand, just as strong, was her allegiance to her job and the Medical Society, which desired to run its own affairs without outside interference.

Donna commented quietly, "This is an important assignment for me, and it is a murder investigation."

The eyes of the two women met. There was no challenge in either. Donna's said that she needed help. Charlotte Waring's said, "I see you're at a crossroad, dear, and I'm going to help you across."

"Will you have to take the documents, or will copies be sufficient?"

"For now, I'll only need copies of the relevant records. If they are needed in court in a trial, we may need the originals." Donna felt an inward relief.

Ms. Waring got up and preceded Donna into the outer waiting area, suggesting, "There's reasonably fresh coffee here. You may want to take a cup along."

At a quarter to five, Donna got up from the conference room table where she'd been working. She'd read all the material and made notes. She had a list of pages she wanted copied. Ms. Waring had remained in her office waiting for Donna to finish—clearly above and beyond the call of duty to the Medical Society. She could have made Donna come back in the morning, or she could have made a like claim that she would need the advice of legal council before releasing the information. Score one for the sisterhood! Donna thanked Charlotte Waring and left.

At five-fifteen, bone-weary, Donna started the long drive north. Once clear of the local Birmingham traffic and onto I75, she began to review what she'd learned.

She had read through many pages of the discussion, at times heated, of the Ethics Committee. What she distilled from her effort came down to this: two women had independently claimed that Derek Marsh had sexual intercourse with them in his office. While neither woman claimed it had been outright rape, both said it had happened without their free will. They were coerced—intimidated—by his authority as their physician. The first charge, brought by Harriet Carter, was dropped by the County Prosecutor's Office, for lack of evidence. Consequently, the Ethics Committee would not touch it for fear Marsh would have grounds for a lawsuit. The second complaint was brought by a fellow psychiatrist whose evidence came from a story told to him by one of his own patients, the sister of one of Marsh's patients. A good bit of the description of Marsh's alleged conduct was reported to the Committee before the Chairman ruled that since the testimony came to the complaining psychiatrist by way of a privileged communication from his patient, the Committee could not hear or consider it. And, since neither of the women, the psychiatrist's patient nor Marsh's patient, had made a complaint, the case was closed and the record sealed.

After reading the report, Donna agreed with this decision on purely ethical grounds, but came away with a strong conclusion that Marsh was guilty. If he was guilty in this case, then he was probably guilty in the other case, too.

Barbara Wilson had been suffocated. Suppose Marsh had made a sexual advance and his expectation that she would go along proved wrong. Suppose she started to cry for help. Maybe the soundproofing in the Peninsular Building wasn't good and he had to silence her quickly. Barbara Wilson had not had intercourse prior to being killed. Her underwear was in place and intact and at autopsy there was no evidence of vaginal entry or sperm. Such would be the case, if she had cried out when he approached her and he'd silenced her.

Marsh had opportunity, the means and the motive. Donna pictured the handsome man, who had produced a flutter in her own heart. How many times had it been easy for him with willing patients? The idea of his taking advantage of their trust was odious to her.

Donna was pleased that her long drive had not been in vain. She might get hell for taking off without getting Hoss's nod, but he couldn't argue with the results.

Thinking of Hoss caused her to consider the wisdom of making at least some contact with headquarters. She got out her cell phone and pressed the auto dial for the number. Kate Schott answered. Donna was determined not to give the dispatcher a chance to pass on any unwanted message to her. "Kate, this is Donna. Everything's fine. I've been downstate to Birmingham and I'm on my way back now. See you in the morning. Bye."

Kate Shott called Hoss at home.

"Deputy Roper checked in, but got off the line before I could inhale."

"Anybody there in the office with you?"

"No."

"OK, exactly what did she say?"

"Said she had gone to Birmingham and was on her way back."

"Birmingham? What was she doing in Birmingham?"

"She didn't say."

"Did she say anything else?"

"Oh yeah, she said, 'See you in the morning, bye.'"

Hoss chuckled. "OK, Kate, thanks."

Hoss had no doubt about why Donna hung up before Kate could speak. But, Birmingham—why go there? He unscrewed the top from the twenty-ounce Coke bottle and took a swig. He had to admire her. She was determined to continue with the investigation. He knew it was partly for her personal satisfaction, but he also knew it represented a dogged loyalty to the Sheriff's Department. And, the way she was doing it said she was willing to take all the responsibility. Gutsy gal. Of course, there was only so long he could let it go on without taking back total control and total responsibility, and they were just about there. Tomorrow morning would be the limit. And indeed, that was what she'd said, "See you in the morning."

Meanwhile, he anxiously awaited the results of the surveillance he'd ordered on Mary and Buddy. If this last effort failed to find Harry, he was ready to fold his tent.

CHAPTER 13

SHORTY KNEW THE MAKE OF the car and the plate number, 1999 Escort, 709 ZKZ. He'd located it at the back of the casino lot where the employees parked. It was blue. He found an empty space nearby for his pick-up truck. Although he couldn't see her car from there, he had a clear view of the driveway Mary would have to use when she left after work.

Quitting time at the business office was six o'clock, but Mary had stayed later doing some free-lance work for the casino publicity department. Shorty was getting very restless; it was close to nine o'clock. When she finally did leave, he desperately wanted her to go straight to see her boyfriend. Hoss needed it, and it would be one hell of a way to top off his own career.

❍

It was difficult to do surveillance on the reservation. About the only place Russ wouldn't be conspicuous was inside the casino. He had a problem. The road where Buddy and Harry lived was half a mile north of the casino and any car parked on the highway with him in it might as well have a sign on it reading, "County Mounty Stakeout". Situated one hundred yards south of their road, however, was the former schoolhouse, which had been remodeled into a fully equipped fitness center. In a good will gesture the

Indians had opened it to everyone. Russ had several friends who came here regularly since exercise machines always seemed to be available, unlike the only other public facility on the peninsula, where waiting for a machine was like being on "stand-by" at the airport.

He sat in his Honda Civic, dressed in workout clothes, a gym bag next to him containing walkie-talkie, cell phone and his weapon. His car was parked in the small parking area on the north side of the building. He'd gone in and asked the young girl attendant if a friend of his had arrived, yet. Getting the negative answer, he said he was going to wait for his friend outside in his car. That would only cover him sitting there for about half an hour, but he figured the girl would forget all about him anyway. To play it safe, he drove up and down the highway when he knew the attendants' shift was changing, and came back and did the same bit all over again. That had been at six o'clock. It was nine-thirty when he saw Buddy's truck edge up to the intersection with the highway.

Buddy didn't look in Russ Preva's direction as he turned south toward the casino. Russ started the Honda and waited until Buddy passed the driveway of the fitness center, before backing out of the parking space and following him.

Buddy's pick-up was now a good hundred yards ahead and there was a car between them. Perfect. Russ's hope ignited; Buddy was about to lead him to the fugitive. He was only shifting into third, when Buddy surprised him by turning left into a side street that ran toward the bay. Russ drove past the street and saw, as he did, that Buddy's truck was stopped at the next corner. Russ made a quick decision and pulled off onto the shoulder of Highway 22, where he got out of his car, grabbed his gym bag, and jogged back a few yards until he was able to look down the sidestreet.

Buddy's truck was still standing where it had been. Russ could see him inside the truck looking to his right into the vacant corner lot. A rusted, faded blue Econovan sat near its center. The abandoned van looked as if it had been there a long time, an accepted and unnoticed piece of the terrain. The lot had been mowed, but the mower had left a two-foot margin of tall grass around the van. Abruptly Buddy drove onto the lot and parked parallel to and on the far side of the van.

Although Russ could still see the tailgate of Buddy's truck, someone driving into the street who wasn't intentionally looking for the truck, would either not notice it at all, or think it was just another discard. Russ waited to see Buddy walk away, thinking he had parked the truck out of the way so he could continue on foot to Harry's hiding place. This didn't happen. Buddy remained sitting inside the truck.

Preva couldn't just stand around on the corner, but was afraid he might miss Buddy if he went to get his own car. So, keeping the Econovan between him and Buddy, he approached the two vehicles.

Slowly, he crept up to the driver's window of the abandoned van and carefully peeked through it at Buddy's truck. Buddy was sitting and staring sternly straight ahead toward the two-story, blue house that faced him across the street. Slowly, Russ withdrew from the window. What to do now?

Again, he couldn't just stand there in his gym shorts. For sure, if someone hadn't already done so, he'd be noticed soon, and that would mean a large guy would be sent to investigate. Instinctively, Russ sank to the ground. If he lay down in the weeds beside the van, he could see under it and be aware if Buddy got out of the truck and stepped on the ground. He opened the gym bag and turned off the cell phone and the walkie-talkie. It was 9:38.

❍

Many questions needed to be answered. Mary McNab had made a start. Like Harry, she had begun wondering why the people at Greenleaf Properties had not simply notified the police about the theft of their truck and computer. And, why try to abduct her at gunpoint? She could imagine some unstable person wanting to exact justice on his own; hadn't she seen enough of those types right here at the casino? But in an organization as large as Greenleaf, wouldn't some cooler heads veto such a reaction? This reasoning led her to conclude that Harry had stolen something that they wanted back very badly—and maybe something they very much didn't want the police to know about. It could only be the computer.

A surge of anger with Harry for his rash, unthinking behavior swept through her. She should let him bear the brunt of his own stupidity! Maybe it would wake him up. At the same time, she also knew she wasn't going to let that happen. She was bound to do what she could to help him.

She needed to learn more about Greenleaf Properties. She called her father. Charlie was a living encyclopedia of Leelanau County politics and had, for years, served this role on the Tribal Council. He told her about Ackerman's Lake County Development Company and the initial resistance it had met with in the county. Charlie held a cynical view of the metamorphosis into Greenleaf Properties.

"It sticks in my throat to say the name. I have no proof, you understand, but I think it's this Ackerman and his cronies who are bankrolling the attempt to defeat Hoss Davis and the rest of the present office holders."

"I hear you telling me we can expect to see the old company emerge if they win the primary election," Mary reasoned.

"That's about it, baby. It won't make a difference to us here on the reservation, but it could mean a lot of changes will occur in the rest of the county."

"How do you feel about that, Dad?"

"I like it the way it is." Charlie didn't ask Mary why she was asking; intruding wasn't the Chippewa way.

"Dad, who besides Ackerman is an investor?"

"I don't know, honey. It's a private investment group, not incorporated in the State of Michigan, so they don't have to disclose the investors."

So after talking to her father, Mary had only one name. She had to think in terms of Jason Ackerman as the man who wanted his computer back—wanted his computer files back—even at gunpoint. The guy in the parking lot hadn't been Ackerman; he didn't fit her father's description. He must be one of Ackerman's goons.

Mary sat at her desk considering the options she and Harry had. It had not passed through any conscious level of decision-making, but she was now thinking in terms of Harry and herself as a unit. How could she and her man survive the present danger and get on with a life together?

Harry had jokingly said he might give the computer back. Was that the answer? Something was wrong with that. She doodled a picture of a computer. She had a feeling of insecurity as she considered the idea of returning it. Why? OK, you give it back and then what? What if Ackerman remains uncertain whether or not you've accessed the files he's concerned about? He would still need to silence you. That was it. If they simply gave the computer back, there would be no protection. Harry and she needed certain assurance that they were safe before they could go on with their lives.

It was way past the time the business office usually closed, but because she had spent so much time looking into the Ackerman business, she hadn't even started to make out the form for the casino's floor manager which listed the personnel present for the evening shift. At 9:30, she went out into the noise and bustle of the casino. Mary had never played any of the games in the four years she'd worked here since returning from college. She regarded the gambling patrons as a strange breed, not understanding their blatant passion, much as a traveler feels about a little understood ritual viewed in a foreign land.

She walked up to a tall blond Californian whose lean face carried a perpetual look of bored skepticism. "Here's the evening roster report, Terry."

"Thanks, Mary. I'll slide it under your door, as usual."

The report listed the station of each dealer and croupier. A strict accounting was made of each table's activity during the shift.

"We go through this labor all the time, yet nothing is ever amiss; do you think it's worth the effort?" Mary asked.

"You better believe it is. Nothing is amiss, because we keep exact records. One little irregularity and that dealer will be through in any gaming house in the country. It's what's known as leverage, my friend."

"See what you mean."

Walking into her office again, Mary suddenly stopped. That was the answer: leverage. She and Harry would be safe from Ackerman for all time if they had some leverage over him. She had a plan and she called Harry.

❍

Shorty almost missed Mary when she drove out of the lot. It was nine-forty and he'd drifted off while thinking of other things. Quickly, he started up his truck and followed. He knew where Mary lived and recognized that's where she was headed when, after driving down Highway 22 for less than a quarter of a mile, she turned into the street that led to her house. This was a disappointment. No straight trip to see her boyfriend.

Shorty was driving his '82 Ford pick-up. He wished it were more beat-up and unobtrusive, but it had a fresh coat of red paint; he'd done it himself three weeks ago with a vibrator sprayer. He followed Mary to the corner. She was just getting out of her car in the driveway of the house where she lived with her great-aunt.

He had to find a place where he could park and still keep her house in view, not an easy thing to do here on the reservation where he stuck out like a Swede in a Japanese steam bath.

Parking on the side street was not a good idea. In no time at all some young bucks like those at the Running Deer would be leaning in his window and wanting to know what the hell he was doing there.

He drove slowly down the road to the next corner where he had a bold idea and turned around and came back. He nosed the truck onto the sandy apron in front of a building a quarter of a block from Mary's house. Shorty remembered that a guy had done some auto repairs there, before he closed shop and took a job maintaining slot machines for the casino. He pulled the hood latch and got out. He reached in under the seat and brought out a set of wrenches, then went to the front of the truck and lifted the hood. Leaning in over the engine, he pretended to be tightening the fan belt.

A black, late model Buick Regal sedan stopped in front of the McNab house. Carl, the man Ackerman had charged with the job of retrieving the computer, turned off the engine. His left hand opened the car door, his right, for reassurance, brushed against the snub-nosed .38 he had inside his jacket pocket. His plan was simple and direct.

He'd learned, from a Chippewa man who worked for him, who the girl and her boyfriend were. He'd also learned that this Harry Swifthawk was wanted for questioning by the police and was in hiding. Carl decided he had to act quickly or the cops would get the computer before he did. Ackerman would not tolerate that!

Carl's plan was to threaten to kill the girl and the old woman she lived with, unless she revealed her boyfriend's hiding place. He'd tie the women up and then go and get the computer from the thieving Indian. It was a wild plan, but time was short.

Carl tied on a bandanna mask and began walking toward Mary's front door.

Preva, lying flat in the grass beside the rusting Econovan, heard Carl's car drive by and then recognized the sound of a car door closing. He began to rise up to take a look, when he heard Buddy open the door of his truck. Russ lowered himself again into the grass and looked under the old van. He could see the grass move as Buddy stepped out and began to walk toward the house across the street.

Russ got up and stood beside the van so he could see Buddy better in the growing dusk. Buddy was carrying a rifle at the ready in front of his chest.

Abruptly the situation had changed. This was no longer a simple surveillance. Russ wasn't sure about his altered role, but he reached down and got his pistol.

The door of the house opened. A young woman was standing in the rectangle of light. A man stood facing her, his back toward the advancing Buddy. The woman tried to close the door, but the man pushed her back into the room. Buddy began running toward the house shouting, "Stop." The light in the front room of the house went out, and Russ heard the young woman yelling something, as the door was slammed shut.

Russ wanting to bring the rapidly developing crisis to a halt, fired a shot into the air and shouted, "Stop! police!"

Kicking the door open, Buddy charged into the dark house screaming, "Don't you hurt her, you bastard!" He was met with a volley of bullets and fell back across the threshold.

A quarter of a block away Shorty heard the shots. He drew his revolver and ran toward the McNab house. Seeing this Russ cried out, "Shorty don't shoot, it's me, Russ. I think Buddy's been hit. He's lying in the doorway. There's a guy inside who grabbed a girl when she opened the door."

"God damn it!" Shorty shouted, and ran on to the front wall of the house and began working his way toward the open door.

Carl had let go of Mary in order to shoot at Buddy coming through the door. She slid along a hallway to the side door and quietly went outside. Carl dashed past the side door on his way to the kitchen at the back of the house, thinking this was where she'd gone. Once outside, Mary took a few steps across her driveway to a tarpaulin her neighbor had thrown over his lawn chairs and crept under it.

A moment later, she heard Carl come out the side door. He walked within a few feet of where she was hiding, but he had ceased to be interested in her. He crouched low behind shrubbery that ran along the side of the house and made his way toward the street.

Shorty waited until Russ took up a position on the other side of the front door, then he swung his gun into the doorway. No one was there. He stepped over Buddy and entered the front room.

"OK, here," he yelled back to Russ, who followed him inside. Russ knelt beside Buddy's motionless bulk, felt for a carotid pulse and called out, "I think he's dead."

"Shit!" barked Shorty as he approached the hallway and looked along it to the side door, then he turned back to concentrate on a move into the kitchen.

Carl made a run to his car. Russ whirled at the sound of the car door slamming. He saw Carl at the wheel and fired two shots at him. Carl fired a shot in return. The bullet missed Russ, but Shorty, standing in the kitchen, groaned and crumpled to the floor.

Carl roared off down the street as Russ hurried toward his fallen friend.

Outside, Mary McNab quietly walked into her neighbor's backyard—from there, to the street behind—then into the night.

❍

A crowd had already gathered outside the house by the time Hoss arrived. Hoss recognized Will Blackbird, who stood near the front steps of the house, illuminated by the light coming from the open front door. Hoss was immediately reminded that he hadn't talked to anyone on the Tribal Council about the surveillance he had ordered on reservation land. That would have to wait. He pushed his way through the gawkers as the wail of the siren of an approaching ambulance came from the highway.

Buddy's body hadn't been moved. He lay as he'd fallen across the threshold, a gory island in a small lake of blood. Hoss made a long step over the body. Russ Preva came up to him.

"Shorty's in the kitchen. He got hit high in the back of his chest—right side. He's bleeding inside and coughing up blood."

"How much?"

"Not a lot. I found some adhesive and put it over the wound, it was sort of sucking air when he breathed."

Hoss went on into the kitchen. Shorty was lying on his right side, covered with a blanket. Hoss knelt beside him.

"Shorty, it's Hoss."

The wounded man opened his eyes. "Isn't this the damnedest thing, Hoss?" Shorty sputtered, fresh blood spitting forth as he spoke.

"How do you feel?"

"I've felt better. Happened so damn fast. Never did...."

A commotion in the front room overrode his answer. The paramedics burst into the kitchen. In a matter of minutes one of them had an IV running with plasma expander, while another checked Shorty's vital signs. Hoss pulled Russ Preva aside.

"OK, Russ, from the top."

Russ reviewed how the events had developed from his point of view.

"What happened to Mary McNab?"

"I don't know. She wasn't in the house after I put in the call to dispatch and did some first aid on Shorty. I asked a neighbor, who came in, to look outside for her. He came back to say she wasn't around. An old lady is upstairs with a guy who came in saying he was Mary's father."

The loud, battering sound from rotor blades fell over the house. The helicopter from Munson Hospital in Traverse City was settling into the space of the intersecting roads.

Paramedics passed Hoss and Russ with the stretcher on which they'd strapped Shorty. Hoss grabbed Shorty's arm. "You're going to be OK, buddy. I'll see that you get the week off."

Shorty managed the beginning of a smile.

Hoss's focus returned to the problem at hand. "Can you ID the getaway car, Russ?"

"I'm sorry, Hoss, but I never specifically looked at it. It was a generic sedan, black or dark blue. Maybe a Taurus. Fairly new."

"How about dark green?"

Russ shrugged, and his eyes did an "I'm sorry."

"Go along the road here and question everybody. You say the guy was burning rubber when he took off out of here; maybe it got someone's attention who can ID the make for us. I'm going upstairs to have a talk with Charlie McNab."

Hoss found Mary's father sitting in a bedroom with a woman who looked to be near ninety. She was very calm as she gave Hoss a steady appraisal.

Charlie looked up at Hoss. "Do you know anything more about Mary, Hoss?"

"No, Charlie. She apparently ran out the side door and made off somewhere." Hoss thought he knew where that somewhere was, but he doubted that Charlie knew about Mary and Swifthawk. "The guy who forced his way in here didn't have her with him, when he got away. My deputy is sure of that."

"What was this all about, Hoss?"

"I don't really know. We were trailing Buddy, hoping he would lead us to Harry Swifthawk. Buddy came and parked across the street...." Hoss repeated the story Russ had related, emphasizing that it had not been a deputy who shot Buddy and that Mary hadn't been hurt.

"How is Shorty, Hoss?"

"He's got a bad injury. Who knows?"

"I'm sorry." Charlie stood up and said to his aunt, "Ill be back in a few minutes." He motioned to Hoss to follow him outside into the hall.

He closed the door to the old woman's room and turned to Hoss. "Now, Hoss, tell me what you know about why Mary is involved in this."

CHAPTER 14

AS SHE LEFT BIRMINGHAM FOUR hours earlier to return home, Donna had decided to call Dr. Marsh when she got near Traverse City. She wanted to confront him with what she'd just learned. She should, of course, wait until morning and discuss it with Hoss, but she wanted to complete the piece, wanted to present the whole package to him.

She was now five miles east of Traverse City, and Marsh's address on Fell's Ridge Road must be about the same distance west of the city. She dialed and got his answering machine on the fourth ring. What message could she leave? She hung up. What should she do now? She knew one thing; she was hungry and wanted company. Becky McConnell, the other woman deputy, lived near Traverse City. She pressed her cell phone's auto-dial. Becky answered.

"Becky, I'm driving through town. Have you eaten?"

"I was searching the refrigerator for something edible. You must be Karnak the Magnificent."

"Karnak the Magnificent is heading for Larry's. How about meeting me there?"

❍

Marti Jensen waited for a car to vacate a space in the jammed lot of Larry's Oyster Bar. Getting dressed to go out for some nightlife with one leg in a cast had been a challenge. Staying alone in her house after last night was a challenge she'd decided to decline. She steadied herself to slam the car door and lock it.

Turning toward the entrance, she noticed the moon, two days on the wane, watching her from just above the rooftops. She and the man up there had shared a chilling moment last night, looking down together on Barbara Wilson's pale face. She knew she'd never look at a full moon again without that memory haunting her.

Larry's was alive—just what she needed. Music blaring, laughter and two TV monitors following a home-run hitter around the bases. She paused to survey the scene and figure out where she could sit. Standing would be more comfortable than perching on a barstool with one leg dangling in the cast, but she couldn't stand for long either without her foot beginning to swell. A seat at a table was best, but they were all taken.

She became aware that a man, who'd been actively engaged in conversation with several men and women at the bar, was looking at her, studying her predicament. He was very good looking and about her age. His dark hair was shot through with gray, his easy smile was friendly and seductive—not blatantly, but experienced. He walked over to her. "Let me help you find the guy who did that to you."

Marti laughed. "If it had been a guy, I wouldn't let you near me."

"Are you meeting someone, or will you join our little band of working poor, girding our loins after yet another day in the trenches."

"There are so many metaphors mixed into that image, I'm not sure just what it is you and your friends are up to, but I'd be happy to join in. The problem is if I stand very long my foot swells up, and even if you could commandeer a barstool for me, I couldn't sit there very long, either."

"How about lying on the bar?"

"That sounds too much like the fate my father predicted for me."

"I like that, I've got to tell the others. C'mon, I'll introduce you, then I'll confer with Larry. Maybe he has a hammock in the back. My name is Ferris Tull, by the way."

Marti pointed toward her chest. "Marti Jensen."

"Didn't I hear that name recently? Did I read it in the paper? I know! You won the one-legged race at the county fair."

Marti met Pete and Grant and Bev and Lacey, although she wasn't sure, through the noise, if it was Lacey or Tracy. She asked the pretty brunette to repeat it, but a wave of laughter from a nearby group drowned out the answer. Introductions made, Ferris Tull went off to find a chair for Marti.

Immediately, the topic became Marti, where she lived and what she did. It took an abrupt turn when Grant associated her name with the newspaper report about the discovery of Barbara Wilson's body. They began pressing her for the details.

In the rear booth of the Oyster Bar, Donna and Becky sat eating their burgers. Donna had just related her day's experience, and they were commiserating about the unfairness of the State Police stepping into the case when Ferris Tull passed right by their booth. He was totally engrossed in his mission for the interesting-looking woman in the leg cast. Again he passed by, pushing a swivel chair toward the front of the bar, not noticing them.

"What are you looking at?" asked Becky, resisting the impulse to turn and look around in the direction Donna was staring.

"Guy I met a couple of days ago when Hoss and I questioned Barbara Wilson's psychiatrist. He's rescuing a damsel in distress."

Becky leaned around the back of the booth and took a look. "Oh, you mean Ferris. So that's where he was going with the chair. That happens to be Ferris's role in life, rescuing damsels in distress. Distressed damsels are easy picking."

"Do I detect a wish to be rescued?" kidded Donna.

Becky gave this some thought, pulling her freckled forehead into furrows. "Hmm. He's cute, and he bought me a few drinks over the years. That's Marti Jensen he just rescued, by the way. It was on her farm that Dr. Wilson's body was found."

"Really!" Donna re-examined the striking, black-haired woman with renewed interest. "Do you know her?"

"No, but I met her when we were all up at her farm this morning."

Meanwhile, Ferris helped Marti into the chair while Grant told him of Marti's connection to the murder.

"God! That must have been awful for you. Tell us about it."

"I'm not sure why, but if I were to talk about it, it would have to be quietly. I can't speak about those feelings in a loud voice and I'd have to in this crowd. Some other time. Sorry."

They all nodded their disappointed understanding and returned to their usual activity at Larry's, swapping stories and flirting. After an hour, Pete and Grant and Bev had made their exits for different reasons, and the guy sitting at the bar next to Tracy—that was her name—had her locked in intimate talk. A couple vacated a small table and Ferris rolled Marti's chair over to it.

"I'll have to come here more often. I've been playing the hermit since I got this fracture."

"How did it happen?"

"A boring, stupid thing best forgotten."

"No, really, I'd like to know."

"How about paragliding in the Alps?"

"Not bad, but you're right, boring."

"How about throwing myself in the path of an assassin's car to save the life of the President?"

"OK, not boring, but stupid."

"You're a Democrat, then?"

"I'm an anarchist. No, I'm not. I just don't think a politician's worth breaking your leg for."

Marti was finding Ferris Tull easy to like. She knew he was attracted to her, but he wasn't pushing it. She sensed her timing and his were in sync. In the meantime, he was bright and simpatico.

For the last half-hour, she'd been thinking about what she would do after she left the bar. She had practically fled from the house and had even thought of spending the night at the Park Place Hotel. On the other hand, she was telling herself that she wasn't going to let last night's experience spoil her feeling for her home. She should go right back there, just as if nothing had happened. Tull read her silence correctly.

"It's going to be hard to stay alone at an isolated farm after what you saw." His voice carried a tender empathy.

Marti wanted to continue in his company. The level of noise in the restaurant had receded by enough decibels to allow conversation in nearly normal tones. Perhaps it would help her if she talked over her experience with a sympathetic listener like Ferris.

"You know, the fact that someone was found dead on my property shouldn't affect my attitude about my place. After all, the land itself had nothing to do with what happened to that poor woman. But one of the flaws of the human mind is that it makes flimsy associations and then treats them as if they're the truth. An event occurred on this spot, or something was the same color, or it happened on this day last year, as if there were a logical connection between what happens today and something that happened a year ago on the same date."

Tull was nodding, but his expression indicated he was puzzled about something. "You said, 'one of the flaws' of the human mind. I gather there are others."

"It's my notion that we go on all the time about how wonderful our brain functions, but we don't like to face the fact that it also malfunctions in some significant and consistent ways. Don't get me started on that. My point is that logically the discovery of the body on my property shouldn't bother me, but I'm human like the rest, and I can't help making this erroneous, morbid association between a helpless person's terror and pain and some soil on my hillside."

"I think anyone would." His face brightened, suddenly. "Ah, I see what you mean. The reason anyone would is because of this shared thinking deficit."

Marti laughed. "You've got it. Anyway, all day long, I've been trying to reason with myself. My being here, instead of at my house, is proof that I've failed."

Ferris gave her a friendly smile. "Then I'm glad you failed, since it gave me an opportunity to meet you." He added sympathetically, "Maybe it would help to go over the experience once again. I know that always helps me, and you wouldn't be boring me, since I share that common human glitch of being fascinated by the details of a murder. Also, I have a small personal interest in Dr. Wilson, because I was on a program with her last year."

"Really, you knew her?"

"I met her then, but only talked to her briefly before the program started. It was on stress management, sponsored by Munson Hospital."

"You're a therapist?"

"My company sets up and runs seminars and workshops on management, motivation, stress management—topics like that. She, of course, was presenting the medical causes and effects of chronic stress."

A man drifted over to them, beer in hand and greeted Ferris. He, in turn, quickly introduced Marti with a subtle communication to the newcomer that a private conversation was in progress. The guy quipped about the cast and drifted away again.

"What was she like—Barbara Wilson?" Marti asked.

Tull thought for a moment. "Fragile, lost, sad. Like she'd been afraid to go to kindergarten by herself, but went so her parents would be pleased with her and has been doing the same thing ever since. It's an impression, you understand, because you asked. Not for publication."

"That's interesting, because I had this idea, looking down at her face in the moonlight, last night, that she was making one last appeal for someone to understand her."

This image visibly affected Tull, who took a deep swallow of his beer and sighed, "Yeah."

"You know," Marti lifted her head, "I think that's what's been bothering me most about being home alone. It's some lingering feeling that she made this appeal and I let her down in some way. Like she charged me with the responsibility of completing something for her."

Ferris could make no reply to that. He offered to get Marti another drink, but she refused. He was still searching for a way to make an intelligent addition to what she'd just revealed when, no doubt relieved by having unburdened herself, her mood lightened.

"Tell me about yourself," she said.

"Ah, what to say?" exclaimed Tull, wringing his hands in mock anguish. "Suddenly his mind is a blank! He would like to tell her a fascinating history about a fascinating person, but all he has to say is, 'There's nothing much to tell.'"

"Oh yeah? I'll bet you say that to all the women."

Tull laughed. "OK, but don't blame me if this puts you to sleep. I was born in Woodstock, Illinois, which is a small city sixty miles northwest of the Loop. It is famous for three things. First, Chester Gould lived and worked there all his adult life. He did the Dick Tracy comic strip, you know. Secondly, the movie Groundhog Day was filmed there, and I played in the high school band. I went on to DePaul University in Chicago and got a master's degree in ed-psych."

"Excuse me for interrupting, but was your playing in the band the third thing Woodstock was famous for?"

Ferris became confused and blushed. "I guess so, because I can't remember what else I had in mind."

"Sorry, please go on."

"OK. My first job was with a company that designed in-service training programs for large corporations, United Airlines, like that. I was sent to Traverse City to do a workshop for Ameritech. It reminded me of Woodstock, so I stayed and started my own business. I play a little golf, ride my bike semi-seriously with friends a couple of times a month and come here too much." He made a gesture with his hands which said, that's all there is.

Before Marti could comment, he continued, "OK, now it's your turn. Tell me about you."

"My life is much too fascinating. It will require a whole evening, two even, and I should be getting home."

"Do I hear you promising to see me again, at least twice more?"

"For biographical purposes, you understand."

"Of course. Are you sure you're cool with going home alone tonight?"

Marti worked her way out of the chair and stood. "I think so."

"I'd be happy to drive out there with you, let you get the lights on and that sort of thing."

"Thanks, but it's not necessary."

"I'd feel better. I'm used to driving up near there to play golf. It's no big deal."

Marti began to consider another need she had, which had nothing to do with turning lights on.

"All right, I'll accept, if you'll agree to come in for a cup of coffee."

"Lady, you've got yourself a deal."

❍

Still engrossed in talking about the Wilson case, Donna and Becky were interrupted when a man rapped on their table.

They looked up at a provocative smirk on the ruddy face of a guy whose upper body said he spent a significant part of his life doing reps. He slid into the booth next to Becky, forcing her to give him room.

Taking in Donna's uniform, he quipped, "Why in the world would a couple of good-looking ladies want to waste their youth playing policeman?" He followed, what he thought had been a playful remark by demanding, "McConnell, introduce me to this pretty lady."

Becky gave Donna an "I'm sorry" look. "Vic Sears. I beg your pardon, Corporal Vic Sears of the State Police."

"And?" Sears prompted motioning toward Donna.

"Deputy Donna Roper—."

"Ah, of the Leelanau County Mounted Marauders, that fearsome gang that strikes fear in the hearts of all evil-doers."

"Don't be such a prick, Vic," Becky shot back.

Donna stared in disbelief, stunned by the guy's raw insolence.

Sears saw that his intended playfulness had missed the mark like a warped arrow. "No offense intended, but you've got to admit your outfit has dropped the ball." He aimed an affirmation-seeking look at Donna.

"I'm not going to comment," she returned. "You're obviously not looking for a discussion."

"Hey, ladies, don't get your feathers up! We're the ones that have the legitimate beef. You should know that the early hours of a murder investigation are critical if there's to be a conviction. Your boss—I assume he's the bozo responsible—has fucked that up. Time has been lost that can't be made up, and now we're asked to go in and repair the damage. It's time you guys left the case to us and went back to getting cats out of trees."

Sears slowly became aware that the booth had become an arctic zone and that the animosity he'd produced was not going to thaw for an eon. There was but one thing to do—leave. His uneasiness, however, caused him to leave with yet another annoying remark.

"You can't agree with me now, but when we crack the case—unless you're just plain stubborn—you'll say, 'Vic, you the man.'"

Donna watched him leave, saying, "What was that all about? I feel like I've been slapped."

"Vic is no prize, but this is worse than usual. It must be the booze talking."

"Booze loosens up, but it doesn't make things up. That guy's got a problem with women police and the Sheriff's Department."

"Maybe it's a superiority problem. The first time I met him here I wasn't in uniform. When he learned I was with the Sheriff's Patrol, he gave a very condescending, 'Oh.' I called him on it and he said seriously, 'I didn't mean anything. Hell, some people are right as fighter pilots and some are suited to be cargo pilots.'"

"He was serious?"

"Completely."

"Let's head on home. We both have a meeting in the morning."

CHAPTER 15

CARL SLOWED TO THE LEGAL speed as soon as he was sure he wasn't being pursued. It was torture to drive slowly when he desperately yearned to get home to the safety of his garage. Fortunately, he met no other cars along the back roads. Once inside with the garage door closed, he turned on the light and examined his car. He had heard what he thought was a bullet hitting the side as he dashed away. Bullet holes would be hard to explain. His heart sank. The metal on the left side of the hood was torn. A bullet had caught it and ripped a long gash. An inch higher and it would have missed altogether. Then, he saw the hole in the rear door, just below the window.

He began taking an inventory of his problems. He was sure he'd hit the guy who was coming through the door at him. Had he killed him? And here he was with a car that cried out to anyone that he'd been shot at. Maybe worst of all, he'd bungled the job Jason Ackerman had trusted to him. It meant the end of his prospects in that quarter. He ran a finger over the jagged rip in the metal. He had two choices; either make a run for it right now, or call Ackerman and tell him what had happened. Maybe Ackerman, who had an uncanny ability to see the larger picture, would see a way out. Carl knew he wouldn't get far on the run. He went inside to make the call.

❍

Remembering she was low on gas, Marti paused as she was getting into her car in the Oyster Bar's lot and told Ferris she needed to stop at the Mobil station in Suttons Bay. He followed.her there, parked and came back to pump the gas for her using her credit card at the pump. As he stood there a State Police car sped by heading north, its siren wailing. He wondered where they were going and what had happened.

Ferris led the way north along the bay to Jacobson Road, which branched inland from highway 22 just south of the reservation, checking his rear-view mirror from time to time to be sure Marti was behind him. Another five miles and the Swede Road sign appeared in his headlights. Here, he turned and in a couple of minutes, pulled off onto the shoulder and waved to her to pass and take the lead. A half-mile farther on, she slowed and turned into the dirt drive entering her farm. After twenty yards, the drive bisected into the driveway to the house and the old road that continued past her house and on up the hill to the old orchard—the road the killer had taken to dump Barbara Wilson's body.

Ferris walked over to help her out of the car and stood by her side, while she got her crutches in place. The sky was nearly cloudless. The white clapboard building shimmering in the moonlight made the unlit interior especially dark and threatening. She was glad Ferris was with her. She paused on the first step to the porch and pointed to a spot up in the field above them made dark by the number of lawmen who had walked over it that day.

"That's where she was," she said, pointing.

Ferris stood for a few moments taking in the macabre scene and then followed Marti into the house. She turned on every light on her way to the kitchen, where she put a kettle of water on the stove. Leaning against the counter, Tull watched with pleasure the way she had of tossing a lock of her long black hair back over her shoulder as she went about making coffee.

"Something you said back at Larry's made me wonder. You said that you thought Barbara Wilson was trying to communicate with you. Did you mean that she was trying to contact you from the dead?"

Marti stopped spooning coffee into a Bokum and looked over at him. "Heavens no. I don't think the dead communicate. I meant the look on her face seemed to be appealing to me."

"Some people think it's possible."

"Communicating with the dead?"

"Yeah. Loved ones, for instance."

"Not me." She poured the boiling water into the cylinder and pushed the plunger in part way. "Do you think so?"

"I've heard some pretty convincing stories."

Marti had taken cups and saucers from the cupboard and placed them on a tray with the coffee. "Do you take cream or sugar?"

"Black's fine."

"Then if you'll bring that, sir, we can sit in the drawing room." She intoned the last words with an exaggerated British accent.

In the living room, Marti led the way to the couch, where she lowered herself part way while grasping one of the crutches and, then, dropped heavily the rest of the way. "Two more days!" she exclaimed with exasperation.

"You're not going to tell me how it happened?"

"I'm going to tell you that I'll never do the thing again which caused it."

"I guess I'll have to be satisfied. I had a broken leg once. Auto accident. Notice, by the way, how freely I share these private details. Anyway, I know what a royal pain a cast like that can be. Hah!" he said, "A royal pain in the cast!"

"Not bad."

"Anyway, for a year afterward, I'd think of the damn cast from time to time and feel so liberated to be out of it."

They were sitting side by side on the couch, their legs touching. "I'll tell you a private bit if…"

"Private bit," Ferris put in, laughing, "Is that like a naughty bit."

She laughed too. "Well, I'm not going to tell you about my naughty bits, only about a dream I had, or a dream I had not."

His voice was still laughing, "Does coffee do this to you?"

She sipped her coffee. "I guess it's just release from tension—feeling safe. Anyway, the night the police think Barbara Wilson was brought here—night before last, when it stormed—I thought I dreamed that a van was backing down the road outside my bedroom window. It's the only road the killer could have used to take her body up to where he left it. I was aware I'd had the dream when the thunder awoke me.

"There was nothing unusual about the dream, but, today, I've been experiencing something very new to me, a kind of flashback. It's as if an internet picture was coming together on a monitor. Little pieces are assembled over time into a complete picture. This is the 'private bit' I was talking about."

"Whoa, I'm not sure I'm getting this," Tull exclaimed. "What is this picture about, the one you're getting little pieces of?"

Marti took his hand in hers. "Getting afraid you're becoming intimate with a loony bird?"

"A loony bird with loony naughty bits," he laughed.

She held onto his hand. "Here's what I think is happening. I think I got up to go to the john that night. I've been doing that lately, and when I do, sometimes I don't remember that I did until morning, when I'll find the light on in the bathroom – a kind of sleepwalking. I think I must have heard something and looked out the window as the killer was backing down the road. The flashbacks I've been having seem to be adding more detail."

"Have you told the police?"

"No. First, because I only started having this flashback thing today. And also I'm not sure it really happened—not sure it isn't just a dream."

"What are the details that have been filled in so far?"

"That's one of the things which makes it dream-like, because the light is on in the van." Marti moved her body around to face him more. "Have you ever had a dream, for instance, where you're outside a building, but you can look right through the walls and into rooms in a way which would be impossible in real life?"

"Yeah, yeah, I know what you mean, but how is that like what you've been experiencing?"

"You see the light is on in the van. I mean the killer would hardly be driving around with the light on in the van, would he?"

"No, I guess he wouldn't," Ferris considered, "But I think you should tell the police about it, anyway. And, I think you should keep this to yourself. If the killer were to hear that you're saying you looked out the window and saw him driving by in a lighted van, well, I don't think it's a wise thing for you to do."

"See what you mean." Marti was touched by his thoughtfulness. She had become so totally independent that she no longer expected this much concern from anyone. She admitted to herself that it felt good.

"Do you think you can make it to work on time, tomorrow, if you start from here in the morning?"

❍

Jason Ackerman listened to Carl's tale. His mind assessed the facts and defined the situation he faced. Carl had screwed up royally, but he and Greenleaf Properties were in no way implicated except through their association with Carl.

"Did anyone see your face, Carl?"

"No, I'm sure, because I was wearing a bandanna across my face. I was wearing gloves, too."

"Good. What about the gun? Do you still have it?"

"Yeah, and that can't be traced to me either. Never been registered." Carl said this with a confident tone, hoping his foresight in this detail would make up for his complete blunder.

"Carl, I can see a way that this can all be handled, but we have to hide your car immediately. Has your wife seen it since you came home?"

"No. She isn't here yet. She's at a meeting at the Historical Museum in Leland."

"Good. Bring the car over here to my house. It will be safest here. I'll load it on a truck and get it repaired out of town. Oh, and bring the gun with you."

"Right, I'll come right over," he said with great relief. Ackerman wasn't angry and had a plan to make it all right. Calmer now, Carl began thinking what to tell his wife about the missing car.

❍

Mary McNab entered the rear kitchen door of the Leelanau Sands Casino restaurant. The two cooks and their two helpers were busy. After first glancing up and seeing her, they paid no further attention.

She pulled a plastic trash bag out of a box and walked into the pantry storeroom, where she half-filled the bag with food that could be eaten uncooked. This she carried outside and left near the rear door. She went back inside and walked through the kitchen and out onto the gaming floor. There she sought Terry, the floor manager.

"Terry, I need some wheels. Mine are out of commission and I need to take care of some business right away."

The tall blond was used to favors being asked without explanation and also used to asking them. He took his keys from his pocket and handed them to Mary. "It's parked next to the fence. It's the-."

"I know the car, Terry. Everyone does. Thanks, and you haven't seen me, OK?"

"You got it."

She drove the red Corvette past her street, where she saw the flashing lights of a police car parked in front of the house and caught the distant lights of another one approaching in the rear view mirror. She continued north on 22 until she came to 112, on which she could climb the hill behind the village to Peshawbestown Rd. Driving south again the wail of more sirens came up from the bay side and she saw the landing floodlights of a helicopter approaching from Traverse City.

Mary purposely passed the overgrown dirt track that led back to Kalcheck's sugar shack and drove a mile farther along to the next intersection. Here, she did a one-eighty and approached the driveway again, this time with the headlights turned off. Slowly, she made her way by moonlight to the stand of sugar maples atop the hill.

Harry had heard the car and was standing behind the trunk of a large tree watching the approach of the low-slung sports car. His hand tightened around the handle of the ax he'd found in the shack. Ten yards from the edge of the woods the car stopped and the door opened.

Mary got out and called, "Harry it's me. Harry are you there?"

Harry stepped out in the open. "Over here, honey. Do you have any food?"

"Yes, I have food and, I'm afraid, very bad news."

It was a deeply pained man who sat listening to the story Mary had to tell. He was frightened that Buddy had been badly hurt. If so, it was his fault—his stupid fault.

"We've got to find out about Buddy," he said urgently.

"Somebody was hurt. I heard an ambulance come, but it might have been the guy who broke into the house. Harry, I'm sure he was the same guy who grabbed me in the parking lot."

"Really? I was afraid of something like this. Shit!" he shouted. But, after thinking for a moment he became calmer. "I've got your phone; we could call someone and try to find out about Buddy."

"Let's wait just a bit. I doubt if anyone I could call would know anything, yet. In the meantime, there's the computer."

"That damned thing. I don't care about that. I'll just give it back."

"Yes, you could do that, but I think we should think through this situation a bit more before we act. We need to see if we can gain access to the files."

"Well, it's inside the shack. I opened up the case and looked inside. There were no drugs… "

"The computer—you looked *inside* it?"

Harry gave a self-derisive laugh. "Yeah. OK, maybe it was a stupid thing to do, but at least that possibility is ruled out."

In the darkness, Harry couldn't see her look of maternal affection. "Yes, that's important," she offered, "but now we have to take it someplace where we'll have electricity and privacy. Any suggestions?"

Harry pondered the question. "It can't be at the house of anyone we know. I'm not getting more friends mixed up in this."

"We need to do it now—tonight," Mary replied. "That narrows the possibilities. Or does it?" She reached out and put her hand on Harry's arm. "I know a place where we'll be private, and … I can return Terry's car at the same time. We'll leave yours here. The police are looking for it."

❍

A sheet had been spread over Buddy's body. Hoss and his deputies waited for the State Police crime lab people to arrive. It was their third trip up into the Peninsula in as many days. The time before that had been four years earlier for a questionable suicide that turned out, in the end, to be just that.

In the kitchen, Hoss sat down at the table. He smelled fresh coffee and saw a carafe of it in the coffee maker. Mary must have started it when she first arrived home from work. He got up, found a cup in the cupboard, filled it and sat down again.

The advent of the gunman opened a whole new dimension to the case, but what did it mean? Who would want to harm Mary? What could he have wanted with her? Could it be connected with the casino? Mary had no direct contact with the gamblers as far as he knew. A crazy, jilted boyfriend? No, Mary wouldn't have stayed away this long. As soon as the guy drove away, she would have been back to see about Buddy.

And, what about Buddy? Why was he watching Mary's house? To protect her? Maybe that was it. Harry had sent Buddy to keep an eye on Mary, because he was expecting the kind of trouble this guy represented. There was definitely something going on here that had nothing to do with the murder of Dr. Wilson.

Hoss detected the sounds of the crime-lab group arriving. He left his coffee and went back into the other room.

"Hi, Hoss. You Leelanau County people trying to replace Las Vegas as the nation's crime capital?"

"I understand how you feel. Must be hell t'have your card game interrupted so much."

The state technician lifted the cover off Buddy. "Was this some kind of shoot-out?"

"Yeah, in a sense. Whoever shot this man got away. That guy's the unknown in this equation. He parked his car out front—late model sedan—then he knocked on the front door and pushed his way inside when it was opened. He was probably wearing gloves, but we need to check the door for prints anyway. He went out the side door, so the same goes for that. He walked up the side of the house to his car, so the footprints. A whole lot of people walked over the area before we could get it taped off. Still, I'm hoping we can find some trace of his tire tracks. There may be spent cartridge casings, and then bullets—several in this man and one in Shorty McQuade. He's in the hospital."

"Shorty was shot? We didn't know that. How is he?"

"He was alive when the helicopter picked him up. I've got to check on him."

The technician turned to his two assistants and began to map out their procedure plan, while Hoss went back to the kitchen and looked into his notebook for the number of Munson Hospital in Traverse City and dialed.

"That's all you can tell me, then. He's in surgery?" He listened. "OK, I'll call back later, thanks."

Hoss noticed his unfinished coffee and warmed it up with more from the carafe. A whole new impression of the case was taking shape in his mind. Maybe Harry had gone into hiding because of his fear of the guy who shot Buddy. Maybe he cut out of work that morning to do something else rather than abduct Dr. Wilson. Maybe he got into another sort of trouble.

What did Mary say about how Harry had acted the night of the abduction? He was very anxious, she'd said, but she would have known if it were about something as bad as kidnapping a woman.

"Damn it, I've been blind as a bat," he blurted out, standing up at the same time, knocking the chair over and nudging the table a foot across the kitchen floor.

The scalping! The damned scalping. K.D. was right, he'd been too quick to go for the stereotype. It was probably just what the killer intended him to do.

Hoss waited at the house and gave the story to an FBI agent, who'd driven up from Traverse City. This shooting was now totally the Bureau's baby; they handled felonies on the reservation. He was going home to get something to eat and then call Munson Hospital to see if there was anything new on Shorty's condition.

Heading north on Jacobson Road, he saw headlights coming out of a side road a mile up ahead and turning in his direction. This was the neighborhood of Kalcheck's hill, so he wondered if someone else also used the hill for rumination. The car passed, a low sports car, its lights blinding him for a moment. He sensed something was wrong about the car having come from the hill—that dirt track was a bit farther on. He slowed down and played his searchlight along the field next to him until he saw the spot where the car had come out. He remembered now. The weed-obscured trail led back toward an abandoned shack. Sudden awareness struck him. He knew who had been in the car he'd just passed.

With wheels spinning he got his car turned around to give chase. The taillights of the other car were not visible now, but he rocketed along until he got to the next intersection. Turning left would take him back to the reservation. He didn't think Harry would be returning there with all the police activity, so he swerved right. After ten minutes he had to admit he had lost the car and his man once again.

Hoss returned to the dirt track and walked back in to the clump of sugar maples at the hill's top. He found Harry's car and evidence that Harry had been staying in the shack.

He mumbled aloud, "What's that saying about being an hour late and a dollar short."

❍

Carl's headlights fell on Jason Ackerman, wearing a warm-up suit and standing in the center of his long driveway. This rendezvous occurred about thirty yards down the driveway from Ackerman's house. Ackerman walked up and shined his flashlight on Carl's face.

"Turn off your headlights and follow me with your car."

Ackerman turned back toward the house, flashlight pointing toward the ground at his feet. At the right side of a large parking area stood a three-car garage and next to it, a separate building that had, earlier that evening, housed the snowblade equipped truck that was now parked along side it. Ackerman motioned to Carl to drive his car inside.

"Leave the gun in the car, Carl. What year is the car, by the way?"

"Two thousand four."

"You're to tell your wife that your car burned out a main bearing and it's being repaired. I think we should be able to do this bodywork and get it back to you inside a week."

Ackerman closed the garage door and said, "I'll drive you back home, but first I've got to get my car keys. Come with me."

Ackerman led the way up onto a side deck and to a door that led directly into his exercise room. He switched on the light and Carl found himself standing in a room that rivaled a professional gym, a Nautilus machine for every muscle group. Against the wall that faced Lake Michigan was a large whirlpool tub. Curtains were pulled, but Carl guessed that large windows were behind them. He imagined how great it would be to lie back, as he imagined Ackerman doing, with the hot water whirling around you and the naked body of a woman in your arms while you sipped champagne and watched the sunset.

"Now, where did I leave my keys?" Ackerman said, then, pointing, he added, in a pleased tone, "Ah, there they are! On that ledge at the back of the hot tub. Do me a favor and reach them for me, Carl."

Pleased that Ackerman did not seem at all angry, but was instead quite friendly, Carl willingly began to carry out his boss's request. He placed one knee on the edge of the tub and leaned out over the water, reaching for the keys.

In the next moment Ackerman was on top of him, forcing Carl's head under the water. Carl struggled but had no leverage to fight Ackerman's grip and position. Soon the struggling ceased. Ackerman held on a little longer just to be sure, then relaxed.

He had just added to his list of things he'd done for the first time. He wasn't happy he had killed a person, but he was satisfied that he'd acted swiftly to do what the situation demanded.

He sat only for a minute on the rim of the tub, waiting to catch his breath before he dragged Carl's body over to an equipment locker and heaved it up and inside. He changed the wet warm-up suit for another. From a small refrigerator he got a bottle of fruit juice, then sat up on a massage table and picked up the phone next to it. He dialed a Chicago number.

"Gene, this is Jason Ackerman, I have one of those *special* jobs for you. I need you to come up here to my place in Michigan. Bring a left rear door and a hood for a 2004 Buick Regal. Black. Oh, and the tools you'll need to take off the damaged parts and install the new ones. I need this done tomorrow and, of course, I'll pay the usual fee."

He sat for a moment, rolling his gold tennis ball between his fingers, reviewing in his mind what needed to be done. He was satisfied that his plan was sound.

❍

The locked room was dark except for the light coming from the computer monitor. The first thing Mary had done before booting up the computer, was to have Harry pull a table against the wall under the surveillance camera and then climb onto a chair placed on the table to put duct tape over the camera lens. Mary sat at the keyboard. Only an occasional sound penetrated from the gaming section of the building into the quiet office.

On the screen the letters IBM were followed by the Windows logo.

"If entry is password protected, which it most likely is, we've got a problem. We'll know in a few seconds."

Harry looked over Mary's shoulder and watched a box appear on the screen asking for the user's password."

Mary groaned, "Damn, that's what I was afraid of."

The user name was already given, "winner". A cursor was pulsating impatiently below it in the empty password box.

"It could be anything," Mary said in a gloomy voice. "The chance that we could hit upon it is about the same as one of those people out there rolling their point twenty times in a row."

"We're fucked, huh?"

"Afraid so."

"Don't people usually choose a number like their birth date or the date of their wedding or some other significant date for alarm codes and stuff like that?"

"True. You're pretty sure you got this out of the main man's office?"

"No question. I asked the secretary."

"For Ackerman's office?"

"No, I didn't know his name. I said I was told to pick up the boss's computer."

"Amazing! What a chance you took. His name is Jason Ackerman, by the way."

"Well, there you are," said Harry, optimistically, "We put in his birth date."

"Do you happen to know what it is, offhand?" she replied, playfully. "Besides, the password doesn't have to be a number, it can be a word or any combination of letters."

"OK, how about his initials?"

Mary typed JA and hit the enter key. A box appeared on the screen informing them, "Invalid password." She tried J.A. and got the same message.

"How about the name of the company. What is it, Greenleaf something."

"Greenleaf Properties," Mary said, and tried it.

Then, Green, then, Leaf...

❍

The eleven o'clock news on Channel 8 reported that the Leelanau County Sheriff's deputies had been engaged in a gunfight at the home of a known friend of suspect Harry Swifthawk. One deputy was critically wounded and the police had killed the former brother-in-law of the suspect.

This announcement was accompanied by an interview with Kip Springer, who stated it appeared that the operation was poorly planned. It was obvious to viewers that he was going to say "bungled," but caught himself.

The Commander of the State Police Post at Traverse City was also interviewed, but said he couldn't comment, because he didn't possess all the facts. To a direct question he acknowledged that, in his opinion, the State Police and the FBI should have been consulted.

CHAPTER 16

JASON ACKERMAN'S SHADOW STOOD OUT sharply on the moonlit sand. He was dragging a kayak down the sloping beach to the water's edge. He slipped inside the narrow hull and using the paddle, pushed off from the shore. A quarter of a mile straight out into Lake Michigan he stopped paddling. Here, he turned the boat to face back toward land. Some lights were on at a neighbor's house half a mile to the south. Apart from this, the whole of the shoreline and the high dunes beyond were dark against the lighter sky. The lake was very calm. Ripples lapping softly against the side of the hull made the only sound. He let the sleek, light craft drift for several minutes. It was calming out here on the water. He needed this reprieve from the intensity of the past hours and those that would follow as he worked to insulate himself from Carl's blunder.

"That dickhead!" he growled.

From the pocket of the warm-up jacket, he took Carl's revolver. He held it in his outstretched hand, its polished, blued surface dully lustrous in the moonlight. He opened his hand and let it fall into the lake, and followed it, in his mind's eye, fifteen fathoms to the bottom.

"Right." he said aloud, and began paddling back to shore.

❍

"It's hopeless. We'll never come up with the password and I don't know how to bypass it. Maybe it can't be bypassed by anyone." Her mood was deflated.

Harry had just hung up the phone after calling Munson Hospital for the second time to be told again that they didn't have a patient by Buddy's name.

"Do you suppose the police won't let 'em give out a patient's name if he's been involved in a shooting?" He wondered aloud. "What was that you just said?"

"Only that trying to guess the password is hopeless."

"I wish we knew the dude's birth date," Harry grumbled.

"Why don't you call him up and ask him? Say you want to send him a present, only you're not sure you have the right date."

Harry laughed. "That's the best idea we've had so far."

"I guess we should throw in the towel," said Mary, resigned to the impossible odds.

"No, let's think this through. You have to type this password in every time you want to use your computer, right?"

"Only if you've turned it off. Many people leave their computers on all the time."

"They wouldn't if they wanted what's in it to remain private. Right?"

"That's right"

"Well, then my guess is that a busy guy like Ackerman would have a short password. He wouldn't want to waste time."

Mary sighed. "You've just reduced the possibilities to around one billion."

"Now wait a minute," Harry objected, pointing to the user name. "What about this user name there on the screen? Do you pick your own, or is it assigned?"

"You pick it yourself."

"OK, then, what does it say about a guy who picks 'winner' for a user name?"

"I'd say he sees himself as a winner."

"Winner of what?"

"In this guy's case, business," Mary answered.

"OK, what word comes to mind about winning in business?"

"Success."

"Try it."

She did with the—by now—expected result.

"What else comes to mind?"

"Profit."

"Try it."

Mary typed the word and hit the enter key. Again the error message.

"OK, what else?" Harry prompted.

"How about you? What comes to your mind about winning in business?"

"Money."

Mary made the entry and got the same message.

Harry leaned over her shoulder, put one finger on the shift key, then hit the dollar sign. Mary hit the enter key and the computer started to click and whir. They both stared incredulously as the Windows desktop appeared on the screen.

"That's it!" she shouted, and spun around in the swivel chair. They kissed and Harry pulled her down onto the thick carpet.

❍

On her desk was the CD containing the files that she and Harry had copied. They were the pertinent files for their purpose, and that purpose was to have a weapon strong enough to stop Jason Ackerman from ever harming them. At this point, Mary had gone out to the restroom in the casino where she overheard two customers talking about the shooting, and about the man who'd been killed.

Harry had been leaning back in her desk chair, feet up on her desk, smiling contentedly when she returned and told him the news. He sat looking up at her for several moments with a puzzled look, and then he took his feet down, leaned forward onto the desk and began to cry. Deep pain was evident in the helpless convulsing of his body.

"It's my fault," he said between sobs. "Buddy was just doing what I'd asked. The whole fucking thing is my fault."

He looked up then, his face shaped by purpose. "I'm going to get that bastard. I will!"

He slumped forward again and began to sob. "I'll get him, but it was totally my fault."

Mary went over to him and put her arm around his shoulders.

"You're not responsible for Buddy's death," she said softly. "You're responsible for taking the computer, but that shouldn't result in a person getting killed. Ackerman is responsible for Buddy's death. But, if you go and do something wild in order to get revenge, then yours will be the blame for whatever follows."

Harry had wiped his face with his hand. "OK, but I'm not going to let him get away with this."

She had never seen Harry this distraught before and was unsure of the best way to help him.

"I'm with you, of course, but we'll have to think of something smart. First, we have to protect ourselves. We have to decide how best to use these files we've copied."

Harry wanted to go straight to the State Police and give them the CD.

"Once the cops have this stuff, there will be no reason for Ackerman to mess with us. And the cops will get Ackerman, and we'll get even for Buddy."

Mary nodded. "It might go as you say, but I see a possible problem."

"Yeah, what's that?"

"There is nothing in the files that connects Ackerman to Buddy's death—nothing that actually proves that the guy who shot Buddy is connected in any way with Ackerman. The documents we've copied all deal with real estate and the things Ackerman and his partners have done to get the present county government replaced. Dirty things, to be sure, but I don't know how illegal they are. I'm afraid the State Police will do nothing about it. Politically, the police could even be on Ackerman's side. That leaves us with Ackerman still knowing we have information which, if made public, could cause him a lot of trouble. Big-time financial trouble, at least, and that leaves us in danger. If, on the other hand, we let him know that we've copied everything in his computer and we've arranged for it to be made public if anything ever happens to us, he'll almost certainly decide it's wisest to leave us alone. And this is especially true if he was behind Buddy's death. He wouldn't know what would be discovered, once people started looking closely."

"That doesn't pay him back for Buddy!"

"We can't bring Buddy back, Harry. The important thing is for us to be able to live in peace." Mary could tell she had won the argument—for the moment, at least.

She relished the power she imagined the two of them now had over Ackerman. Harry always knew Mary was smart, but he didn't know she had the balls this situation demanded. He chuckled. "You're one helluva woman Mary McNab. What else have you planned for us?"

Mary's dark eyes glowed from the admiration she heard in Harry's voice. "I'll be safe here tonight, but you'll have to hide a little longer until Ackerman has a chance to realize we've got him in check. After that it will be safe."

"I guess I can do a couple more nights in the sugar shack and when you agree to marry me we'll go there on our honeymoon." He became serious. "Mary, I want you to know I appreciate your sticking by me in this mess. And, I'm aware of what I've caused... you and Buddy." More words would not come.

❍

Harry walked for an hour before he came to the place where he could leave the road and take a shortcut through the field to the shack. Only two cars had come along and he hid each time until they passed. He felt a mixture of very strong, clashing emotions as he climbed toward the copse of sugar maples at the top of the hill. His heart was filled by the growing love he had for Mary. The future, a thing that had held no meaning for him earlier, had become like a newly discovered continent, one rich with new possibilities for him and visions of unending joy with her. At the same time, he knew deep loss and hatred over Buddy's death. Mary was content that they should be able to live their lives out without worry. It wasn't the same for him, and he decided this was one of the differences between men and women.

Freedom from worry wasn't as important to him as settling scores. Settling scores had been a force within him ever since his Uncle Joseph had told him how his father was fired from the lumberyard and about the events surrounding his father's murder. He wasn't consciously aware, however, of just how large a part this had played in his refusal to participate in the white world around him and in his constant need to provoke symbols of that world like Hoss Davis.

Thirsty from the walk, he approached the dense trees hoping there was a beer left in the shack. He froze, suddenly, as a deer might, hardly breathing. He had seen, in his peripheral vision, a tiny flash of light coming from the woods. Slowly he sank to the ground. Someone was in the woods. Had they seen him? The moonlight was bright enough. There was the chance that whoever it was would be looking in the other direction, watching the dirt track, waiting for him to return to the shack for his car.

He crept through the weeds, until he reached the first large maple. Raising himself, he peered into the darkness of the woods.

Immediately, he understood the situation. A car painted with the familiar insignia of the Leelanau County Sheriff's Patrol was parked out of sight of anyone entering the woods from the dirt track. They had discovered his hiding place and were waiting for him.

"So much for spending the night here," he thought. Where could he go? Then, he knew. It was the perfect place given certain strong, new feelings that filled him. He retreated back down the hill, then set a course across the field toward another hill that lay five miles to the northwest.

The moonlight, filtering through the overarching trees, cast patterns on the road as he walked along it. On a moonlit night such as this, Harry loved to be walking alone on deserted roads or cutting through fields or sitting by the shore of the big lake. He had not done this for some time, and he wondered how he could have forgotten the pleasure. It was times such as these that evoked a feeling of knowing the Great Spirit. On a night such as this, the Strawberry Moon full, he once sat motionless at the point where tiny Gill's Creek entered Lake Michigan and watched the deer come down to drink. They were only several yards away, and they had looked around at him but then went on drinking, unafraid. At that moment, he'd felt that the Great Spirit was watching and was pleased to see these creatures of his realize they were brothers.

He decided now he had not been good to himself most of his life. He had strayed far from the harmony with the Great Spirit that his uncle, Joseph, had spoken of. Mary was his gateway back to that harmony.

A cherry orchard covered the crown of the hill toward which he'd been walking. The cherries were almost ripe and would be picked soon.

In answer to an impulse he didn't understand, he took off all of his clothes and stood naked in the moonlight. Raising his arms above his head, he stood a long time, bathing in the silver light, gazing into the heavens.

At length, when he dressed, he felt as if some change had occurred in him. He walked to the edge of the high orchard. From there he could look down onto the ribbon of road and the farmhouse and barn. He had reached his destination, one where he hoped to be accepted as a brother.

CHAPTER 17

FERRIS AWOKE TO FIND HIMSELF alone in bed. Pale, early morning light touched the room's few, spare furnishings. Immediately, he remembered the night and its pleasures—her cast notwithstanding. But where was she? There was movement in the light, causing him to look over his shoulder toward the window that faced the dawn. She stood there with her hands lightly holding each side of the frame, looking out. Her gaze was not directed toward the farmland, but toward the horizon and above. He could just see the side of her face and the corner of her mouth. She seemed to be saying something, inaudibly.

Marti heard him move and turned partly to look back at the bed, the dawn's glow softly modeling her body.

"Good morning," she said, cheerfully.

"Good morning. What were you just saying out the window?"

She laughed. "Nothing, really."

"Another evasion."

"OK, it's my little ritual, an orientation."

"Religious ritual?"

Her answer was a gloss. "Ah … no. Ready for breakfast?"

"Ready for something else," he said, reaching out toward her.

Later, seated at the small table next to the kitchen window, he studied her as she sat opposite him, wrapped in a thick, yellow, terry-cloth robe. His usual confidence with women was shaken because he remembered that she wasn't just a pick-up, but in fact was the one who'd been in charge. She was an unusually beautiful woman–exotic even. Morning sunlight glinted in her hair, gathering no other color than pure jet black. The skin of her face was deep copper and taut over high cheekbones. Her eyes were as dark as her hair, large and almond-shaped.

Disturbing too was his awareness that, although she had been pleasant and complimentary to him, there was a lofty, worldly air about her that hinted she was more experienced than he.

He needed something to change the direction of these thoughts before he lost his confidence. "Seriously now, you called what you were saying to yourself upstairs an 'orientation ritual.' What was that all about?"

Marti, holding an oversized coffee cup with both hands considered how much of herself she'd reveal to this stranger. Her hesitation did not spring from any tendency to withhold but from repeated experience that most men did not find her non-physical self to their liking.

"Last night at the bar, I warned you not to get me started on this subject, so now you have no one to blame but yourself. You see, I happen to think that we humans are flawed creatures, flawed in the very quarter for which we generally give ourselves so much credit, our brains. We usually can't put three thoughts together, even when trying, which don't become contaminated by self-centeredness. We constantly overvalue ourselves personally, our families, our organizations, our nations, even our plumbing." She paused to see if he was still with her, or if he had taken to the barricades when she'd put forward the idea that *we* overvalue and not *they*. He was listening, still, but she thought she'd better keep it short.

"Before one starts any job, one does well to stop a moment and review the realities of the situation. That's what I do every morning. I remind myself that this universe is a very huge place, and of my realistic importance in it."

"Realistic importance?"

She laughed lightly. "No importance ... except to myself and my friends."

Ferris Tull did not like this last bit. Marti had expected he wouldn't. He shook his head. "No. I couldn't begin my day if I thought there was no purpose, if we hadn't been put here for a purpose. I don't believe you really think there's no purpose."

Marti wasn't going to argue. She heard that tone in his voice that meant he wouldn't entertain an argument.

"You asked me, I told you, but don't tell me I don't believe what I just took the trouble to tell you I did." This was said in a playful way. She didn't want to continue her explanation, but she wasn't going to have her position dismissed without pointing out a breach of parliamentary rules.

He glanced at the kitchen clock. "I'd like to prove you wrong, but my life purpose calls."

He started to rise, but she delayed his move by saying with a serious tone. "Thanks so much for insisting on coming back here with me last night. I think my fear of ghosts has about disappeared now."

"I think your fear was of more than ghosts." He looked to her for confirmation.

She nodded. "I was, perhaps still am, afraid the killer will return. I know it makes no rational sense, but maybe my feeling that the dead woman was communicating something to me there in the moonlight would cause the killer to wonder if she revealed his identity to me. Crazy, I know but something is making me afraid."

"Our minds can do a real job on us," Ferris agreed, "Actually, as I said before, this is the last place the killer would ever go again. This, in fact, is probably the safest place on the whole peninsula.

It's like a shopper avoiding a store after it's been held-up, when that's really the safest time to be there; the robbers already have what they wanted, and the police have been shaken out of their sleep and are alert for a while."

Marti was nodding and smiling as he talked. "Thanks again."

❍

Col. Mel Pollock had driven to Traverse City from the State Police Director's office in Lansing in order to talk to Lt. Lyle Steele alone and unrecorded. Lyle, the Commander of the Traverse City Post, had not been moving fast enough to satisfy the political needs of Boyd Steward and the others. He now knew who one of those was; Mel had gotten a call from the big man himself. The governor had a skill for delivering an ultimatum in an unmistakable tone, but harmlessly worded if quoted. He'd said, "Mel, I want to be able to tell the guys at lunch that this is taken care of."

Hoss Davis had so far bungled his attempt to catch the Indian, but the voters would still see him as doing something. What Mel had heard from on high was a demand that the State Police must immediately snatch that image from Hoss.

Mel suggested to Lyle Steele that they go for a walk.

"You're telling me you haven't been moving to catch this Harry Swifthawk, because you have no reason to think he's the perp?" Mel said with the tone of a skeptical father listening to his son's explanation for not bringing home a better report card.

"The woman was scalped, that is a piece of her scalp about four inches in diameter was removed. As far as I can see, it's the only thing that might cause Davis to think of Harry Swifthawk. That and the fact Swifthawk is hiding."

"That's a pretty big point, don't you think?"

"No, I don't. This guy has been in chronic trouble with the police, and he's a Native American to boot. A guy like that is used to having the law look his way whenever there's an unexplained crime—always afraid he's going to get something hung on him that he didn't do. And he's got reason to fear it. It's not hard to understand why he'd make himself scarce."

Pollock didn't have a rebuttal. He still needed Steele to take immediate action.

"OK, then, Lieutenant, what's your plan?"

Lyle Steele didn't like being pushed, but he suspected it would take a source much higher up the chain of command to cause the top man in the State Police to drive all the way up here to talk to him. He counseled himself not to take Pollock's attitude personally.

"We've concentrated first of all on the physical evidence. There's not much, but some. The guy who did it was very careful. There are no prints on the van. We recently identified a few cotton fibers taken from the driver's seat—almost certainly blue jeans. Unfortunately, not new jeans. The amount of dye left on the fibers is like that found on the jeans of roughly fifty percent of the general population.

"There were several black dog hairs on the driver's seat, but the Wilsons have a tan dog. The hairs found are curly and short. Examination revealed that one end was the natural end of the hair, but the other end had been cut with a sharp tool—a groomer's clippers, probably. A dog breeder we consulted believes the hairs are from a black poodle. We don't have a DNA on the breed yet. The breeder made a guess, based on the length of the hairs, that the owner has it groomed regularly."

Mel Pollock had dropped the attitude of the critical father and was listening now with respectful attention. He commented, "You've checked the records of local dog groomers for customers that fit that description, I take it."

"We have and we have a couple of leads. Checking them out is on the agenda for today. There is one groomer who's on vacation and isn't due back in town until tomorrow."

"Good," Pollock commented, "anything else?"

"The husband. We found out he was having an affair with a neighbor—a possible motive for murdering his wife."

"You think it could be the husband, then?" asked Pollock.

"No, actually I believe it will turn out to be someone who kidnapped her with a motive of robbery. She may have had over six thousand dollars in cash on her."

"Yeah, but what casual carjacker would know that?" Mel inserted. "That's an angle you need to look into. Who would be likely to know she had the money on her?"

"It's a very good point, Colonel." Lyle wondered whether to leave Pollock with the impression that his suggestion was original, or tell him that he already had two people investigating this angle. It irked him to have Pollock go away thinking and saying he had gone up to Traverse City and "put those guys on the right track". It was, however, the perfect way to get Pollock off his back, so he let it stand.

"I'm glad I came up here, Lieutenant. I can see you're working hard on this matter, but there is a need for the public to see us as being more active. They need to be reassured that we're on top of things. It makes them feel more secure."

Sure, Lyle thought, but it's not the public that needs reassurance.

"I understand," Lyle said. "I'll call a press conference: 'Leads from physical evidence found in the van are being pursued and we expect to make an arrest soon.'"

Mel Pollock put his hand on Lyle Steele's shoulder. He almost said, "Good man," but caught it in time to say instead, "You're doing a good job, Lieutenant. Handle it your own way. I'm sorry I bothered you."

❍

A very tired Hoss Davis faced the deputies of the morning shift. "First of all," he announced, "Shorty did well in surgery. He's listed in serious condition, but the doc told me that barring any unforeseen complication he'll be all right."

Clapping and cheering commenced. "I never had any doubt," chimed in David Wick, "He'd never die with me owing him money."

When the kidding and comments subsided, Hoss reviewed the events of the previous night. He went on in his tired voice, "Well kids, I've got to confess I was wrong about Harry Swifthawk. He probably had nothing to do with the Wilson murder. He's involved in something serious enough to cause him to hide, all right. But he's not hiding from us. He's probably hiding from the guy that killed Buddy and shot Shorty. That guy was apparently after Mary McNab and wants her badly enough to commit murder to get her. As you know, the killing on the reservation belongs to the FBI, but the way I figure it, Harry and Mary are still in real danger and they may be hiding anywhere in the county. That's our territory."

"Donna—." Hoss, about to give her an assignment, paused. "By the way, Donna, it's a real pleasure for you to pay us a visit—. I want...." He had to wait again until the kidding stopped. "As I was saying, I want you to talk to Mary's friends. See if they can think of any place she might go if she thought she was in a jam—an old haunt, perhaps. And convince them Mary's life might depend on their telling us if Mary contacts any of them. If any of you can think of another approach, toss it out here on the table."

"Did the crime lab come up with anything?" asked Russ Preva.

"Not much about last night as far as I know. By the way it's pretty clear the State lab boys in Gaylord are in no hurry to keep us informed. Ordinarily we'd have had a call by now. Don Silver, however, pulled a bullet out of the woodwork and thinks it's .38 caliber—no casings left behind, so it was a revolver.

"Your question about the crime lab reminds me of a development in the Wilson case. Lyle Steele, being the decent guy he is, called me. They're pretty sure now that the hairs we found in the van came from a black poodle that had been groomed recently. They're interviewing groomers in the area."

He stood looking around the room for a few moments. "No other questions? OK, let's get out there. Donna, come into my office for a moment."

Hoss sagged into his desk chair, while Donna remained standing.

"What did you learn in Birmingham?"

"I learned, or rather I re-confirmed that it pays to make friends. Otherwise, I may not have learned much. The Executive Secretary of the Medical Society was cooperative and saw to it that I got all the relevant information they had." She laid a manila envelope containing the copies of Oakland County Medical Society's records on Hoss's desk.

"The details are in there, but it comes down to this; two of Marsh's patients claimed he coerced them into having intercourse with him during one of their therapy sessions. He was charged, in the first case, but the case was dropped for lack of evidence. After reading about both cases, however, it's my judgment the women were telling the truth."

Donna waited for Hoss to digest this. His heavy lids lifted and he studied her face. "How did Marsh reply to the charge?"

"He denied it, of course. Claimed the woman was delusional. He gave an example of a time when his wedding ring was lost and the patient noting this, firmly believed it meant he was wanting her to leave her husband and run away with him. Marsh, by the way, refused the polygraph."

"Interesting. Good work. I'm going to call Lyle Steele and tell him what you found. However, I think we can do the most good right now by finding Harry and Mary McNab before they get hurt. Understand?"

Donna saluted.

"Good. Go talk to Mary's friends."

❍

Mary was at her desk when her boss, Gladys Tallfox, came in at eight.

"Mary! I didn't expect to see you this morning after that awful shooting at your house last night. In fact, I heard they were looking for you." Gladys thought for a moment then asked, "Does your father know you're here?"

"No." Mary knew Gladys was giving her a silent reprimand. "You're right, Gladys, I should call him."

She had left a message on his answering machine last night to tell him she was safe, but had not told him where she was. He was home when she called now, and she told him she was at work. He asked if she thought she was safe and she said yes. "I'll sit down with you, Dad, and tell you the whole story in a couple of days."

"Whenever you're ready."

❍

Donna's assigned task was completed very quickly. Instead of going to interview Mary's friends, Donna decided to stop at the casino office first and question those who worked with her. Lo and behold, there was Mary sitting at her desk.

Donna pulled up a chair. "So, you're the elusive Miss McNab."

"Elusive? I've never thought of myself that way before, but it's better than what I have thought."

"Which is?"

"The plain Mary McNab."

Donna appraised the young woman. It was true, one wouldn't instantly think of her as attractive. Her figure was a little too full and her face lacked the structure we generally term beautiful. Her eyes were very expressive, however. There was integrity there and wit. What little Donna knew of her behavior, promised an independent and attractive personality. And, thought Donna to herself, there was a lot Mary could do to improve her appearance, if she wanted to.

"I'd say your former opinion was faulty."

Mary pondered the situation. She anticipated having to make this agreeable and very beautiful woman, whom she was sure she would like, angry with her.

"I'm Donna Roper, by the way. Deputy Roper, as you can see."

"And what does Deputy Roper want with the elusive Mary McNab?"

"It is our collective opinion that you and Harry Swifthawk know the identity of the man who killed your friend Buddy and seriously wounded Deputy McQuade. We … earnestly want this information." She was smiling, but it was like the smile of the weightlifter whose seat you've occupied, who says, "I'd like my seat back."

"I don't know the man," Mary answered. "He was wearing a handkerchief over his face."

"Yes, so we've heard, but why do you think he was after you?"

"Was he after me? How can you be sure of that?"

"He doesn't fit the profile of a petty burglar, so the only other explanation is that he was going to carry your aunt away to be a love slave in the sultan's palace."

Mary smiled but remained mute.

"You must have expected him to try what he did, or why else was Buddy watching and guarding your house?"

Mary said nothing.

"One would think you'd want our help. After all, the guy is still out there."

Donna looked at Mary, frustrated. "I'm about to start calling you 'the bullheaded Mary McNab.'"

It was what Mary had anticipated would happen. She hated treating the woman this way. "Nothing personal, OK?"

"OK. Tell me where Harry is then. He's no longer at the sugar shack."

Mary was clearly surprised, but remained mute.

Back in the patrol car, Donna called Hoss. "I don't think she really knows where he is. I'm sure it surprised her when I said he wasn't at the shack."

"So, we're back to the old business of finding Harry Swifthawk," Hoss groaned. "Damn, but he causes us a lot of trouble. Well, he's not going to spend his life in hiding. We'll just wait until he surfaces. He knows the danger he's in. If the man doesn't want our help, so be it. I think I'll give a call to the Tribal Police and tell them I believe they need to post a guard on Mary, then I'm going to the hospital to talk to Shorty. Why don't you come on back here and be on call at headquarters."

Being on call at headquarters usually meant an opportunity to catch up on paperwork. Donna sat down to a report sheet and began writing up the required report of her trip downstate. The effort was a waste; the State Police may be interested in the records she'd brought back from Birmingham, but no one would read her report.

David Wick came over the intercom. "Donna, call for you, line two."

"Deputy Roper speaking."

"Donna?"

"That's right."

"This is Derek Marsh."

Donna was startled. His calling at this moment was surreal.

"I hope it's all right to call you at work," he continued.

"Yes, of course." Her interest flared. What could he want?

"It's not a professional call. It's personal. I was wondering if you would have dinner with me?"

It was the last thing she had expected. And, he was probably the last person on earth she'd like to dine with, but something prevented her from giving a quick, negative answer. It was the challenge that a meeting with him held out. Hoss had as much as ordered her to forget her investigation of Derek Marsh, but no one could object to her accepting a dinner invitation from an eligible bachelor. If she were able to lure Marsh into betraying himself, it would be a great victory for her side. An additional element stood just behind this motivation; such a victory would wipe the smirk off the face of that arrogant State Trooper she'd met in Larry's Oyster bar.

"Yes. I'd like that," she answered in a pleasant tone.

"Great. It may be an unusual suggestion for a first...uh date, but cooking is a hobby of mine and I'd like to cook a meal for you, if you'd be willing to come out to my place. If there's a problem with that," he hurried to add, "we could eat in town."

Last night she had been ready to stop at his house on her return from Birmingham. Now, by the light of day she paused at the thought of being alone with Derek Marsh. But, at the same time, she wanted to get him to talk without the restraint he'd feel in a public restaurant.

"OK, if you'll let me help."

Marsh laughed. "My salad chef is on vacation. I'd welcome your help. Now that you've agreed to come, I've got to turn right around and warn you that it's very hard to find this place. It's really in the middle of the proverbial nowhere."

"That's all we do in the Sheriff's Department, drive around and find houses we've never been to before."

After she put down the phone, the question occurred to her: Why had he asked her to dinner at his house? It was naïve to think he merely had a social motive. Was he hoping to learn the direction the investigation was taking? Yes, as the killer she suspected him to be, he must be very anxious to know what the police had discovered.

❍

She'd carried the easel about thirty yards straight out toward the barn and was absorbed in sketching the simple, clean lines of her farmhouse. Marti needed a fresh point of view, since the view of the hillside had been spoiled for her. As she worked the right side of her brain sketched, the left thought about Ferris Tull. Her initial response to him was familiar to her. How many times had she met attractive, interesting men, ones with whom she could … frolic. Yes, that was the word that came to her mind, frolic, in the sense of working together to make life fun. And wasn't that enough for her in a relationship? Yes, it was. In the past, the trouble began when the frolicking ended. After an initial period in which all the man would seem to want from her was good times in her company, he'd begin to impose new conditions that contradicted his earlier, avowed priorities. His career now would come first, their relationship second, and these new priorities were expected to become hers. She'd witnessed such an accommodation to occur with many of her women friends. What was different about her, she wondered, that seemed to make that kind of accommodation impossible? She had no objection to a man pursuing his career or avocations with vigor, but she refused to allow this to subordinate her own needs. She needed a relationship founded on the strict respect of the other partner's personality, style and goals. But so far in her experience, what started with mutuality became invaded by the man's push to prevail. In this case, it wouldn't be Ferris's career that would take precedence; he would let her paint—encourage her even. But she feared he would demand that she think as he did.

The brief exchange they'd had on the subject of life's purpose told her that they were as different as chalk and cheese. Could he respect her point of view completely, or would he press for her to change her ideas in exchange for harmony? She'd have to wait and see. The bold line she drew on the canvas that accompanied this thought said there would be no compromise on her part. Some things, to save one's soul, couldn't be compromised. Marti wanted very much to have a soul mate, but she had resigned herself to the likelihood that it would never be. Still, if one chose carefully, moments of pure frolic were possible. Better to conserve one's resources for the occasional bottle of Romanee Conti than to settle for a steady diet of a poor table red.

Hoss Davis had been her first candidate for soul-mate. She realized now that had been because he had respected her individuality. Also, he was kind. These were two qualities she had not experienced from either her father or her brother, who treated her like an unwelcome stranger in the family. Her father had been harsh and critical. She could never discover why he didn't like her, encouraging her older brother's endless expressions of obsessive jealousy. Since she was the only one in the family with black hair, her brother loved to call her "Black Sheep". This seemed to delight her father, to which he would contribute his own demeaning and at times sexually suggestive remarks. He'd made good work of disowning her, and her mother had not been strong enough to intervene. That had been her adolescence.

She knew Hoss had been interested in her, but he was years behind her in the kind of relationship he was ready for. She would have had them run away together; he was interested in working on his car and dreaming of college football.

The other night, she had tricked him into coming to her farm in order to discover what might be possible between them. He'd obviously been tempted to satisfy his old longings for her and might have even wondered what it would be like to live with her, but he'd held back. He wouldn't betray K.D. and thereby himself. In spite of her personal disappointment, Marti respected his loyalty to K.D. Still, if he decided to get his old longings off his chest, she was not in the ranks of the thought police.

In the meantime, maybe she was jumping to conclusions about Ferris. Part of the previous evening had been very pleasant. She decided she'd call him and see if he was interested enough to make the drive back up to the farm tonight for dinner. She put the brush down and took up her crutches and went inside.

"What would you say if a very sexy woman called you up and said she desired your company this evening."

"I'd ask if she were sure she had the right number," Ferris answered.

"You would not."

"You're right, I wasn't thinking, but then how do you expect me to think at all when you call with such a proposal?"

"I'm still waiting for an answer."

"The answer is yes, of course. And where is this meeting to take place?"

"I'd be happy to cook something here at the farm, but I know it's a long drive for you. Maybe you'd rather meet again at the Oyster Bar."

"I'd much rather eat your cooking."

"Sevenish, then." She began thinking of what to wear. She'd wear the new, white sundress.

❍

"I can't be sure, Hoss. Everything happened so damn fast. An' I was more concerned with who was shooting and was any of it comin' my way. It was a sedan, though, and dark in color. I couldn't swear to it, but I'd say new, or only a couple of years old, kinda rounded lines. Like I said, I never actually saw the guy."

Shorty looked weak and ten years older. His few strands of hair he let grow long so he could wind them artfully around his bald scalp were spread up on the pillow like an aura. There was a rectangular plastic container half filled with a pinkish fluid on the floor into which a chest tube extended. The fluid level in the tube rose and fell with each of Shorty's breaths.

"Too bad about Buddy," he added. "He was an ornery son-of-a-bitch, but I kinda respected him just the same. He was tryin' to protect the girl, you know. I heard him yell, "Stop!" at the guy. That was just before the shooting started."

Shorty repeated and worked through the scene in his mind, trying to master it.

"You don't know this yet," Hoss said, "but Mary McNab took off while all the shooting was going on and hid for the night—with Harry, we think. This morning we found her. That is, she came out of hiding and showed up at work. Donna talked to her and believes Mary knows the identity of the guy who shot you, but won't talk. Not about where Harry is either. It's like those killings you read about in the inner cities where nobody knows nothing."

"And we got nothin' else to go on, right?"

"Zero," Hoss replied and fell into silent rumination.

"I was just talkin' to a nurse," Shorty commented in a disinterested tone, "who told me Lyle Steele just come on the tube to say the State Police were working on some important new evidence in the Wilson case, and were expecting to make an arrest soon."

The words stung Hoss. Did Lyle have something he hadn't told him about? His spirits sank. Hell, maybe it's true that they are better able to handle this case than his group is. Then a cynical thought occurred to him.

"Was Kip Springer standing at Lyle's elbow, grinning, while Lyle made this statement?"

"Nurse didn't say."

Hoss saw his job fading rapidly away. If the State Police, with Kip holding onto their coattails, can make a credible arrest, his chances of winning the primary election were small. Rapid results in the killing at the reservation possibly might have balanced the books, but without Harry or Mary's stories he had nothing.

"Do you think Charlie McNab can convince her to talk?"

"Good idea," Hoss said, even though he had already thought of the possibility and rejected it as unlikely. He rose to go and gave a high five that Shorty met weakly. "What the hell, you're going to be good as new. What else matters?"

❍

The phone rang on his bathroom extension. Ackerman stepped out of the shower and answered.

"Mr. Ackerman," It was the maid's voice. "There's a call from a Mary McNab. She said I was to tell you, 'the password is the dollar sign.'"

A sharp fear gripped his heart. He paused, steadied his voice. "I don't know anyone by that name, Claudia, but put her on, I'm curious." Nervously he reached toward his neck and the gold tennis ball.

"This is Jason Ackerman," he said in a supercilious tone when he heard his extension click.

"This is Mary McNab. Harry Swifthawk and I have copied the files out of your computer. Your password is the dollar sign."

He tried for a disinterested attitude. "I'm sorry but I think you have the wrong person."

"Listen to me or we'll turn the files over to the Sheriff right now." There was no protest from Ackerman. "We have made several copies," she continued. "We each have one. Three will be given to three different people to be sent to the police if anything ever happens to either of us, and I do mean anything. I've put one copy in an envelope and addressed it to you, care of General Delivery, Pshawbestown."

"I really don't know what you're talking about. I could care less about anything you have copied."

"Have it your way," Mary continued in an even voice. "Just keep in mind that the post office only keeps letters a certain length of time and then they open them. Inside the envelope is a note that reads, 'If undeliverable to the addressee, it is urgent that this be given to the Leelanau County Sheriff. It contains information about the murder of Buddy Delcorte of Peshawbestown.' We have included a file of our own that accuses you of being behind the shooting last night. Have a good day, Mr. Ackerman."

CHAPTER 18

THE DIRECTIONS DEREK MARSH HAD given Donna led her into a deeply wooded area eight miles west of Traverse City. It is, Donna concluded, an intrusion-proof location selected by a person who wants total solitude.

Donna had thought through her objectives more soberly than the wild impulse of the night before. Then, she had been ready to throw what she'd learned in Birmingham in the doctor's face and hope for the best. She surmised his reason for inviting her to his house tonight was to subtly probe the direction the investigation was taking. The fact she had accepted a dinner invitation must reassure him that he is not a suspect. To avoid arousing suspicion, he should, of course, show no curiosity at all about the investigation. She'd see if that were true, but her plan tonight extended further. She intended to feed his curiosity by revealing bits of information about the case, hoping his responses would show he knew more than had been revealed to the general public.

Dusk grew as she found the driveway entrance in a break in a dense pine forest. She drove for a tenth of a mile through a meandering, pine tree tunnel, emerging into a clearing where a very large log structure faced her. The wood shingled roof, deeply overhanging the front and side walls, soared up and back, giving the impression of a game bird preparing to take flight. A canopy supported by heavy log posts sheltered and darkened the entrance. In its shadow, Dr. Derek Marsh waited for her.

He had mixed feelings, watching her alight from her small coupe, her dark hair, freed from the braid, bouncing about her shoulders. Re-ignited was the attraction she held for him, but opposing it was his fear of the potential harm to him that her investigation represented. Tonight he must ascertain how great the danger was and act accordingly.

"You didn't exaggerate, when you said this place was remote," Donna said nervously, holding out her hand.

Marsh took her large, supple hand in both of his and asked, "Were the directions OK?"

"No problem, but without them I'd never have found you. Travel must have been like this before maps and signs."

"I'm sure it's part of the attraction this place has for me—far from the madding world. There's a beautiful river that runs past the rear of the house. I'll show you later."

Marsh's natural manner unnerved Donna. She felt very much like the fly about to enter the spider's parlor. It was then that she realized she had told no one about her plan to meet Marsh here at his house. Her second thought was an admission to herself of just how frightened she was to be here alone with him in this isolated spot, or she would never have had the first thought. She steadied herself with the reminder that Marsh didn't know she'd told no one.

Marsh put a hand on her back and turned her gently toward the open door. "Dinner is at a perfect stage to allow us time for a drink."

They passed through a low-ceilinged foyer walled by logs the color of rich maple syrup. The flagstone floor was covered with oriental rugs as in his office. She gasped as they entered the living room. The space suddenly opened up, the ceiling vaulting upward to open rafters and huge, log cross beams.

"Fabulous," she uttered.

Marsh smiled with pride at this appreciation of his home. "Yes, isn't it. I feel so fortunate to have been at the right place at the right time to buy it. What can I get you to drink?"

"White wine would be fine."

Marsh took a bottle of wine from a refrigerator below a wet bar on one wall. "I found this Chilean sauvignon blanc that I think is very good." He held up the bottle. "OK?"

She walked over to him as he filled two glasses. He showed her the label. "And, it's—how shall I phrase this? It's not pretentiously priced."

"Do you mean it's—?"

"Cheap."

She laughed. "Ah, a familiar quality of the wines I usually drink." She sipped it. "You're right, it's very good."

"Yes, excellent," Marsh thought. "Excellent for my purpose."

He motioned toward the large leather couch, "Please sit down." He sat down himself, pulling one knee onto the cushion so he could face her.

"How long have you been with the Sheriff's Department?"

"Only six months. I was in sales before that."

"That's quite a switch. What caused you to make that move?"

"I got tired of selling cereal. Felt guilty, too, all that sugar-frosted stuff. Like pushing tobacco to minors."

Marsh studied his glass as he swirled the liquid. "So, you came to law enforcement with a zeal for public service?"

"I guess you could say that."

"Have you lost any of that zeal by now?"

"Actually, not."

"I believe you. You seem dedicated and thorough. Retailing's loss is the public's gain." He made as if to toast her and drank some of the wine.

In an offhand way, he added, "How's the murder investigation going?"

All right, she thought, here it comes. The form of his question seemed to mean he didn't know about the State Police. Good!

"Interesting new developments," she began. "We have reason to doubt that our previous prime suspect is guilty. This has caused us to look into other possibilities."

Marsh wondered what that meant, a deeper investigation of him?

"By previous suspect, do you mean the Chippewa man?"

"Yes."

"Who does that leave?"

She looked directly into his eyes. "Just about everyone."

"That's a lot of people. You must have to start somewhere."

"True." Donna left the subject hanging. She wanted to find out how urgent his curiosity was, to let his questions confirm what she suspected.

On his side, Derek Marsh was cautious about appearing too curious.

"I think we'd better become chefs for a few minutes and then I'd like to know more. You have to understand, I'm very interested because it's the first murder that's touched me personally."

He led the way to the kitchen. Donna followed, suspecting exactly what "personally" meant in this case, and a wave of awareness again passed through her of how foolish it had been to come here without letting headquarters know about it.

❍

"My God, you've got a shotgun in your pantry closet!" gasped Ferris Tull in mock horror from the pantry, where Marti had sent him to get peppercorns. "Do you load shells with poppy seeds and shoot them at rolls and muffins?" he said returning with the pepper. "That thing isn't loaded, is it?"

"No, I just unloaded it this morning and put it in the closet. I kept it loaded and behind the kitchen door after finding the body."

"I'm glad to see that you're feeling more secure."

She nodded. "I finally realized that the murder had nothing to do with me."

She handed Ferris a jar of peppercorns. "Crack a couple of tablespoons, would you? You can use the flat side of that cleaver".

"Am I right to think we're having *boeuf au poivre*?"

"Could it be that you were tipped off by those two steaks on the cutting board?" Marti threw some salt in a frying pan. "After you crack the pepper, please spread it on the steaks and press it in with your hand. The steaks will have to rest for half an hour before we fry them, so we can go to the living room and have a drink."

"I like that—the steaks 'have to rest.' Sort of readying themselves for the ordeal of being sautéed. By the way, I think *boeuf au poivre* should be sautéed, not fried."

She looked at him with mock amazement. "I never would have guessed you were a gastronomic snob, and a picky one at that."

"What can I say? I've been known to challenge someone to mortal combat over a mispronounced sauce."

Marti laughed. "Was that a man or a woman you challenged?"

"Wait just a minute. That was an uncalled-for attack on my manhood."

"You're right, and I apologize. How about if I buy you a drink?"

❍

Tossing the salad was calming. How could any harm come to a person who is doing such a domestic thing? Besides, Derek Marsh looked like anything but a vicious killer peering, as he was now, into the oven checking on the progress of the *coq au vin*. Donna found herself drifting into a dangerous reverie, one in which this charming man was just that; a charming, handsome man who was alone and in need of companionship, and one who seemed to be very interested in her.

In the next moment, she remembered that just such fantasies had brought down his patients' guards.

"How's the salad coming?" he asked. "The chicken is about ready." He strode past Donna into the dining room, where he adjusted the lights with a dimmer and lit the two candles.

Donna followed him with the salad bowl and placed it on the table. She took a moment to look around the dining room. It was a hexagon. Two adjoining sides were glass. Opposite these a huge stone fireplace took up most of a wall. The remaining walls were of logs. Above the table hung a chandelier made up of elk horns. Marsh had adjusted the lamps to a romantic glow.

Donna raised her voice so Marsh could hear in the kitchen, where he'd returned to get the chicken, "This room must be great in the winter when there's a fire."

Marsh came through the door carrying a platter of *coq au vin* and a dish of parsleyed potatoes. "You're right, that's when it's at its best, but now is not bad either." He went to a wall switch and turned on the lights to dramatically illuminate both the river that ran swiftly a few feet from the window, and the solid pine forest beyond.

"What can I say? It's so beautiful," Donna murmured, truly thrilled by the effect, in spite of the circumstances.

Marsh poured each of them a glass of wine and held a chair for his guest. Before he sat down he went to a cabinet and pressed a switch and soft jazz filled the background.

It would ordinarily be too much to resist, Donna thought. She had been programmed over the years by subtle messages from every form of media to respond romantically to a setting like this. She felt the urge all right, but that wasn't what this night was about.

Marsh passed a basket of bread, saying, "Police procedure must be very much like that followed by a good diagnostician. First of all, you know your subject, anatomy and physiology in the physician's case, human nature and the mechanics of crime in your own case. That would include the well-known triad of motive, opportunity and means."

Marsh seemed genuinely absorbed in this reflection, and Donna had to remind herself of the deliberate plan she suspected he had to pick her mind about what they knew about him.

"With this background of knowledge, you begin to collect data. The doctor looks for physical signs and symptoms from which he can conclude what is going on anatomically and physiologically. You, on the other hand, look at the evidence and arrive at conclusions about motive, opportunity and means." He smiled, pleased with this construction. "What do you think?"

Donna nodded. "Yes, that's right and we each use the laboratory to help us understand the data we've collected."

"Ah yes, of course. Very good. And has there been data you've sent to the laboratory?"

If she hadn't been anticipating his questions, she may well have been lulled into thinking they sprang from the efforts of a good host to make conversation in his guest's field of special interest.

She swallowed. "This chicken is delicious." She touched her mouth with her napkin and sipped her wine before answering his question. "Yes. We sent several items to the crime lab."

He looked at her, a fork full of potato poised at his lips, eyebrows lifted in inquiry.

"Well, to begin with," she continued, "we asked the lab to go over the Wilson van for fingerprints." She concentrated on her chicken. "You're very good, you know."

"What's that?" Marsh looked up, startled. "Oh, the chicken. Thank you."

Donna imagined he was searching for a way to get back to the subject of fingerprints without it being too obvious.

"Let's see, you were telling me.... Oh yes, fingerprints in the van. What were they able to find?"

He must know the lab techs were unable to find any prints, because he had worn gloves. "They were able to tell us that the crime was well planned."

"Really? How could they determine that?"

"Because the killer made sure we would find nothing. He wore gloves. He was very careful not to leave anything incriminating. He even wiped all of the surfaces, just for added insurance."

Was that relief which Donna saw on Marsh's face? She was sure of it.

He sipped his wine thoughtfully. He put both elbows on the table and leaned forward with renewed interest.

"The good clinician assembles all his data, including laboratory findings, before he begins to hold it up to a comparison with what he already knows about anatomy and physiology. So, is there other data we should consider?"

Nicely done, Donna thought. He even attempted, with his 'we,' to manipulate me into thinking I was actively working with him on developing this analogy between medicine and detection. Now, to manipulate the manipulator! But how much was it wise to reveal to him? The cards she held were these: the cause of death, the shape of the scalp wound, the missing six thousand two hundred and sixty in cash and finally the poodle hair found on the van seat.

"I found out that Dr. Wilson had a considerable amount of cash on her the morning she disappeared—six thousand, part of which she got from an ATM before her appointment with you."

Marsh suddenly looked stunned.

"Does this have any meaning to you, doctor? You look as if this information troubles you."

"Ah, no," he said making an effort to maintain his composure.

Donna was certain he was lying. She had given him the wrong amount, hoping he would slip at some point in the evening and say six thousand two hundred and sixty.

Subliminally, Donna heard a sound coming from another part of the house, but she was focused on Marsh's reaction.

"The money wasn't on her body," she added.

"It was taken from her, then?"

"Most likely."

"How much can one get from an ATM, not six thousand, surely?" Marsh asked, seeming perplexed."

Donna hesitated. "No, only two hundred sixty came from the ATM."

"Five thousand seven hundred and forty came from another source, then?"

"She withdrew it from her bank the day before. What are you thinking about?" Donna asked, because he seemed to be working with the numbers.

Marsh shook off his rumination. "Nothing. Nothing, really."

There was a sound like scratching at a door.

Marsh went on, "You said you have eliminated your prime suspect, the Indian. How did you arrive at that?"

Donna swallowed the last of her salad before answering. "The main reason we suspected him, of course, was the injury. Unlike your logical clinician, we were guilty of jumping to the wrong conclusions. But, tell me frankly wouldn't you have thought the same as we did?"

"Uh, I'm afraid I don't know what you're referring to. Maybe I missed something. Did you say 'injury'?"

Well, that attempt at tricking him didn't work, Donna thought, now to back out of it.

"Oh, it's unimportant. But, the guy acted very strangely. He ran and hid when we came looking for him, confirming our suspicions. It seems he was involved in something else, no doubt illegal, and he no doubt thought that's why we wanted him."

"I saw on the news there had been a shooting on the reservation. One of your deputies, I believe, was shot. Is that the business your Chippewa friend was involved in?"

"So it seems."

"But what was there about Barbara's injury that led you to suspect him?"

She hadn't mentioned whose injury... but maybe that was obvious. Also, he had used Dr. Wilson's first name – a slip revealing the nature of the relationship?

Marsh was waiting for an answer. She was stumped. She couldn't reveal the scalping, it might be an important part of a State Police interrogation.

"It's nothing really."

Marsh, with a quizzical expression, went on, "OK, aside from this unmentionable injury, do we have all the data on the table, now?"

Wishful thinking? "No, there are a few more things. We looked at all those who had opportunity - those whom we knew about at least. It was a short list."

"Yes?"

She had somehow gotten herself to a point in the progression of the conversation that would have alarmed her earlier. She was impulsively stepping beyond the limits of her reasoned plan for this meeting.

"Well, there's yourself, of course," she said, trying to make it sound like a playful tease.

"Me?"

His heart sank. So they would be investigating him, after all! He tried to cover his acute discomfort by nodding vigorously. "I understand, of course, it's logical. I was the last known person to see her alive."

Donna saw that Marsh had come to the point he'd been angling toward since he first called and invited her to dinner. Certainly it was his wish that the police had overlooked him, but he must have been experiencing unbearable tension wondering if it were true, or if in fact we had been quietly gathering evidence, preparing to pounce.

Marsh had regained his composure. Once again he managed a tone of neutral intellectual inquiry. "Following our analogy, how would you say I fit the required triad of means, opportunity and motive?"

Donna matched his cool objectivity. "Means: the killer used his hands, strong hands." Donna looked at Marsh's hands. They were gripping his napkin tightly. "You have strength in your hands equal to that requirement."

Marsh made an effort to relax his grip.

"Opportunity: you could have killed her in your office. A witness saw her going to your office that morning, but no one saw her leave. You could have hidden the body in a closet until the night, and then disposed of it and the van. That was done the night she disappeared. To look into that aspect of opportunity I'd have to ask you where you were that night."

Marsh tried to appear comfortable. He took up the wine bottle and started to pour more for Donna, who put her hand up, stopping him.

"I'm driving," she said.

He poured himself another glass. "And why haven't you asked me that question?"

"I think I already knew what you'd say. You'd say you were home alone reading a good book."

"You're right, I was."

"See."

Marsh laughed, attempting to continue the notion that they were playing a pleasant parlor game but there was tension in his voice. "So, that only leaves motive."

Donna was looking directly into his eyes. He wanted to look away, but couldn't afford to. As he continued the union with her brown eyes, he wanted her thoughts to be much different than what he feared they were.

A voice within her was warning her to go no further, but the implied challenge that Derek Marsh had initiated by comparing the work of a "good clinician" with the task facing a detective seemed to have introduced an element of competition into their dialogue. It was the impulse to win that had canceled out her voice of reason.

"Birmingham. I drove there and looked at the records of the Oakland County Medical Society's Ethics Committee."

The silence between them was so complete it seemed audible. Clearly now, against this silence, came the sound, coming from the direction of the kitchen, of an animal scratching at a door.

"And, what did you find out?" In spite of his best effort, it came out sounding like a patient asking, "What did the lab report say?"

"Before going to Birmingham, I'd learned you had only been in Traverse City for eight months. Before that you'd been in practice in Birmingham. I wondered why you had moved here, so I went to the Grand Traverse County Medical Society. There is a letter in your file that states that, while in Birmingham, a patient had accused you of sexual misconduct, a charge that had been dismissed. On an impulse I made the trip down to Birmingham."

Donna was still looking directly at Marsh, who averted his gaze to look out the window. "And?" he said.

"I read the Ethics Committee's file."

"Those files are confidential."

“Not when you come with a subpoena in your hand.”

“And, you learned—what?” Marsh asked, tersely. He was angry now.

Again there was scratching coming from the direction of the kitchen.

“What’s that? Do you have a dog?”

“Yes, that’s Frieda. I put her in the utility room, because she tends to be overly friendly … especially with pretty women.”

Was the added compliment meant to change the subject? Then, out of her own need to delay confronting him with the rape charge, she said, “She’s going to scratch the door down. Let her out, I don’t mind.”

Marsh went through the kitchen and opened a door. Moments later a large black poodle happily ran into the dining room and straight over to Donna.

❍

“Great meal!” Ferris studied Marti approvingly. “Is there anything you can’t do?”

Marti pretended to seriously apply herself to the question. At length she shrugged with mock apology. “Can’t think of anything.”

“I’ll bet you can even out-run me when you get that cast off.”

“Now, why did that come to mind? Are you planning to give me reason to run?”

“Yo no, senorita.”

“Good. As it happens, I can run pretty fast. I could beat my brother. That’s one of the reasons he couldn’t stand me.”

“What were the others?”

“There were many, but the main one was that I had him figured for just what he was.”

“Which was, if you don’t mind telling me.”

"Not at all, I told everyone. He was, and I imagine still is, a sadistic jerk. I haven't seen him since I left home after high school. My parents have both died, and I've lost track of him."

"You are about as far from that description of him as I can imagine. Funny how two sibs can be so different."

"It was quite simple in our family. I took after my mother even though I didn't look at all like her, and he was a clone of my father."

Ferris refilled her wine glass. "A bad man, I take it, your father I mean."

Marti stared into the red liquid as if she could see her childhood written there. "A troubled man. It was as if he had received a terrible hurt at some time and was blaming my mother and me for it. Early on I could never understand what it was I had done. I tried hard to please him, but it just seemed to make him hate me more. Later, when I got my feet under me and said, 'fuck you' through my attitude, he did have reason to dislike me, but I was beyond caring by that time."

Tull's expression became very serious. "It all happened before, you know."

The statement took her aback. "What do you mean?"

"I mean that you arranged to have him treat you badly, because there is something in one of your former lives for which you feel you need to be punished."

Marti stared at the man sitting opposite her as if he had just announced that he was Zorg from the planet Krypton.

CHAPTER 19

DEREK MARSH NOTED DONNA'S ALARM when she saw his dog. He didn't know what it meant, but he knew it wasn't because she feared dogs; she'd asked him to let Frieda out.

Donna was frightened. She'd been treating this like a game—a game of tag. She'd catch him off base and she and Hoss and the whole Sheriff's gang would be the winners. Here was the kind of slip she'd hoped for - the source of the black poodle hair. Suddenly, her eagerness to pursue the game vanished. This man was a cold-blooded killer and she was alone and unarmed. He had invited her to his house to discover just how much she knew. Should he decide she knew too much, he'd silence her. All that saved her right now was the fact that he didn't know whether she'd told anyone else about the dinner date.

Marsh stared at her angrily. Had she, Donna wondered, given herself away by her reaction to his dog?

Derek Marsh was angry because the beautiful woman sitting opposite him was intending to ruin the life he'd managed to create for himself here in Traverse City—his medical practice, his reputation here, this rustic paradise where they sat opposite each other.

"So, you know about the misconduct charge," he said levelly. "And, I suppose you have concluded that because someone once made a wild charge against me, I'm prone to raping my patients?"

Donna didn't know how to answer, didn't want to have to answer. She only wanted to be safely away from this house.

"Yes, of course," he continued, "I see what you've put together. You believe I made a sexual move toward Dr. Wilson and she started to scream. I clamped my hand over her mouth to stop her and she accidentally suffocated—or not so accidentally. No, you wouldn't think it had been an accident, since you'd know that if I allowed her to live, her story would destroy me."

So he knows Barbara Wilson was suffocated. Strangling had been the cause of death released to the media, and just a few minutes ago she had only said the killer had used his hands. Nervously, she stroked the poodle's head, it licking her hand whenever she stopped.

A strange contemplative mood settled over Marsh and he stood up and walked over to the window. "I've been very blind. You think I'm a predator who preys on people who trust me." He glanced her way. "Then why come out here for dinner?" This last was posed almost inaudibly to himself. "Bearding the lion in his den. Is that it? Never a wise thing. Never."

He turned suddenly to face her. "What did it mean to you, when you saw Frieda?"

Donna's mouth was dry. For months now she had been merrily playing the role of law enforcer, feeling strong and powerful with her Smith and Wesson strapped to her side. At this moment, she felt like one of those teenagers who fly along the highway, secure in their mistaken belief they can respond adequately to any situation at any speed until they discover there are forces operating at seventy miles an hour that they'd never dreamed of.

She was out on a limb. There was nothing she could do. She couldn't call for help. No one could hear her. Her gun was in the glove box of her car, but she could never get to it. Marsh was much larger and stronger than she. He probably had even locked the doors when she first arrived.

"The dog hair," Donna answered, in an impulsive, instinctive move to throw him off balance.

"Dog hair?" Marsh echoed.

"Frieda's hair was found on the van's front seat."

"Frieda's hair?"

"They must have been on the seat of your pants."

Marsh considered this. "Black hair, I presume."

"Yes. Black poodle hair."

"They can tell that it was a poodle? Yes, of course they can." Marsh was pensive. "I recall Barbara Wilson mentioning they had a dog—a puppy for her daughter." There was a question in his expression.

"A tan dog."

"I see," he murmured. "The hair may have come from anywhere—mechanic, car wash attendant."

Marsh sounded like someone trying to think of arguments to use in court.

He continued, "DNA. Of course, you're thinking, a DNA match would convince any jury." He laughed cynically, "Except a California jury, of course."

Marsh studied Donna for a long moment, his handsome face drawn down flaccidly. Deep disappointment was written there. "No, Donna, yours was not logical thinking on a par with a good clinician. You've jumped to conclusions based on possibilities, not even probabilities and certainly not logical inevitabilities. If this were a serious illness, someone might have died because of your sloppy thinking. And my reputation may yet die because of it."

He thought for another moment, then stated with feeling, "I'm damned angry with you, Donna, and that's not what I want to feel toward you."

Donna's head swirled. He was bawling her out, but it didn't seem to be because she'd discovered his guilt. Gradually, she realized that he was saying he was innocent and was angry with her for thinking he wasn't. She felt confusion, anxiety and, to her surprise, embarrassment.

Marsh shook his head. He sat down opposite her again and looked into the candle flame with the weary expression of one who is accepting an unwelcome reality. At length he said, "From your point of view I can see it all fits— particularly if you believe I raped my patient."

"It wasn't just that patient," Donna inserted as if to justify herself.

"What do you mean?"

"There was the other woman."

"Other woman?"

"I don't know the patient's name, but one of your fellow psychiatrists—he was treating the sister of this patient of yours—lodged a complaint against you." She watched his face for a sign that he knew what she was alluding to, but all she saw there was a troubled puzzlement.

"He said that his patient was told by her sister that you had seduced the sister—had sex with her in your office."

"Why did I hear nothing of this?" His anger mounted again.

"The committee wouldn't—that is, the chairman, with the support of a couple of the committee members—wouldn't hear the complaint, because it involved an unethical revelation of material told to a doctor in confidence."

"Well I'll be damned," he uttered in astonishment. "It was in the minutes of the committee?"

"The minutes were sealed," Donna explained, "But I had a subpoena."

Marsh was nodding. "Good ole Jack. It took some backbone to stand up to some of the vultures on his committee." Derek Marsh met Donna's eyes. "Who was the psychiatrist?"

"I'm not allowed to say."

Marsh laughed out loud. "Deputy Roper, you're not allowed to say almost everything you've said here tonight."

Donna took a deep breath, letting it out slowly "Coller. The name was Eugene Coller."

Marsh thought about it. "Sure," he allowed at last, his gaze focusing beyond Donna. "I know whose sister was seeing Coller." He interlaced his fingers behind his head and leaned back. "My patient's problem was she'd been telling any lie to get attention since she was a kid. Her sister knew this. It's hard to believe she wouldn't know that a tale of my screwing her sister was just another lie. Coller. It was Coller, of course, who wanted to believe it."

"If these accusations weren't true," Donna challenged, "why did you move away? It appeared like you were running away."

He laughed derisively. "I *was* running away. Running away from a stigma that would never have been erased. And don't tell me that people would realize in time that I was innocent … it never happens. That's why my wife left me. Yes, I was married, but I suppose you found that out, too. She left me not so much because she believed I was guilty, but because she knew the stigma would be associated with her also. She was too deep into the local social scene to risk that. Her family had been top drawer Birmingham since her great grandfather invented an automobile steering gear or some such device. By divorcing me she cleansed herself of stain. But, of course, it was seen as proof positive to everyone—not legally, but practically—that I was guilty."

Donna was still wondering what to believe. If he was manipulating her, he was the most adroit con artist she'd ever met. Suddenly, she realized that her case against him was more of an emotional position than a rational one. Take away his earlier sexual crimes and what was left… only that he was the last known person to see Barbara Wilson alive and his poodle was black. She became aware that he was staring at her with a very sober air.

"You came here this evening hoping to catch me in some guilt-revealing slip?"

She didn't answer.

"I see." Regret was in his voice. "I'm surprised. That's an impulsive kind of thing to do… shot in the dark sort of thing. I had you figured for a more thoughtful, patient woman."

Donna felt chagrin.

"And," Marsh added, "if I were the killer, haven't you put yourself at considerable risk?"

She managed a wan smile.

"Why did you do it this way? I don't think I've judged you wrongly. Why this desperate attempt?"

She felt impelled to answer truthfully. "You apparently haven't heard, but the State Police have entered the case—started their own investigation. Since they realistically have greater resources than we, our Sheriff has decided to concentrate our effort on another issue. I was told, in effect, to drop my investigation of you."

"Why was the case given to the state cops?"

"Politics."

Marsh smiled. "I understand now. My calling you and asking you to have dinner here with me was an opportunity for you to continue questioning me without disobeying orders."

Donna shrugged in answer.

"And your boss doesn't know you're here. Right?" He could read her silence as a confirmation. "I've just formed a new appreciation of your courage. Your judgment, however, in coming here alone, while believing I was the killer, sucks, my friend."

Both broke out in a laugh of relief. Both were quiet for an interval. Marsh looked Donna in the eyes. "I didn't kill Barbara Wilson." He paused to let the statement settle in her mind. "Something you said a moment ago, however, might help you. Help us, because I want to find out who killed her as much as you do. When I talked to you before and said I knew nothing that could explain her absence, it was true. Now, I'm not so sure, but there's a point that troubles me. It's the money; are you sure Dr. Wilson was only carrying six thousand dollars?"

Embarrassed, Donna admitted, "First of all, we don't know what she actually had on her when she was killed, but we know she withdrew six thousand from the bank the day before she was abducted and another two hundred and sixty from the ATM just before her appointment with you."

"And was that another attempt to lure me into a slip?"

Donna blushed.

"Ah well, it's important you cleared that up, because, you see, that morning was to be our last treatment session. She was quitting her treatment with me. I can't go into the details, but she had been depressed for a long time, and I thought we were getting to material in her therapy that could have helped her, but she was discouraged and impatient and wanted to find a quicker solution. She had heard from a friend of hers about a therapist who claimed to be able to cure emotional problems by enabling people to recover memories of a 'former life.' According to him, it would be some event in her former life that was causing her present depression. She went to see this man—I don't know his name. I was too furious with his kind of quackery to even dignify him by asking her. Also," Marsh confided with a smile, "my pride was hurt that she would choose this bozo over me and all my training.

"I was reminded of something I'd heard," he continued, "when you mentioned the sum of six thousand dollars. A couple of months ago a psychiatrist friend of mine told me about a guy in this area calling himself a therapist who was guaranteeing people a ten-session cure for the flat, up-front fee of six thousand dollars—paid in cash in advance, like some cosmetic surgeons demand. That's all my friend knew, but he was going to try to find out more about him."

Donna became hyper-alert. "She must have had an appointment with him that morning after she saw you. That's why she drew that amount out of the bank the day before. But, just a minute, it doesn't mean he killed her. She could have been picked up by a carjacker before she had a chance to keep her appointment with him."

"True, but it's a new possibility. By the way, the thing that troubled me when you said the total sum was just six thousand was that she had given me two hundred and sixty dollars that morning to pay me for the two sessions we'd had this month."

For a moment Donna became excited hearing this new information, but then sighed. "Yeah, it's a very interesting new angle, but it comes a little late for me. The State Police should be told, however."

Marsh smiled impishly. "No one said I couldn't continue the inquiry. I'll call my friend and see if he learned anything."

❍

Marti knew Ferris Tull was serious about what he'd just claimed about events in a "past life" returning to cause problem. She wasn't sure how to respond. What came to her mind was, "You've got to be kidding," but she intuitively knew he couldn't handle that.

"That's a new idea to me," she said.

"It's not new, really. There have been many brilliant people who have known the truth of rebirth over the centuries, but there have been powerful interests working to keep the truth hidden."

Tull had completely dropped his guard. His manner was now that of a zealot, a true believer. They were the types she feared most. They couldn't tolerate other points of view. Other points of view were dangerous.

She began, "I'm not much of a philosopher. I'm afraid I've never been able to understand anything except putting one foot in front of the other." She hoped that this non-challenging position would allow Tull to throttle back and get control of his feelings.

Tull did visibly bring himself down. He smiled. "You've been brainwashed, of course. I don't blame you for finding these ideas new and a bit frightening, but I think I can bring you around, in time."

Marti was thinking that there wasn't going to be any "in time" for them. She only wanted to end the evening as soon and as smoothly as possible.

"You'd be spending your time more profitably with someone smarter than I," she offered.

"No, I don't think so. Your reaction is very like that of others. It isn't until I'm able to demonstrate the truth by helping them regain memories of their previous lives that they really become convinced." Tull now seemed to be his charming self again. The driving, insistent edge had gone from his voice.

"For instance, you told me last night about a dream you had of a van driving on the road outside your window on the night when Barbara Wilson's body was brought here. You thought you must have awakened and gone to the window and looked out just as the killer was passing by. But, it remained vague, you couldn't remember the details of his face, in spite of the fact that the car's interior light was on."

Marti was surprised at his memory of the details.

"That kind of description is very typical of previous life memories. It couldn't really have happened in the present. After all, as you said yourself, what killer would drive around with a body in his car with the interior lights on? It's the distortion that's the clue to this being a breakthrough from a previous life."

"But aren't most dreams distorted?" Marti countered.

"Yes, of course, and most dreams represent intimations of past lives. Your dream really dealt with something from one of those lives, something you're afraid to remember. And, because you're afraid, you've made that something into a killer's face."

Marti was baffled. How could she move him off the subject and out the door?

"Am I right? Wouldn't you be afraid if you thought the killer knew you had remembered what he looks like?"

Marti gave a nervous laugh. "You're right about that."

Tull reached across the table and took one of her hands in both of his. "Close your eyes and describe a scene in which you are wearing a long dress, a dress from years before you were born."

Marti joked, "What makes you think I was a woman? Maybe I was one of Napoleon's marshals."

"One does not change sexes with rebirth," Tull stated emphatically.

Touchy, touchy! Marti thought, but didn't say it. She decided she'd better pretend to go along with his suggestion.

"OK, I'm wearing a full skirt and I'm talking to ... an Indian. He has paddled his canoe in close to shore and has handed me something." Marti laughed. "It seems like he's a delivery man, sort of a birch-bark UPS."

"Yes," Tull intoned in a low, sedating voice. "You've turned the canoe into a van in your dream—a van, because they are used for deliveries today. How do you feel in this scene?"

"I don't seem to feel anything. It seems quite natural."

"Again, that's what we do to hide our feelings, we turn them into their opposites. You felt anything but natural. You did something with the Indian. His handing you the object represents a sexual contact. Not necessarily intercourse, but maybe the desire for it. Can you feel any of the guilt, now?"

Marti could identify guilt feelings, but she thought they might have originated from her mother's warnings about the danger of becoming involved with people other than her own kind.

“Your mother would have been angry.” Tull’s words caused her to jump. “You were thinking that, weren’t you?”

“Yes.”

“It frightened your mother when she found out about the Indian, and she said you were bad and could easily have been raped! This made you very afraid.”

Where was all this leading? Marti wondered. God forbid he should think she was a convert!

“Now, think of the man in the van. He is as harmless as the Indian you talked to. He doesn’t want to hurt you. He doesn’t want to scalp you like Dr. Wilson was scalped. That’s what brought this old memory through from that time long ago. You had heard of settlers being scalped, and your mother was hinting that it would happen to you.”

A shock passed through Marti, taking away her breath. She tried to hide her reaction. She hoped he hadn’t noticed, but she couldn’t be sure. Hoss had said that Barbara Wilson having been scalped was a fact he was withholding from the public. Only those few directly involved in the medical examination would know. She was certain there had been no mention of it in the papers. She attempted to cover her reaction by asking him to pour her some more wine.

Ferris Tull had discerned her alarm. “I can see that you recovered part of that memory from your former life. It always affects people this way.”

It appeared he was too taken by his own bizarre theories to have guessed her thoughts. Good. She tried to calm her growing fear by counseling herself that there may be another explanation for his knowledge of the scalping. Maybe someone in the crime lab or the Medical Examiner’s office had a loose tongue.

Her initial shock receded enough to permit her to wonder how Ferris could have a connection with Barbara Wilson. It didn’t seem likely. What would be his motive? She could think of nothing.

And that night at the Oyster Bar he hadn't known about the body being found on her farm. He didn't even know where she lived. She began to relax.

"Now, describe the Indian in the canoe." Tull prompted.

"I don't think I can."

"Does he look like anyone you know?"

At that instant she realized he was really after her description of the man in the van. Her breath caught again, as a clearer image of the van driver came together in her mind. He *did* look like Tull.

"Yes, you were saying that the Indian did look like someone you knew. Why did you stop?"

It was Tull she saw in the van! He was looking at her, waiting for her answer. She was unable to speak.

"Yes?" Tull insisted.

Marti put her best acting effort into her reply. "It's just that it doesn't make sense. I mean, I've never seen a blond Indian."

"Blond hair?" Tull was not expecting this.

"Yes, the Indian looked like my brother."

"And the driver of the van?" Tull pressed.

"Yes, you're right about a previous life memory breaking through in dreams, because the driver also looked like my brother."

"I'm not sure what you're saying. Exactly what does your brother look like?"

Any answer to this question was blocked by a thought that hit her like a blow to the gut. Picturing Ferris driving the van had brought it out. It was that Ferris had known where she lived last night, driving here from the Oyster Bar. She recalled a moment of confusion she'd felt at the time. She'd overlooked it because of her sexual excitement. Ferris had led the way in his car right up to her driveway before he pulled over to let her take the lead. How did he know to pull over right there? Her address hadn't been in the paper, or on television. Hoss had personally requested that it be omitted. There was only one way he could have known exactly where her house was.

"So, what does your brother look like?"

"Nothing like you," she blurted, then realized her blunder.

Tull studied her face, thinking of her reply.

She, in turn, studied him to see if he'd caught her fatal misstep.

"You're saying he's short and blond, not tall and dark-haired like me?"

Was she right in concluding he'd missed the meaning? She wasn't sure. If he isn't convinced that he's safe—that I don't know he drove the van—.

A sinking certainty took hold of her. She would never get away from this man. It was then that she thought of calling Hoss.

CHAPTER 20

WITHOUT AWARENESS, HOSS WAS DOING the caged grizzly imitation again. He crossed his office to the filing cabinets and then marched back to look briefly, unseeing, out the window at the Carp River before pivoting and, with his head down, charging back toward the cabinets as if he were bound to walk straight through them and the wall beyond.

It had been a wasted day. They were no closer to finding Harry. Hoss felt the sand running through the hourglass of his career as Sheriff. If Lyle Steele wasn't bullshitting and the State Police really were nearing an arrest, he'd fast become as relevant in the county as a month-old copy of the *Leelanau Clarion*.

In addition to the stress of his own professional demise, a new—and possibly very serious—problem had been placed on his plate, –and it demanded his immediate attention and resources. Mrs. Carl Brock had called in the late morning to say that her husband was missing. She hadn't seen him since he went to work the previous morning. There had been several signs of his having been home in the evening after work at a time she'd been away from home at a meeting. He'd been home but had gone out again. Atypically, he hadn't left a note saying where he was going.

David Wick had taken the call and when he'd heard this much information he'd transferred the call to Hoss's phone.

"Where does your husband work, Mrs. Brock?" he'd asked after she'd repeated the story to him.

"Greenleaf Properties. He's the General Manager."

The name startled Hoss. According to K.D., it was this outfit and its leader, Ackerman, who were backing Kip Springer. Mrs. Brock went on to say she had assumed her husband's absence had something to do with his work; he'd had to make overnight trips on short notice in the past. But when Mr. Ackerman called her this morning to find out why Carl hadn't come to work, she called the Sheriff's Department.

Hoss had immediately put out a bulletin on Brock's car, a 2004 black Buick Regal sedan. He'd also sent Russ Preva to interview Ackerman, to see if he could supply any information to help in the search. To Mrs. Brock, Ackerman had supplied nothing beyond surprise at her husband's absence.

Hoss ceased his pacing and leaned against the jamb of the window and watched the lights dance on the river. He decided he'd done everything he could that day and might as well go on home to be with K.D.

He stopped at the dispatch office on the way out. "I'm heading home, Kate. Be sure and call me if any killers come into the office and give themselves up."

❍

"Hi Jim, it's Derek Marsh. I hope I'm not calling at a bad time … I see. Well, what's a friend for if he can't help you avoid work? What I'm calling for is to find out if you ever learned anything more about that guy who was promising cures for six thousand cash. Something has come up which is relevant…. You did? Good. Did you learn his name? … Ferris Tull?"

Marsh said the name in Donna's direction. Her face registered pure shock.

"I have to excuse myself, Jim. This information is very important, and I need to follow something up immediately. I'll call you and fill you in just as soon as I can."

Marsh hung up and faced Donna. She was shaking her head in disbelief. "We never even thought of him," she said. "You must know him—he has an office on the same floor as yours. Hoss and I talked to him just before we interviewed you. He said that he'd only seen Dr. Wilson once before. They were on the same program at the hospital a year ago."

Donna's body stiffened as if shocked. "My God, I saw him in the Oyster Bar just last night with Marti Jensen. It was on her farm the body was found." She pondered. "Could they be in this together? No, that's not right; I'm sure they had just met last night in the bar."

When she fell silent, Marsh commented, "Actually, I've never met him. I've seen his name on his office door, and someone told me he was a management consultant."

Donna wasn't paying attention. Her thoughts raced ahead. "Yes, he must have thought he'd dumped the body off on a deserted road, then discovered it was on her farm. Did he want to find out if she'd seen anything? I've gotta call Hoss."

Marsh stepped aside so she could dial.

"Kate, this is Donna. Is Hoss there? Just left? I'll try his car phone."

❍

It felt like another one of those turning points in his life, so Hoss obeyed his urge to go up to Kalcheck's Hill on his way home to think things over. He got out of the patrol car and wandered across the stubble of the freshly mown hay under the waning moon.

Back in his office he'd been irritated. Something was being taken away from him and he'd felt helpless to prevent it from happening.

He'd been angry at those responsible for this change in his life. His thoughts had become mean and small. He didn't like the feeling. Breathing deeply of the fresh, hay-sweet air, he relaxed. He had walked more than a hundred yards before he turned to face west towards the big lake. The night was clear and the moon still bright enough to cause Manitou Island, eighteen miles away, to stand out against the water. The night was warm and the residual heat of the sun was still rising from the ground. A pleasant, modulating lake breeze cooled his face.

He began thinking of K.D. and Kristen and the happy life they had together. This led to good memories of his companions at work. Many years of good times. Slowly his state of mind shifted from regret to appreciation, from irritation over loss to anticipation. There was this idea he'd had of starting a ferry service from Northport across Grand Traverse Bay to the mainland, only a ten-mile stretch of water, but a two-hour drive if one followed the road all the way down the peninsula to Traverse City and then up the opposite shore of the bay. Back when he'd first considered the possibility, there hadn't been enough traffic to make it pay, but times had certainly changed. Times change. Go with the flow. That was an admonition from his youth. Suddenly he laughed out loud, his deep voice shattering the stillness. "If the son-of-a-bitch ever comes out of hiding, I'll hire him to run the ferry."

Standing where he was, Hoss didn't hear his phone ringing in the patrol car.

❍

"This kind of talk is much heavier fare than I'm used to. Let's take a break. You find some soft music in that pile of CD's, and I'll put on the coffee," Marti said lightly, taking up her crutches and rising from the couch.

Tull, lost in thought, nodded and watched her closely as she started off down the hall.

Marti went into the kitchen and turned on the water in the sink and made some clatter with the kettle. She quickly looked up Hoss's home number, then, waited until she heard music from the living room before dialing. K.D. answered.

Barely above a whisper Marti announced herself. "K.D., this is Marti Jensen. I need to talk to Hoss, right away."

K.D. bristled. She had always been annoyed by Marti's brashness, but just calling with not so much as a "how are you" and demanding to speak to her husband was really outrageous.

"Hoss isn't home yet. You might want to try him at his office if you're in such a hurry."

Marti seemed to have missed the dismissive anger in K.D.'s voice. That was also like her, K.D. thought, ignoring insults and barreling ahead toward the thing she wanted.

"If he comes in, tell him to come to my place immediately, OK?"

K.D. hesitated for several counts. "I'll give him the message."

Marti hung up the phone and picked up the kettle to fill it. She felt a presence behind her and turned to see Tull standing in the doorway, soberly staring at her.

"What were you doing?" he asked, his tone icy.

"Oh, I was letting the water run until it was hot. What did you find to play?"

Tull didn't answer immediately. His steady gaze into her eyes froze Marti's heart. Had he overheard her call? Her mind couldn't find the words to continue her ruse.

Tull hadn't overheard, but he'd had a fleeting impression that her hand was moving away from the phone as he came to the doorway. He decided that her reaction when he asked her what she was doing was too natural for her to have just made a call for help. His whole routine of questioning her about her dream, as if it were an emanation from a past life, had been an attempt to find out how much she remembered about the driver of the van. Her answer that her brother looked *nothing* like him had not gone unnoticed—too quick and emphatic a denial. What Tull heard was, "The driver looked like you!"

Tull didn't want to kill Marti. He hadn't wanted to kill Barbara Wilson, either. That had been an accident. He'd come here this evening, however, knowing he must make a decision as to whether Marti remembered or would likely remember the face of the van driver. He'd made a stupid mistake that night. He'd backed down the hill with the door open in order to see in the heavy rain. That, of course, had put on the interior light. He hadn't noticed it in his excitement. Apart from that he'd made no other mistake. He'd even ad-libbed the brilliant ploy of the scalping that had sent the police off looking for the Indian.

He had decided, already, that if it was likely she could identify him as the van driver, there was but one thing he must do. Her saying her brother looked nothing like him strongly suggested she had identified him.

Marti's anxiety grew as she waited for Tull's answer about the music. Relief flowed over her like a cool stream when he finally answered, "I see you've got Harry Goldson's big band album. I hope that's OK."

"Perfect, but then if it isn't, it's not the end of the world is it? You seem so serious."

"I guess I wasn't ready to change the subject so abruptly a while ago."

"It's plain that you're a person who thinks deeply about things. I'm afraid we're not very compatible on that score."

Her breathing returned to normal. So, he hadn't overheard her on the phone. She busied herself getting coffee out of a cupboard and spooning some into a coffee maker.

"Oh, I forgot to ask if you wanted decaf."

"Regular's fine. I wasn't thinking of sleeping soon," he replied with sexual innuendo.

Marti's heart sank. This was going to be very difficult—repulsive. She had never feigned sexual feeling. She only became involved with someone if the feeling was genuine, never when it wasn't. This was a principle she'd never compromised. She had no desire to involve herself further with this man, but she had to keep him occupied until Hoss came.

She poured the boiling water into the cylinder. "You take yours black, don't you?"

"Yes, black."

Swinging easily around the kitchen on her crutches, she assembled the tray on which she'd placed the cups and coffee carafe. Tull took up the tray, while she tried for a very chatty manner as she followed him back to the living room. "That CD was on top of the heap, because I just bought it. I haven't heard it yet, myself."

Tull put the tray on the coffee table and turned to her. "The bathroom's down the hall past the kitchen, right?"

"Right."

"Pour me some coffee, please, I'll be right back."

Tull was pretty certain Marti had not—yet—called anyone. He had to make sure she didn't.

❍

"K.D., please ask him to call this number just as soon as he gets home."

Donna hung up and turned to find Derek Marsh watching her closely. He was intensely interested in what she was saying but even more interested in her.

"He doesn't answer his car phone and he isn't home. While I was on the phone just now, I realized I had the desire to call Marti Jensen and warn her."

"Why don't you?"

"It's like being a loose cannon. Perhaps Barbara Wilson's withdrawing six thousand from the bank had nothing to do with Tull. Maybe it's only a coincidence he charges that for a quick cure."

"True, but it's quite a coincidence."

Donna chewed her lower lip. "OK, but it doesn't mean he killed her. Maybe she left your office, went to see him, gave him the money and was abducted by someone else afterward."

"That would at least mean he was one of the last persons to see her alive, and you just said he denied knowing her except for their meeting on that hospital program. Why would he lie?"

"That's true. I know, I'll call the Oyster Bar and see if he's there. I heard it's the center of his social life. If he's there, it would at least eliminate the urgency where the Jensen woman is concerned."

Donna jabbed in the information number on the phone, listened a moment, and then pressed the "1" button for immediate connection. A shouting voice told her she had the Oyster Bar. She shouted back, "That you, David? This is Donna Roper. I don't want to talk to him, but can you tell me if Ferris Tull is there?"

"Haven't seen him all evening."

"Thanks, David,"

Donna faced Marsh again indecision on her face. "He hasn't been there tonight."

"Call her, then," Marsh said.

"Right. I will."

She got the number and dialed. She waited through eight rings, then hung up.

"No answer." She became more agitated. Intuitively she sensed danger. She dialed again.

"Operator, this is Deputy Roper of the Leelanau County Sheriff's Patrol. I need a check on a number. It rings, and there is no answer. What would I get if the line has been disconnected at the house?" Donna began nodding. "I would hear a normal ring. In that case, can you check to see if the line has been disconnected? You say you can determine if the problem is in the home or on the line. Great, please do that for me." Donna gave the operator the number and turned to Marsh. "She's having the line checked. I know it's been pulled out of the jack, I just know it." Her attention went back to the voice on the phone. "The problem's in the home."

"Thank you very much, operator."

She looked up at Derek Marsh and said urgently. "I just know the line's been disconnected."

Donna dialed again. "Hello, Kate, this is Donna. Can you tell me who's out on patrol?"

"Ryan and Moore. They're both at a fatality accident at 72 and Bugai Road. They just got there. If it's important, of course, I can call in the man on back-up."

"No, at least, not at the moment. Thanks, Kate." Donna hung-up.

"What was that about?" asked Marsh.

"I hoped someone would be available to go by Marti Jensen's and check to see if she's OK. Both men are tied up and I don't want to call in the person off duty."

"Why not?"

"A guy having to leave home and his family for what turns out to be a false alarm is going to be quick to spread the word that I'm a 'typical hysterical female'. I've got to go up to her place right now and check on this myself."

"Right, and I'm coming with you."

"You can't; the rules say I can't have a passenger."

"The rules don't say you can't hitch a ride with a citizen. Let's get going!"

His determination was overpowering.

"Do you have call-forwarding on your phone?" Donna asked.

"Yes."

"Then, put in my cell number in case Hoss calls."

Donna went to her car to get her gun and her cell phone and got in the car Marsh had backed out of his garage.

❍

Through the kitchen window, K.D. watched the lights of Hoss's car come up the drive. These had been hard days for him—for both of them. She yearned to have their tranquil life back, the days before the doctor's murder, the days when Hoss's job was secure—the days before Marti Jensen came back.

K.D. met him at the door. He was smiling. He wrapped her in his arms like old times and kissed her warmly. She had him back now. She wouldn't give him up again!

"Is there any of that chili left? I'm as hungry as a lumberjack?"

"There's some, but there's also lasagna in the oven."

"Have I had any calls?" Hoss asked looking in the refrigerator over K.D.'s shoulder for a cold beer.

"Donna Roper left a number for you to call."

"OK, any others?"

Taking out the pot of leftover chili, she hesitated for a moment before answering, "No, there haven't been."

❍

"If you're not afraid I'll step on your toes, let's try dancing."

"What, with that cast?"

"I've been putting my full weight on that foot. I'm just faster on crutches."

"When does the cast come off?"

"Couple more days. C'mon, we can dance to this music."

Marti put all her effort into moving smoothly, trying to keep Ferris occupied a little longer.

Tull wasn't sure yet what he was going to do, but he was reminding himself that if he decided he had to kill her, he must make sure to remove his fingerprints from everything he'd touched tonight and last night. There were also tire tracks to be erased. He had to calmly go over every detail. He was no cold-blooded killer, yet he had proven he was capable of keeping a cool head and doing what must be done. He delayed that final decision because he didn't want to kill her. Then it came to him: he would have her one more time. The decision could wait that long.

"Have you heard Cheikh Lo?" Marti asked. "I'd like to know what you think of him."

Sensing that Tull's attention was no longer on dancing, she let go of him and stumped over to the CD player, keeping up her chatter.

❍

Passing slower cars at every opportunity on the two-lane road up the peninsula, Derek Marsh concentrated on the business of driving fast.

Donna was thinking aloud. "Tull must have parked her van in the garage under your building all that day, and her body must have been in his office at the time Hoss and I talked to him. But how could he have driven it all the way up to Marti Jensen's farm without being seen by our surveillance?"

Marsh laid on the horn as the lights of another vehicle approached the highway from a side road. He slowed to make a turn onto County Road 637, then sped on as fast as the curving road allowed.

"What makes you so sure he's there with her now?" asked Marsh.

"I can't explain it rationally, I just feel it."

"At times strong feelings have a rational basis."

"I hope this turns out not to be true in this case. I'd much prefer to be wrong."

"Amen." Then, he asked seriously, "What's our plan if we find him there?"

"I've been thinking about that. I'll sneak up to the house and take a look inside. If I find that she's not in immediate danger, then I'll wait for Hoss. If I find otherwise, then I'll have to act as the situation dictates. I need to try to get in touch with Hoss again."

On her cell phone, she dialed Hoss's home number.

"Hello," answered K.D. guardedly.

"K.D, this is Donna Roper again. Has Hoss come home yet?"

"Yes. He tried to call you but got the message that your phone was off or out of the area."

"We were probably in one of those many cell phone dead spots on the peninsula. May I speak to him?"

"Of course, but he's not here right now. He's walking the dog."

"I need to talk to him as soon as I can. It's very important. He can reach me at this mobile number."

K.D. wrote down the number. "I'll tell him, Donna."

❍

Marti didn't know what was on Tull's mind, but she began to feel a definite chill in his attitude toward her. She needed to try Hoss's number again. He may have come home and it may have slipped K.D.'s mind to tell him to come.

"Gotta go. Nature calls. Why don't you find some more music we can dance to," she said and started off down the hall toward the bathroom. She opened and closed the door noisily and then came back down the hallway to the kitchen.

Marti froze when she went to the phone. It had been moved from the place she'd left it. It had no cord! The cord had been pulled out of the wall jack and it was nowhere in sight. Tull must have disconnected it, when he said he was going to the john.

Tull must have overheard her when she'd called Hoss's house. If true, he wouldn't be waiting much longer to deal with her. She had to get away!

Marti swung herself over to the pantry, took up her shotgun and left her crutches leaning against the pantry wall. From the kitchen drawer where she kept the shells, she snatched up four shells and jammed them into her pocket. Quietly, walking on her cast, she went to the back door, opened it and went outside, gently closing the door behind her. Where could she hide? In the moonlight, her white sundress almost glowed. Looking around, her gaze fell on the barn, its partially open door shouting, "Hide here!"

❍

"I don't think it's much farther," Donna said. "I haven't been here, but I overheard another deputy giving directions on the phone. He said the drive is off Swede Road directly across from a stack of cherry lugs."

"Cherry lugs?"

"Those boxes the pickers put cherries in."

"How about up ahead there?"

"Yes. This must be the drive."

Marsh turned into the dirt road and drove along it until he came to the place where another dirt track joined it. He stopped and turned off the headlights.

"Park here. I'll walk the rest of the way." Donna said.

"I'm coming with you."

"No way, this is a police matter. I can't allow a citizen to get into the middle of this."

"This happens to be a citizen with a profound interest that nothing bad happens to you."

"I never should have let you come along. Please don't make it difficult for me. Here, take my phone, in case Hoss calls."

Marsh didn't answer.

She reached for his hand and squeezed it.

"Come when Hoss gets here—I'll take care of myself."

❍

Marti desperately hobbled across the yard to the barn. Slipping through the doorway out of the moonlight let her feel safe for a moment, until she reminded herself that Tull would quickly find out she had not gone to the toilet and come looking for her. The neighbor boy, who had been mowing her grass since her injury, had put the mower away without closing the sliding door completely. It now stood open about four feet.

Marti laid the shotgun down and tried to slide the door shut. She discovered why the boy had failed to close it. She couldn't move it.

Glancing at the house, she saw movement inside. Tull was passing along the hallway toward the bathroom. He would be looking for her. She had to find a place to hide inside the barn. It was dark, but she knew the interior.

Immediately inside the door was a room wide enough for a horse-drawn wagon to enter. Above each of the eight foot sidewalls of the room were the open haylofts. Opening into the rear wall was a narrow passage to a back door. Along one wall of the passage were two stalls once used for horses. Instinctively, Marti made her way toward the small closed space of one of the stalls. By the time she shuffled back to the first stall, her eyes had accommodated enough for her to find and lift the latch. The wall of the stall that faced the barn door was composed of railings set six inches apart. She leaned against the wall and listened intently. She heard something that sounded like a door slamming at the house.

Marti opened the shotgun's magazine and slid in the four shells, then pumped one into the firing chamber. She had only fired this gun once, years ago. It had been at clay pigeons and her marksmanship had been surprisingly good. Could she shoot a person?

❍

K.D. stood with her back to the kitchen counter. Hoss had just come through the side door into the utility room. She listened to him talking to Charlie, their dog. Now she was feeling guilty about not telling him about Marti's call.

She opened the door and said, "Donna Roper called again and left another number."

"OK, I'll call her."

"Hoss, I didn't tell you the truth when you asked me earlier if there had been any other phone calls. You had one call from Marti Jensen. She wanted you to come to her place as soon as you came in. It sounded urgent."

Hoss was astonished that K.D. had lied to him. "When did Marti call?"

"About half an hour before you got home." She held out the paper on which she'd written the number Donna had given her.

Hoss dialed and listened through eight rings.

"No answer," he muttered to himself. "I've got to go to Marti's farm."

"Can't you call her?" protested K.D.

"I think she would have said to call. There must be a reason she said to come to her place." Hoss started to open the door and then reached back and grabbed his holster with its Barretta automatic.

He glanced at K.D. before he closed the door. He saw the pained look of apology. He knew why she'd lied to him.

"I shouldn't be long."

❍

The moment it occurred to Ferris Tull that Marti had been gone a little long for a trip to the john, he went to the bathroom door and knocked. He opened the door, then quickly went to the kitchen. Through the open pantry door, he saw her crutches leaning against the wall. He checked for the shotgun and found that it was gone. He noticed the open drawer and the box of shells.

Now what? She was out there in the dark with a shotgun.

He switched off the kitchen light and opened the back door cautiously. Was she poised, waiting for him to come out? He swung the door shut, letting it slam noisily. At the same time, he hurried through to the front door and out onto the dark porch. He heard no sound, saw no movement. He waited for his vision to adjust then stepped out onto the lawn. It was then he noticed the barn and the dark rectangle of the open door.

Marti peered through the rails of her wooden bunker toward the barn door and the relative brightness of the moonlit yard. Where was he? Had he thought of the barn, yet? Icy fear shot through her. She heard a slight sound. She strained to hear, then saw a dark object down low in the doorway slowly moving along the ground. He was trying to crawl around the door and into the barn. With a pounding heart, she gripped the shotgun, aimed and fired.

The noise of the blast in the confined space was deafening. The smell of burnt powder filled the narrow horse stall. The form she had seen was still there, but it was no longer moving. She'd hit him. Was he dead or only wounded? Might he have a gun and would he shoot her if she came out of her hiding place? He was lying very still. Marti struggled clumsily out of the stall and into the passageway.

"Ferris?" she said tentatively, as if making an inquiry. Fool, she thought to herself, as if he would answer if he were playing dead. The safe thing would be to fire again, but she couldn't bring herself to do it.

Suddenly, a strong arm encircled her, holding her tightly, while a hand grabbed her gun.

"You're a dangerous lady," said Tull's victorious voice in her ear. "But you were a sucker for the old decoy trick, and you forgot your barn has another door." He wrenched the gun from her hand and pushing her forward, jammed the barrel into her back. "Now, let's go back to the house and finish what we started."

❍

Donna heard the shot as she reached the open area where two cars were parked. The shot had come from inside the barn. Her gun was already in her hand. She pushed the safety off. Crouching low, she ran toward the barn, approaching the open doorway from the side. With her attention focused on the doorway, she failed to see the shaft of the old hay-rake lying hidden in the deep grass. She tripped and landed hard outside the door.

A loud, "Shit!" ripped through her mind. Had she given herself away?

Ferris Tull heard the sound of the fall and slammed his hand over Marti's mouth and pulled her back against him. He held her tight and settled back in the deep shadow beneath the overhanging hayloft.

Donna got up immediately and checked her revolver to be sure the safety was still off and started side stepping along the wall toward the open doorway. Only then, did she begin to think of the situation confronting her. Did Tull fire the shot? Most likely. If it had been Marti, she would have come out of the barn already. If he were the shooter, was Marti dead? If not, it would jeopardize Marti's life to go through the door shooting. Whatever she did it should be done now, because if Marti were injured she would require immediate aid.

"Tull!" she shouted. "Do you hear me? Come on out."

There was no answer. "Tull, I know you killed Dr. Wilson. There's no way you can get away, but it will go easier for you if you allow us to get help for Marti if she's hurt."

Marti struggled to get out of Tull's grip, kicking back at his shins, but he held his hand firmly over her mouth and brought the barrel of the shotgun down hard on her skull. She groaned and sagged in his arms.

"Please help me," Tull called out to Donna in a pitiful voice. "I've been shot."

"Where's Marti?" Donna called back.

"She's here. I knocked her out. But I'm bleeding to death...." His voice trailed off to a whisper.

Derek Marsh had had no intention of letting Donna go alone to the farmhouse, but he knew it was useless to argue. He let her get a head start and then, leaving her cell phone on the car seat, followed close behind. He was close enough to hear the exchange between her and Tull. He didn't believe what Tull said, and he assumed Donna wouldn't, either. He was horrified when he saw her begin to step into the doorway, and he ran and dove at her screaming, "Get down!"

Donna was thrown forward onto the barn floor as the flash and thunder of the shotgun filled the room. She didn't know for an instant what had happened, but instinctively began raising her gun to fire, only to realize her hand no longer held a gun. It had skipped several yards into the darkness of the barn when she fell.

"Don't move," barked Tull, "or I'll shoot your buddy!" His command was accompanied with the sound of another shell being pumped into the firing chamber.

Donna looked behind her. Lying on the ground in the moonlight at the doorway was Derek Marsh. He was trying to crawl toward her, but was obviously hurt.

"OK, OK. I'm not moving," Donna called out.

"Now, both of you get up and stand against the wall——very slow and easy like."

Donna's eyes had adjusted enough to the dim moonlight coming through the doorway to see Tull holding Marti and see the shotgun pointed at Derek Marsh, who got up stiffly and limped to stand next to her.

Ferris Tull was presented with a huge problem. If what the woman deputy said——"I know you killed Barbara Wilson"——meant that others knew, then killing these three would accomplish nothing. But if it had only meant that she and this guy knew…. But how could he ascertain that? It would be useless to ask; the deputy would lie. So all three would have to die. He'd take the chance that no one else knew the truth. Now how could he stage it to avoid a manhunt? Could he kill them in such a way that it would appear they had killed each other?

At that moment, Tull saw a flashlight beam playing across the porch of the farmhouse. He knew Marti hadn't seen it. She had recovered from the blow he'd given her and was standing on her own, so he shoved her hard toward the others at the wall. Tull stepped out from under the loft overhang to get a better view of the porch and at the same time watch his three captives.

Tull saw that the person had switched off the flashlight and had gone into the house.

In a low voice, Tull told his three captives that he didn't want to hurt anyone and how everything could be worked out. He needed to keep them calm and quiet while he waited to see what this newcomer was going to do.

The porch door opened and the guy came out of the house and stood on the porch steps. Tull was sure he knew who it was. A guy that big had to be that damn bear of a sheriff. Hoss left the steps and started walking toward the barn, flashlight still off. Tull couldn't afford to let him get into the barn. There would be too many of them, even if he did have a shotgun. He'd wait until the Sheriff was right at the doorway, then blast him. He took a quick look at the three against the wall. They were quiet and had no awareness that Hoss was only a few yards away.

Once again Tull said softly and reassuringly, "Don't worry, we can work things out." He shifted his concentration to the door, his hand tightening on the gunstock.

Donna's eyes sought out and located her pistol lying fifteen feet from her on the barn floor.

Suddenly Hoss's silhouette filled the doorway. Tull brought the shotgun around and leveled it. In the same instant a bale of hay flew down from the loft, hitting Tull in the back of the neck and knocking him to his knees.

Donna dove for her gun, her fingers desperately seeking the trigger. She turned the barrel toward Tull just as he recovered from the blow and was raising the shotgun. Their eyes met for a second. She squeezed the trigger twice. The force of the shots threw Tull's body backward to remain lying face up on the barn floor.

Hoss was turning on his flashlight, preparing to enter the barn, when he was startled by the shots. He fell to one knee, drawing his weapon and shining the light on the incredible scene.

"Donna! Jesus!"

Donna was shaking uncontrollably. "Hoss, Oh Hoss!" she cried. Derek Marsh came and put his arms around her, holding her head to his chest.

Marti yelled, "Hoss, for God's sake, where the hell have you been?"

Hoss leaned over Tull's body and checked for a pulse.

It took several minutes for them to reassure each other that they had escaped certain death before they faced the fact that it had been the hay bale that had saved their lives. Hoss shined his light up at the loft and called out, "Who's up there?"

There was no answer. The four stared up into the empty darkness of the loft.

"Who's up there?" Hoss called again. They all thought they heard a stealthy footstep, then silence.

With flashlight in hand, Hoss rapidly mounted the loft ladder.

The others waited, looking up, saying nothing, until Hoss walked back to the edge of the loft. "No one up here," he reported. "Is the loading door at the end of the loft usually open, Marti?"

"No. No, it isn't."

"It is now."

CHAPTER 21

IT WAS MID-MORNING ON SATURDAY. Life was humming as usual along Main Street in Leland. The summer visitors were getting started on the many activities planned for their day. The hot dog buns were nearly sold out at the Leland Mercantile Co.

At the office of the *Leelanau Clarion*, however, things were not as usual. The regular weekly edition was not due until Tuesday, but Gerald Gibbs and Mary Beth Holding, who together made up the owners, publishers, editors and two of the three reporters on the paper's staff, had just made a decision to come out with an extra edition. The last time an extra edition had been published was when Suttons Bay won the state basketball championship for its division. The time before that had been VJ Day. There were two reasons for this exceptional move. Last night had seen a spectacular finale to the sensational Wilson murder case. Gerald had been called by Kate Schott, the Sheriff's Department dispatcher, and told about it right after it happened. Gerald called Hoss at home this morning. Hoss had asked K.D. to refer any calls from the media to his office, but he took Gerald's call and told him enough to give the Clarion a genuine scoop, a story the national services would buy.

By itself, the story of a Traverse City psychotherapist killed in a gun battle with the police would not generate an extra edition of the paper. However, a story of even greater interest to the readers in the peninsula had been dropped, in the form of a CD, into the mail slot at the paper's office during the night. The disk was wrapped in a rubber band bound note, which simply stated. "Very important. Read right away." Mary Beth had immediately loaded the three files on the disk into the newspaper's computer.

The first file was labeled "Explanation." It stated that the material contained in the two other files had been copied from the computer of Jason Ackerman at Greenleaf Properties and contained the organization's development plans for Leelanau County. The file labeled "General Aims" consisted of meeting agendas and memoranda written by Jason Ackerman and concerning his plans for bringing about zoning changes by various means. Included were direct quotes of promises made to Ackerman by the candidates backed by the syndicate. The file designated as "E-mail" contained the correspondence between Ackerman and various others revealing the day-to-day ways these aims were being pursued.

It was the "E-mail" file Mary Beth looked at first.

"If this does belong to Ackerman, he's a guy who never deletes anything," she said in the direction of Gerald, who was watering the ficus plant in the corner of the office. "There are 85 messages in the 'in box.'" She clicked on one of the messages and began reading.

After several minutes, Gerald began reading over her shoulder. Mary Beth uttered an occasional, "Can you believe it?" and several times "That son-of-a-bitch!" came out of Gerald.

"It looks authentic as all hell," said Gerald. "There are just too many details for anyone to make up. And, all those e-mail addresses."

"Of course, the addresses may be pure fiction," said Mary Beth soberly. "I know what we can do, though. We can send a message to a number of these addresses saying we're awarding a prize to the first person to respond to our e-mail with the correct answer to a contest question. It will be a simple question like, what state is surrounded on three sides by fresh water?"

"And what will be the prize you'll tempt them with?" asked Gerald.

"We can give them a free subscription to the Clarion."

"I'm certain it's to their discredit, my dear, but many may choose to pass up this golden opportunity."

"OK, I hear your sarcasm. How about a weekend in Chicago?"

"That's more like it. As a matter of fact, I think I'll enter the contest."

Mary Beth ignored the remark. "Seriously, if we get answers, we'll know the addresses are authentic. That will mean there's a good chance the rest of the information is accurate, also. So, we go to press."

Gerald hesitated. "We can make sure the addresses are genuine much more simply than that. We'll send a message to a dozen addresses and see if the message is delivered. But even if we determine to our satisfaction that all this is genuine, where do we stand legally? Could we be sued for invasion of privacy? Also, if this disk is a hoax, we could be sued for slander."

"I know what we can do," said Mary Beth brightly. "We include a disclaimer: 'The *Clarion* makes no claim for the authenticity of this material at this time but is printing it in the hope that someone can help identify the person who left it at the paper's office.' How does that strike you?"

"If I thought for a moment that you weren't kidding, I'd start looking for a new partner. But let's do that checking to see if the addresses are real and if they are, I'm for printing an extra."

An hour later, Gerald picked up the phone on his desk and began dialing the number of Ben Watkins, the paper's press operator.

❍

A sleepless, hungry Jason Ackerman had returned home from a strenuous pre-dawn project. He was in the act of spearing a sausage with a fork, when Claudia came into the room with a portable phone. She knew Ackerman would take the call as he'd done before.

"This man says he knows a dollar sign from a wooden nickel."

Ackerman waited until Claudia left the room. "Yes?"

"Those files of yours are all in the paper today, all except the part where we accuse you of Buddy's murder. That part we're saving, unless you're a bad little boy. Keep that in mind, Dude."

Ackerman's feelings went from alarm at hearing about the newspaper story to rage at being referred to as a "bad little boy." No one had ever used those words with him before! He began to tell the guy this, then realized he was talking to a dead line.

❍

Hoss combed his hair before the mirror in the small bathroom off his office. He wasn't comfortable with these press interviews. He didn't like having to be so very careful about what he said. In ordinary conversation, misunderstandings can be recognized and cleared up as the talk goes along. Invariably, in the few televised interviews he'd participated in, some unfortunate and false impression had been created. Thousands of viewers who'd see the broadcast could get the wrong idea, and there was no way to get back to them to set them straight. And, if you did try later to say that it wasn't what you meant, it sounded defensive, as if you were lying. He believed that much of the time an interviewer is not trying to get the true story anyway, any more than an attorney in court is trying to get at the truth; both are only out to make their biased points. Hoss would have liked to read his statement and leave, but as an elected official—an elected official facing re-election—he was obliged to appear to be open to questioning.

He looked at his face and saw his tension reflected there. He tried a few forced, exaggerated smiles to loosen his facial muscles then went to his desk where he picked up the statement he'd written and left his office. Waiting for him in the hallway outside was Gerry Gibbs of the Clarion.

"Hoss, this just came off our press. It's an extra we're getting out about the fracas last night, but also there's a part about a plan that Jason Ackerman and his pals have for exploiting the County. There's a bit about their putting Springer up to run against you in the primary."

Gibbs held out the extra edition and a preoccupied Hoss took it from him.

"We're ready to start taping," a bored looking news director said to Hoss from the doorway to the conference room.

Hoss turned back toward Gerald Gibbs. "Thanks Gerry, I'll talk to you later."

The reporters from both local television stations were simultaneously recording their on-the-scene introductions to the news briefing when Hoss entered the room. The director asked him to sit down at a conference table flooded with bright lights.

Present, in addition to the two local stations, were a couple of free-lancers and two stringers for national wire services. Hoss wiped his forehead with his handkerchief and furtively glanced at his prepared statement and notes, while the two cameramen finished their preparations. He looked up when he heard his name and saw the director bring his arm down to point emphatically with the gesture Hoss had seen so many times in films, the sign that said, "You're on!"

He made an effort to compose himself and began his spiel.

"Last night at 11:30 P.M. two members of the Leelanau County Sheriff's Department, Deputy Donna Roper and I, attempted to arrest Mr. Ferris Tull of Traverse City for the murder of Dr. Barbara Wilson of Elmwood Township. Mr. Tull resisted arrest and was shot and killed when he attempted to use a shotgun to shoot Deputy Roper, myself and two other people who were present. There is abundant evidence in our opinion that Ferris Tull was guilty of Dr. Wilson's murder. Details of that evidence will be revealed at the inquest scheduled for Wednesday."

Hoss looked up toward the two reporters. "That is our statement at this time."

"Sheriff Davis," the man from Channel 8 quickly said, beating his rival out. "Who was it who shot the suspect?"

"Deputy Roper," Hoss answered tersely.

"This was in self-defense?"

"That's right."

"How did Tull manage to get a shotgun——I mean, with two armed officers present?"

Hoss recognized the reporter from the evening news. He was the same one he'd also seen interviewing Kip Springer outside Kip's campaign headquarters and again at the State Police post. K.D. had commented that the guy seemed to think he was the Mike Wallace of Traverse City, flavoring his questions with innuendo meant to let the viewers know they were watching the unmasking of yet another scoundrel.

"Ferris Tull was in possession of the gun when Deputy Roper and I arrived on the scene. In my judgment, he was about to use the weapon."

"And what led you to conclude that, Sheriff Davis?"

"He had already shot at Deputy Roper and missed." Hoss looked over at the other reporter and nodded to him, as if to acknowledge his question. The viewer at home couldn't see that the man had made no move to get Hoss's attention.

"For how long a time had you suspected Mr. Tull of the murder?" the man from Channel 4 managed.

"Actually, I didn't suspect Tull. It was Deputy Roper who broke the case. I came as back-up at her request."

"How did she work it out?"

"She will testify at the inquest. You will get an answer to your question then."

Hoss made a move as if he were about to say that was all, but before he could speak the first reporter asked, "Sheriff Davis, a few minutes ago I was given a copy of an extra edition of the *Leelanau Clarion*. There is an article that alleges to be a copy of computer files taken from Greenleaf Properties. I understand the text is supposed to outline a plan whereby the firm intends to manipulate local primary elections to put people in office friendly to their land development plans. One of these primary races is between you and Kip Springer for Sheriff."

At this point, a smirk appeared which announced that he was about to force the interviewee into a cleverly conceived trap. "Did you know that this was going to be printed by the Clarion today? Did you know that before you called this press conference?"

"No, I didn't."

"Sheriff, isn't that a copy of the extra edition that you have right there under those notes of yours on the table?"

Hoss was stunned by the guy's open attack on his honesty. "Yes, it is, but just what is it you're implying?"

"Nothing." The reporter said with a knowing look toward the camera.

"You seem to be implying that I was lying when I said I had no knowledge of the article you're referring to. The first I knew about this story was just now—from you. I was handed this copy of the paper not more than five minutes before this interview began. I haven't yet even glanced at it, so naturally I have nothing to say about it."

Gerald Gibbs was smiling broadly. This ass of a reporter, in his stupid belief that he was so clever, had very nicely presented the very meaning of the article that he and Mary Beth hoped people would get, at the same time giving the *Clarion* article enough publicity to insure a record sale.

Hoss said "Thank you" to the TV audience and rose from his chair, causing the cameramen to adjust their cameras upward to take in the whole man.

❍

Wes Haldeck dropped the hoist after draining the crankcase for an oil change and glanced at the wall clock. It was five after three. The sign over the garage entrance said, "Authorized Employees Only," but a man was walking in anyway and straight up to him, with his hand extended. He was holding out some money to Wes, which Wes automatically accepted.

"My name is Harry Swifthawk, and I owe you this for some gas." He turned on his heel and walked out.

Wes Haldeck looked at the seventeen dollars he now held. Earlier he'd imagined all the things he would say to this guy if he ever met him, but now he was speechless.

❍

There was a message from Donna on Derek Marsh's answering machine when he finished a therapy session at three-thirty. He immediately called her at the number she'd left.

"How's your knee?" she asked after the greetings.

"Much better, thanks. I can envision the day when I will even be able to bend it. No, seriously, it's fine today. How about your own bruises?"

"Did I mention to you that I put Motrin at the head of my list of the greatest advances of the last thousand years? I'm fine. So fine, in fact, that on my day off I've decided to do something I haven't done for a long time and prepare a real meal. It's not intended to compete with that great dish you made last night, but it will be nourishing. I want you to share it with me. It would please me very much if you'll come."

Donna's voice and her message thrilled him. His feeling soared way above anything he could think to say, but he made an attempt.

"And, I won't pretend that this isn't one of the three best things I've heard in my entire life."

"Really? What are the other two?"

"The first was the time I overheard my mother tell my aunt, 'I know I shouldn't have favorites, but I really favor Derek.' The second was when the teacher said, 'Boys and girls, today we're not having our regular class. Instead, we're having a movie'."

Donna laughed. "I get it, what you want is undivided attention and self-indulgence."

"Close, but not quite right. What I prize is the combination of an unexpected pleasure and a compliment coming from the one person from whom I really want to hear it."

Donna was touched. "I don't know what to say."

"You don't have to say anything."

"But I do want to say this: thank you again for saving my life."

❍

On the six o'clock news, as she put the finishing touches on one of Hoss's favorite meals, morel stuffed ravioli, K.D. watched Kip Springer announce his withdrawal from the primary.

"Certain facts which have come to my attention today make it impossible to continue my campaign. I want to thank the friends who have worked for my election and I want to say that I am giving my full support and effort toward the re-election of Hoss Davis as Sheriff of Leelanau County."

An interviewing reporter attempted to get a detailed clarification. Springer, who gave the decided impression that he was hurrying to a cocktail party at the White House, handled these probes adroitly and humorously.

K.D. wiped her hands on a dishtowel and neatly folded it and hung it up, smiling to herself.

❍

Jason Ackerman put down the phone. He'd just been talking to the largest realty broker on the peninsula. He mixed a pitcher of martinis, poured two glasses, and went to join his wife on the deck overlooking the lake. The sunset was spectacular.

"Lauren, you've been wonderful the way you've pretended to like it here as much as I. I know you'd prefer to be back in Chicago, or better yet New York. I want you to know that after this last sunset, I'm ready to go, too. I just called a realtor and told him to sell the house. We'll leave Claudia to supervise the movers and we'll take off in a few days for a vacation in Europe. Maybe your father's Paris apartment is available and I can buy you some great new dresses. How would you like that?"

Lauren Ackerman was confused. Usually Jason's moments of expansive generosity followed his triumphs, yet she'd heard no boasting and neither was there evidence of that other invariable accompaniment of his successes, sexual desire. A disturbing thought crossed her mind. Maybe she had lost her appeal. But in that case, she knew intuitively, he'd be telling her he was leaving her, and here he was talking about showering her with gifts instead. Most confusing.

"I'd love that, darling. But what about Greenleaf Properties?"

"The investment climate has changed here. I can get a better return on my money by shifting it to our projects in Montana and Cabo."

"What will you tell your partners?"

"I don't have to tell them a damn thing. They're lucky I'm letting them invest their money with me."

This thought aroused him. He pulled Lauren closer and kissed her neck. She responded, parting his shirt at the neck to return the kiss.

"Darling, your tennis ball is gone," she said, surprised.

His hand went to his neck. "So it is. The clasp must have broken in bed last night. Ask Claudia to look for it will you?"

❍

"Russ just drove in," David Wick said to Hoss, who had himself just arrived back at Headquarters and was standing next to Wick in the dispatcher's office. "I've been waiting to hear what he saw. About an hour ago, this cyclist stopped at the bridge on Soder Road and looked over the railing. Down there—rear end sticking out of the water—is a car. Turns out it's Carl Brock's car—with him in it."

"Carl Brock? That must have scared the bejesus out'a the guy who discovered it."

"You know it did," said Wick. "You should'a heard him when he called in here. The guy goes down the riverbank so he can see inside, an' there's this guy in the car lookin' very dead. He tore outa there and set some kind'a record gettin' to a phone—Willard Johnson's place. Russ went out to be there as they hoisted the car out."

"Maybe Brock fell asleep and left the road. There is a curve right there, or maybe he'd been drinking." Hoss speculated.

Preva walked in and recognized the questioning looks that greeted him. He began relating a description of the scene.

"I took a quick look over Brock's body, but I saw no injuries," Russ said. "One thing I did find was this gold chain and charm. It was on the floor by Brock's feet. Funny, but I think I've seen this thing recently." He took it out of his pocket and held it up. "But, I can't remember where?"

"Looks like a baseball or a tennis ball," Hoss said. "The clasp is broken; it must have happened in the crash. Give it to me, Russ, and I'll give it back to Mrs. Brock. I have to go and see her now to tell her the bad news."

Hoss took the chain and put it in an envelope, then left the office.

"At least," Preva observed, "That's *one* person we can quit looking for."

EPILOGUE

THE CAST HAD BEEN OFF two days, but she was still walking with a slight limp. Marti crossed the porch and went outside and stood on the steps in the dark. A breeze coming off the lake rustled a nearby cottonwood tree. She waited there until her eyes adjusted to the darkness. Her gaze fell briefly on the barn. She hadn't been back inside since that night. More time had to pass. She turned to look up the hill. It was there that she intended to go tonight.

She heard the phone ring and decided to ignore it, let the machine take it. There had been many calls in the four days since the shooting. Most had begun by asking her if she was all right after what she'd gone through. Several of the callers were old high school friends—acquaintances really. She had few friends from that time. They had sounded warm, holding out the offer of a relationship if she desired it. She'd responded positively but wondered if she could spare the time for more involvement with people. She was eager to get back to the canvases she'd been waiting to complete.

In the afternoon she'd walked to the top of the hill and reawakened the mood expressed in those paintings. Passing the place where she'd looked down on Barbara's face in the moonlight she'd sensed, again, that something was unfinished—unfinished between them. She'd paused in the bright sunlight at the spot, trying to recapture the feeling of communication she'd had that first night, but failed. She'd decided to return after dark and try again. She left the porch steps now and began to climb. The waning moon, filtering through high clouds, cast but a dim light.

Marti came to the place in the grass where Barbara Wilson's open eyes had seemed to look into her own. She could call up an image of Barbara's face clearly, so strong was the memory. After several minutes she spoke aloud.

"I wanted you to know that he's paid for what he did to you." A sudden breeze moved the grass, almost as if in response. Marti's voice was earnest. "What happened to you was one of those things that can happen to all of us. You weren't at fault. Our world hasn't changed. It's still filled with good people. Have peace."

Marti looked up at what remained of the Strawberry Moon. She hated violence. She loved the beauty that the night and the breeze and the moon represented. She felt an understanding love for all the people who, like her, had difficulty at times letting themselves live in harmony with this beauty.

She sensed a nearby movement. There had been no sound, yet she knew someone was there in the darkness with her.

"I know you're there," she said and was surprised to find she was unafraid.

A figure moved toward her now until he was only several feet away. She could sense she was not in danger. Calmly, she took him in—his long black hair, loosely held together in back, his high forehead, his erect bearing. She looked into his dark eyes, finding something very familiar there—as if looking into her own face. She laughed lightly.

"It feels like I know you, do I?" she asked.

"Not yet, but now that I've found you, you will ... little sister."